SLEEPING ALONE

Barbara Bretton

W9-BBF-109

BERKLEY BOOKS, NEW YORK

SLEEPING ALONE

A Berkley Book / published by arrangement with
the author

PRINTING HISTORY
Berkley edition / April 1997

The Putnam Berkley World Wide Web site address is
http://www.berkley.com/berkley

ISBN: 0-425-15717-2

BERKLEY®
Berkley Books are published by The Berkley Publishing Group,
200 Madison Avenue, New York, New York 10016.
BERKLEY and the "B" design
are trademarks belonging to Berkley Publishing Corporation.

PRINTED IN THE UNITED STATES OF AMERICA

10 9 8 7 6 5 4 3 2 1

Berkley Books by Barbara Bretton

ONE AND ONLY

MAYBE THIS TIME

SLEEPING ALONE

ONE

∽

London, England

Alexandra Curry Whittaker was debating the relative
merits of the jazzy red suede Filofax against the more
sober black leather model the day her world exploded.
She didn't need a new Filofax—truth was, she didn't
need anything new at all—but it was a rainy September
afternoon, and shopping was the traditional outlet for
lonely American wives with too much time on their
hands.

"Go out and enjoy yourself, darling," Griffin had said
to her that morning, barely glancing over the top of his
Times. "You deserve it."

He left a bouquet of credit cards on the mahogany
hall table, and she gathered them up as if they were
roses. In the beginning there had been roses, dozens of
them, long-stemmed American Beauties, perfect white
teas, armloads of pale yellow and peach and ivory, but
the roses had long ago been replaced with credit cards
and cash. She supposed she should be grateful she had

such a generous husband, even if she didn't quite understand how that was supposed to make up for the fact
that she was sleeping alone.

Her closets bulged with Thierry Mugler dresses, Armani jackets, slinky Hervé Leger outfits that Griffin
loved her to wear to theater premieres when he knew
the paparazzi would be out in force. "American businessman Griffin Whittaker with his beautiful young wife
Alexandra." He clipped every mention, no matter how
small, and filed them away "for posterity," he said.

Posterity. The word made her think of manor houses
with clipped privet hedges and dour-faced nannies pushing prams the size of VWs. If she closed her eyes she
could envision an endless daisy chain of babies, linking
each new generation with the one that had come before.

"Don't think of this as a failure, Alexandra," her doctor had said after the last series of painful and expensive
tests had turned up neither a pregnancy nor a reason why
there wasn't one. "Nature has her own timetable. Her
own reasons."

She had nodded calmly, as if her heart broke in two
every day of the week. "I understand," she'd said. "It's
no one's fault."

But that wasn't true. She knew whose fault it was.
Her uterus was a clenched fist, defending its walls
against all invaders, and not even Griffin's seemingly
endless funds could pry it open. Sometimes she wondered if her doctor wasn't right and if nature didn't know
exactly what she was doing, protecting an innocent child
from a marriage that had long ago lost its sense of joy.

Still she longed for a child. She'd struggled to accept
the fact that pregnancy might not be an option for her
and turned her dreams toward adoption. "We have so
much," she'd said to Griffin one night before they
started sleeping alone. "Why not share it with a child
who needs us as much as we need him?" There were

times she physically ached with longing for a child to love.

Griffin wouldn't hear of it. He wanted a child of his own, a child who shared his blood and background, and nothing less would satisfy him.

"Mrs. Whittaker?" The salesclerk's voice broke into her thoughts. "If I might be so bold, the red suede is produced in limited quantities, while the black leather is more readily available."

Snob appeal, Alexandra thought. How well the Brits knew their former subjects. She flipped through the calendar section of the red organizer and was mentally filling in all the tidy little squares with upcoming appointments and social engagements when she saw her husband's mistress.

Alexandra had known about Claire Brubaker for three years. Claire was one of the reasons they'd moved from New York to London. Griffin had assured her that the affair was over, that Claire had been a brief midlife aberration that wouldn't happen again. Because she needed to, Alexandra believed him. Her marriage meant everything to her. If she wasn't Mrs. Griffin Whittaker, she wasn't certain she existed at all.

Claire was admiring a rose-colored silk scarf. Her dark red hair was pulled back in an intricate French braid. She said something to the salesclerk, something low and urgent and endlessly amusing, and the salesclerk laughed out loud. Claire wore a strand of pearls at her neck, a chunky Rolex on her left wrist, and a chic navy maternity dress.

Alexandra's stomach lurched as a wave of dizziness swept over her.

"Are you all right, ma'am?" the salesclerk asked, all courteous solicitude. "You're terribly pale. Let me fetch you a glass of water."

Pregnant. Claire's belly swelled beneath the fine wool

of her dress. Five months along? Maybe six? Not that it mattered. Claire Brubaker was pregnant, and Alexandra knew there was only one man who could possibly be the father. "Oh, God," she whispered, as pain swallowed her whole. "Oh, God . . ."

"Ma'am, please let us help you."

A knot of salesclerks gathered around her. One pushed a chair against the backs of her knees to force her to sit down. Two elderly matrons in matching chesterfields peered at her curiously.

"Poor dear," clucked the taller of the two. "You're pale as cream."

"Please," Alexandra managed, "I'm fine. "

The buzz of concern around her grew stronger.

"I'm going to call for assistance," the salesclerk said. "We can't have you fainting on us."

"I'm not going to faint," Alexandra protested, standing up.

"You *are* terribly pale," the first salesclerk said. She lowered her voice. "Might you be enceinte?"

"No!" The word rose up over the buzz of the crowd. "I'm late for an appointment. I really must run. . . ."

Claire was still absorbed in examining a Hermès scarf. Alexandra had to get out of the store before she looked up. She tossed the Filofax down on the counter, then dashed for the exit. She heard voices calling after her, a symphony of voices, all of them begging her to come back. *Mrs. Whittaker! Mrs. Whittaker! Don't go!*

Her face burned with embarrassment, but she kept moving. She'd never be able to shop at Harrods again, not in a million years. She'd always tried so hard to blend in, to adapt, to be as invisible as possible, and now she was making a scene the salesclerks would talk about for days. *Don't think about it,* she told herself as she elbowed past a knot of customers and pushed open the door. *Just keep moving.*

All that mattered was putting as much space between herself and Claire Brubaker as she possibly could. A blast of wind-driven rain hit her full force as she stepped outside. She stood in the middle of a dark sea of umbrellas and wondered if you could die from a broken heart. Rain puddled at the curbs and splashed up from the sidewalk, turning everything gray and ugly. London was a filthy city, every bit as dirty as New York. She'd be spattered with mud from head to foot by the time she got home. Griffin hated it when she looked anything but perfect. The thought was almost enough to make her laugh. In the space of a second, her entire life had been turned upside down, and she was worried about mud stains.

She began to run, slowly at first, then gathering speed as she dodged angry taxis and curious businessmen in Savile Row suits that defied the weather. Maybe if she ran fast enough, far enough, she could make it all go away.

But Claire's face danced in front of her, laughing. Pregnancy had softened the woman's angular features, making her look more beautiful than ever. She wondered how long Claire had been in London. Had she been here from the start or had she flown into town specifically to see Griffin?

Certainly his behavior had given away nothing. He'd been his usual composed self, solicitous of Alexandra but emotionally distant. Once upon a time she'd been too young and trusting to know the difference. Now that she did, it came close to breaking her heart.

She ran until she couldn't run anymore. Gasping for breath, she leaned against a lamppost at the entrance to the park across from their flat. Usually the park teemed with fresh-faced nannies and their young charges, but they were all inside today, safe and warm. How many sunny afternoons had she sat at her bedroom window, watching the children play . . . listening to the sweet sound of their laughter as it rose toward her on the wind? Things would be different in London, Griffin said. There would be more time for each other, more space. And, she'd prayed, maybe a miracle was waiting for them there.

Pain knifed through her middle, and she sank down onto a bench and lowered her head. Even miracles needed some earthly help. She couldn't remember the last time she and Griffin made love. Three months? Maybe six? She didn't know. More often than not, he slept in his study. He claimed late nights and an unwillingness to disturb Alexandra, but she knew it went deeper than that. Disappointment had taken its toll on them both, turning sex into something joyless and pathetic. She missed being held. She missed the comforting weight of his body next to hers. She missed waking up in the morning and seeing his familiar face.

Griffin was fifty-five years old, and time was running out. He wanted a child more than anything, a son to carry on his name. "I'll give you sons," Alexandra had promised him on their wedding night. "As many as you want." He had been there for her when she needed him most, and she would do anything to make him happy.

Ten years later she was still trying.

She placed her palms against her midsection and tried to imagine how it would feel to carry a child within her own body, to watch her belly grow bigger with each month that passed—to share it all with a man she loved.

The thought brought her up short. Did she love Griffin any longer? Once upon a time, loving him seemed as natural as breathing. She depended on him. She respected him. He was responsible for everything in her life—the roof over her head, the food she ate, her clothes. Without Griffin she would have nothing. He was the one who had helped her make sense of her life after her parents' tragic death, shielding her from the legacy of bad debts and lawsuits they had left behind for their only child. She'd been seventeen years old, left with no home, no family, no one to turn to . . . except for Griffin.

But was that love? She'd thought so once. The sound of his footsteps on the other side of the door had been enough to brighten her day, but his infidelities had taken their toll. No one could sustain a marriage on gratitude alone. She'd often had the sense that she was a visitor in her own home and that one day he would look up from his *Times* and tell her that it was time she moved on.

She looked across the park at the place she'd called home for the last two years. Her passport was tucked in her purse, along with an inch-thick stack of credit cards. She could grab one of those big comfortable cabs London was so proud of and head for Gatwick. Planes left every hour of the day, for every corner of the globe. All she had to do was pick a destination and within hours she'd be there, ready to start a new life. Griffin had already started a new life—it was growing deep inside Claire Brubaker's body. Maybe it was time for Alexandra to do the same.

But how did you start a new life? She hadn't a clue.

She wondered what Griffin was doing right now. He was one of those men who managed to cram twenty-five hours into every day. He was probably busy with one of his multinational deals, immersed in details she'd never understand. All these years he'd waited and hoped for a child—you would think he would be shouting his news from the highest rooftop. Instead, he acted as if nothing had changed, as if he wasn't about to become a father.

But what if she'd jumped to the wrong conclusion and nothing *had* changed? Maybe Claire's pregnancy had absolutely nothing to do with Griffin. Claire could have taken a new lover, or maybe even found a husband of her own. She was a beautiful woman. The odds of her being alone were a million to one. Besides, it wasn't as if Claire's belly bore a sign that read, "Courtesy of Griffin Whittaker." Maybe she'd let her imagination run away with her and there was really no cause for alarm.

She dashed for home across the rain-swept park to find out.

ALEXANDRA DRESSED CAREFULLY FOR DINNER in a flowing pants suit of coppery silk. Her hair was swept off her face in a loose French twist. She looked calm, sophisticated, in control.

"I saw Claire today," she announced casually over dinner. They were seated at opposite ends of the mahogany refectory table, separated by a wall of candles, cutlery, and crystal. "In Harrods."

"Claire told me," he said. "You left your credit card on the counter."

Claire told him? Her hands began to tremble, and she quickly placed them on her lap. "I'll pick it up tomorrow."

"You must be more careful, darling," he said evenly. "Not every establishment is that honest."

"I had other things on my mind," she returned, just as evenly. "I was . . . surprised to see Claire at the scarf counter."

"I didn't invite Claire to London," he said, pouring himself more wine. "She came of her own accord."

"That's interesting." She drew in a breath. They sounded as if they were discussing the price of eggs. "How long has she been here?"

He met her eyes. "Why do you ask?"

"Because she's pregnant." She hadn't meant to say it so bluntly, but there it was.

He nodded. "Claire wasn't sure you'd noticed."

"My God, Griffin, I'd have to be blind not to notice her belly." She barely recognized the sound of her own voice: strident and much too frightened.

His brows drew together as he met her eyes across the table. Griffin hated loud, pushy, angry women. For the first time in their marriage, she was all three.

"Is the baby yours?" She struggled to moderate her tone, but failed miserably.

Griffin glanced down at his medallions of veal, but not before she saw the expression in his eyes. She wished he'd reached into her chest and ripped out her heart, because that couldn't have hurt her any more than that look of naked pride. This couldn't be happening to her, not to her safe and protected life. She had given him her loyalty and her love, but Claire had given him the future. There was nothing she could do to compete with that.

"How long have you known?" she managed.

"I was with Claire when the doctor told her."

She felt herself shrinking in her chair like a frightened child. *Months,* she thought dully. *He's known about it for months.* "I'm your wife," she said, trying to sound as if she believed that meant something. "I deserve better than this."

"There's no need for moral outrage, my dear. You've known about Claire for a long time now."

"Yes, but you said it was over. I thought . . ."

"Nothing has changed," he said, between bites of veal and sips of wine. "Claire and I had a brief reunion, with unexpected results. The situation needn't affect you." His voice was soothing, almost hypnotic, and she wanted to believe him, needed to believe him. "Claire and the child will be well taken care of, and you and I will go on as before."

"Go on as before? You'll have a child, Griffin. You'll be someone's father while I'll be—"

"My wife," he said smoothly. "For now and always."

OVER THE NEXT FEW WEEKS, her moods ran the gamut from white-hot anger to an almost placid acceptance of the situation. There were times she wanted to force the issue, make Griffin choose between his barren wife and his fertile mistress, but she wasn't fool enough to believe she would come out the winner. And if she wasn't the winner, who was she?

In mid-October they hosted a dinner party for Griffin's French business partners. Alexandra wore a simple Oscar de la Renta sheath that garnered almost as many compliments as the food and wine. But it was the approval on Griffin's face that spoke loudest. *See?* his look said. *Our life is the same as it ever was.*

She wanted to believe that, but the image of a radiant Claire Brubaker was never far from her mind.

Their guests left a little before midnight. Griffin had arranged for a private plane to jet them back to Paris in time to get a good night's sleep.

"Antoine found you charming," Griffin said, locking the door to their flat.

"I'm pleased," Alexandra said as she slipped off her spindly high heels. "He and Monique are delightful."

"Did I tell you how lovely you look?"

"No, you didn't," she said, "but thank you." There had been a time when those words would have been enough to warm her heart.

He led her back into the front room, then gestured toward the sofa. "Sit down, darling. We'll have a brandy."

He poured them each a snifter of Drambuie, and they settled in front of the fireplace.

"Thank God for this," Griffin said as he stabbed at

the logs with a poker. "I doubt if the English will ever master central heating."

"I'm glad. If they did, our flat wouldn't have three beautiful fireplaces."

He reclaimed his seat next to her on the sofa. "It's been a long time since we enjoyed a fire together."

"I've been here," she said lightly. "Where were you?"

A flash of annoyance appeared in Griffin's eyes. "That is something—"

The ringing of the telephone stopped him.

"It's after midnight," she said. "Who would call at this hour?"

Griffin set his brandy down on the end table. "Bates can't seem to master the time difference between here and L.A." He excused himself to answer the phone.

She placed her glass next to his and sat stiff-backed in the corner of the sofa. Griffin's voice, low and urgent, drifted toward her, but she couldn't make out his words. She found her anger flaring up at odd moments lately, burning through her veneer of composure and surprising her with its heat. Anger unnerved her. It demanded a resolution. It demanded change, and change scared her more than anything. She'd spent the first seventeen years of her life searching for the safe harbor her parents had never provided, and she'd thought she found it when she married Griffin.

She took a deep breath, willing the tension from her body. Griffin could talk to Sam Bates for hours. Over the years she'd grown used to his devotion to work. It was that devotion, after all, that had saved her from disaster after her parents' unexpected death. She rested her head against the back of the sofa and closed her eyes. She wondered what Claire thought when he interrupted a tryst to take a business call or schedule a meeting.

The fire sputtered weakly. It had been roaring when

Griffin left the room. How long had he been on the phone?

"Griffin," she called out, but there was no answer. She stood up and started for the foyer. He wasn't in the study, the bedroom, or either of the bathrooms. She checked the closet. His camel's hair coat was missing, and so were the keys to the Mercedes he kept in the car park.

An hour passed, and then another. The fire died out completely, and she wrapped a lap robe about herself for warmth, but it couldn't begin to reach the chill deep inside her bones.

Claire, she thought with growing certainty. Fertile Claire with the growing belly. Where else could he be? London was a civilized town. Few businessmen conducted meetings after midnight on Saturday morning. He'd said Claire's pregnancy wouldn't change anything between them, but he was wrong. Claire was between them every hour of every day, and she would be for the rest of their lives.

Whether or not Griffin realized it, he and Claire had forged a bond that nothing, not even his marriage to Alexandra, could ever break. First cries, first teeth, first words—there was so much ahead for them to share together, and Alexandra knew that as the weeks turned into months and the months became years, she would be reduced to a shadowy presence with no future of her own. Grant would have a child to love, and Alexandra would have no one.

One day last week Alexandra had forced herself to sit down and take a look at her situation. She didn't own property or blue-chip stocks. Their investments were in Griffin's name. All she owned were the clothes in her closet and the jewelry he'd given to her during their marriage. Emerald and ruby bracelets. Sapphire rings. A treasure chest of diamonds and gold. Oh, yes—Griffin was a generous man who bought only the best. An establishment like Sotheby's in New York would pay good money for her jewelry. Enough to give her a start at building a life away from Griffin and Claire and their child. She could buy herself a little house somewhere, a house that would belong to her alone. A home that nobody could ever take away from her.

She'd pushed away the thought, feeling guilty, although she didn't quite know why. Griffin and Claire were the guilty ones, weren't they?

She dozed for a while, curled in the corner of the sofa, until she was awakened by the sound of a key scratching in the front door lock.

"Griffin?" She sat up and pushed her hair off her face. "Is that you?"

His lean silhouette filled the archway. He was still wearing his camel's hair coat. The unexpected stench of whiskey surrounded him like a humid cloud. A series of alarms went off inside her skull.

"Where have you been?" she asked, rising to her feet as he crossed the room toward her. "I—"

The first blow caught her off guard. Her head snapped back, and she fell against the arm of the sofa, more stunned than hurt.

"What—"

The second blow landed against her jaw. She tumbled backward, striking her hip against the desk chair as she crashed to the floor. Ferocious waves of pain tore across her jaw and down her right leg. She scrambled to her knees and tried to dodge the next blow, but he trapped her between the desk and the sofa, then pinned her with his body. She could smell the rug freshener the maid used when she vacuumed, a powdery smell that made her want to vomit.

"Griffin, please . . ." She bucked sharply, trying to knock him off, but she couldn't topple him.

He gripped her shoulders, fingers digging into her flesh as he clung to her. "Jesus," he said, his voice harsh and raw. "Jesus . . ." He started sobbing, ugly tearing sobs that sounded almost like screams.

Sweat broke out under her arms. "What's wrong, Griffin?" She struggled to gentle him with her voice. In all the years she'd known him, she'd never seen her husband lose control, and the sight of his face twisted with emotion was shocking. "Talk to me, please."

The high shriek of ripping silk filled the air as he tore the front of her dress from neckline to hem.

"No!" She swung at him with her fists, but he didn't seem to notice. He was looking past her, through her, those drowning eyes of his fixed on something only he could see. Her dress was bunched over her hips and he shoved her legs apart with his knee. "You don't want to do this, Griffin. Tell me what's wrong. I can help you. I can—"

She heard the scratchy rasp of his zipper, and her body jerked with raw terror. Tears poured down his cheeks, dropping to the bare skin of her breasts. His anguish dwarfed everything but her fear as he fumbled between her legs.

"You don't know . . ." he mumbled, his voice thick with pain and booze, ". . . shouldn't happen . . . never happen . . ."

"Not like this, Griffin," she pleaded, desperate to make him stop before it was too late for them both. "We have a wonderful bed . . . we can—"

"My son," he cried out as he drove into her tight, dry body. "My son is dead."

GRIFFIN LAY DEEPLY ASLEEP ON the floor near the sofa. He was still wearing his topcoat, but his trousers were pulled down and twisted around his knees. Alexandra stood over him in the first light of morning as a strange sense of relief washed over her. No more hesitation. No more guilt. For the first time in weeks, she understood exactly what she had to do.

Her bags were packed and in the hall. The sides of her Coach tote bag bulged with her jewelry. The car and driver would be there any minute to take her to Gatwick, and by this time tomorrow she would be back in the States ready to start a new life.

Funny how the thought no longer scared her. A thousand other emotions battled inside her, but fear wasn't one of them anymore. She mourned the baby who had been born too soon. She even felt compassion for Claire. But when she looked at her husband she felt nothing at all. There had been hope for them right up until the last moment. If he'd turned to her for comfort, she would have offered it gladly. She would have opened her heart to him one more time and tried to find a way to make their marriage work.

She touched her chin gingerly, wincing at the pain. She'd done her best to cover up the blossoming bruise, but there was nothing she could do to disguise the swelling. In a way she was glad. Any time she lost her nerve and wondered if she'd done the right thing, all she had to do was look in the mirror.

In a strange way Griffin had given her a gift last night. He'd given her back her future, and she wasn't going to waste another second of it.

The doorbell rang. "Your car is here, Mrs. Whittaker. Anthony will fetch your luggage."

She pressed the intercom. "Thank you, Michael."

Griffin stirred slightly, but he didn't wake up. She slipped off her wedding ring and placed it on the end table near the phone. Her finger looked strange without the ring, but she would get used to it, the same way she had gotten used to sleeping alone.

She gathered up her things, walked out the door, and didn't look back.

TWO

❦

Sea Gate, New Jersey

The first time John Patrick Gallagher's old man disappeared, he only made it as far as the intersection of Spring Street and Soundview. Mrs. Mangano, who lived in the corner house with the view of the water, found him sitting on her back porch eating a bagel and waiting for dawn. She gave him a cup of coffee, then called John.

"Take a load off," Eddie had said when his son got there, patting the seat next to him as first light gilded the ocean. "It doesn't get much better than this."

John didn't think too much about it that time around. Eddie had spent all of his life in fishing boats, watching the sun rise over the Atlantic, and after sixty-eight years it was a tough habit to break. He'd lost his driver's license last summer after an unfortunate run-in with an Atlantic City–bound stretch limo, and everyone in Sea Gate had gotten used to seeing Eddie walking around town at all hours of the day.

Eddie showed up two more times at Mrs. Mangano's house that month, and once he almost made it to the highway before Dan Corelli, one of the local cops, offered him a ride home.

"He's sleepwalking," Dr. Benino said, scribbling a prescription. "Lock the doors and don't worry about him. Sooner or later it'll stop."

John locked the doors and continued to worry. Eddie strayed a few more times, then stopped, but just as John started to believe the problem was over, his old man took off again the Tuesday before Thanksgiving.

He woke up in the gray early-morning light to find Bailey, his huge sweet-faced mutt, pushing against his hand with a cold wet nose.

"Can't it wait?" he muttered. "Ten minutes more, Bailey, and we'll—" Bailey whimpered insistently, and John came awake. "Something wrong, girl?"

She trotted toward his bedroom door, her tail at half-mast, and whimpered again. John threw back the covers, then swung his legs out of bed. He grabbed his jeans from the floor, yanked them on, and pulled a fisherman's sweater over his head. The only times he'd ever heard Bailey whimper were when his father disappeared on one of his nocturnal rambles.

"Shit," he mumbled as he shoved his feet into a pair of Nikes. The front door was wide open. Dead leaves tumbled across the living-room floor and came to rest in front of the television. He scratched Bailey behind the ear. "You stay here, girl. One of us might as well get some sleep."

He wondered if this was how his old man had felt twenty years ago. How many times had Eddie turned up in some rathole of a bar down the Jersey Shore to drag John home by the ear? Turnabout was fair play. It was John's turn to track down his father and return the favor.

He pretty much had it down to a science at this point. He didn't bother with the car. Sea Gate was small enough that he could cover it on foot and never break a sweat. A cold gray rain was falling, and the wind was beginning to pick up off the ocean. It didn't take a degree in meteorology to know some major weather was on its way. He turned left at the corner onto Mullica Drive, then headed toward the center of town. He used to take this route to school, down Mullica, across Ocean, then down to Soundview. He knew every shortcut, every dead end, every hiding place, and so did his old man.

Connie Mangano's house was dark and quiet. There was no sign of Eddie at the park or the beach or the ball field, so he headed for the marina.

Gallagher's Marina was an institution in Sea Gate. His parents had bought it the year before John was born, and Rosie Kelly Gallagher went into labor at the big desk to the right of the office door. Rosie ran the marina while Eddie fished the Atlantic. She managed to give preference to townies and fishermen who made their living on the sea without ever once taking advantage of the weekenders whose money kept the whole enterprise afloat. They should have known it was too good to last. Rosie died, the nor'easter came, and the town began its downhill slide. After a while Eddie quit going out in his fishing boat and for the most part avoided the marina and its memories—yet that was where John found him that morning, sitting at the end of the dock with his bare feet and legs dangling into the Atlantic Ocean.

It was so damn cold John could smell the ice forming on the water, but his old man didn't seem to notice. Weather had never mattered much to his father except when he was taking the boat out into the ocean. Eddie wore a faded pair of blue flannel pajamas Rosie had given to him twenty years ago and a shapeless old fishing hat with a fly lure pinned to the dent in the top. A copy of the *Newark Star-Ledger* was spread out on the dock next to him, and it looked to John as if his father had peeled shrimp on top of Doonesbury.

Eddie was leaning forward, elbows on his knees, looking out to sea the way he used to when he piloted the *Kestrel*, as if the secret to life was just beyond the horizon.

"I can't give you much," he used to tell his sons when they worked on the boat with him during school vacations, "but there ain't much better than what I *can* give."

It had taken John almost thirty-five years to understand what he meant.

A cluster of Canada geese bobbed in the gray and choppy sea. Whitecaps crashed against the stretch of beach that curved to the east of where they sat. The only sound was the cry of a gull circling overhead.

"Pop?" He placed a hand on Eddie's shoulder. "It's freezing out here. Let's go down to the Starlight and grab some breakfast." The Starlight was the local diner, the place where everyone gathered to drink Dee's coffee and shoot the breeze.

"Hey, Johnny boy." Eddie motioned for his son to sit down. "Hendrickson took his boat out this morning." He shook his head and chuckled. "Fat lot of good it'll do him, going out so late in this weather. You'd think he'd know better, wouldn't you?"

"Hendrickson?" John crouched down next to his father and peered out at the angry gray ocean. "You sure you mean Hendrickson?" Frank Hendrickson had been dead at least half a dozen years. Eddie had been pall-bearer at his funeral.

"Who else is gonna go out in *Lucky Lady*? Sure it's Frank, and no other."

There wasn't a single boat out on the water, and with

good reason. Only a fool would venture out with a storm ready to slam into town.

"I don't see him, Pop."

"Damn right you don't. Frank's halfway to Ambrose Light by now."

"So what are we doing here?" John asked with false good cheer. "I don't know about you, but I could use some coffee right about now."

"No use sitting here waiting for Frank," Eddie agreed. "He won't be back before nightfall."

John helped his father to his feet. He considered suggesting that Eddie stop by home and change into something besides his pajamas before they went to the diner, but it was early enough that Dee would be the only one around. And Dee was practically family. Hell, she would have been family if his brother Brian hadn't been too goddamn stupid to recognize a good woman when he found one.

"Will you look at this?" Eddie stopped in front of the slip where Dick Weaver's dory was moored.

John whistled low. "Someone must've taken an axe to it." The starboard side of the steel vessel had sustained a series of two-foot gashes and dents from stem to stern.

"Damn kids," Eddie muttered. "Too much time on their hands, if you ask me."

"I'm not so sure kids did this, Pop. It's been happening too often lately." He'd noticed that it was always fishing boats that were hit and never pleasure craft, but when he mentioned that to the sheriff last week, Mike hadn't thought much of his suspicions.

"One day I'll catch one of the little bastards redhanded," Mike had said around a big unlit cigar. "That'll put an end to this shit soon enough."

Truth was, Mike didn't much care what happened at the marina. Sea Gate's economy didn't revolve around the marina any longer—hell, most people said Sea Gate didn't even have an economy. Fifteen years ago Gallagher's had done turn-away business with everyone from locals who depended on the sea for their living, to weekenders in their plush cabin cruisers, to charter boats ferrying sportsmen out for some deep-sea fishing.

Bed-and-breakfast inns popped up on both sides of Ocean Avenue, and before long they were booked a year in advance. Travel guides lauded Sea Gate as a contender for the Cape May crowd, the perfect place for everyone from honeymooners to senior citizens. Far enough away from New York and Philadelphia to be quaint, yet close enough to Atlantic City to be glamorous, Sea Gate enjoyed a boom that even the most jaded townies believed would never end.

A monster nor'easter took care of that. A full moon, high tide, and fifty-mile-per-hour winds had destroyed the beach and most of the businesses. Now, almost eight years later, the town was still reeling from its effects. Half the shopkeepers had closed their doors permanently and moved to sunnier climes. One family after another said good-bye and followed the jobs to Somerset and Monmouth. Pollution took its toll on the fishing industry during the bleak summers of the late 1980s. The weekend crowd abandoned Sea Gate for Cape May, and sometimes John wondered if it would have been better if the damn storm had just leveled the town.

The weathered boards of the dock glistened with sea spray, making the surface slick as a skating rink. Eddie had a tough time keeping his footing. His bare feet shot out from under him, and twice John just managed to grab him before his butt hit the ground.

He yanked off his Nikes and pushed them toward his father. "Put these on," he said. "I don't feel like carting your sorry ass to the emergency room when you break your leg."

His father grumbled loudly, but he put on the shoes. "Where's the car?" he asked as they crossed the parking lot.

"Home."

"What the hell's it doing there?"

"It was easier to look for you on foot."

"Look for me?" Eddie sounded puzzled. "Why were you looking for me? I wasn't lost."

"You took off in your pajamas at four in the morning, Pop. What was I supposed to think?"

"A man's got the right to go wherever the hell he wants whenever he wants."

"Not in your pajamas," John said, trying to hang on to what remained of his self-control. "Next time you feel like going out, try getting dressed first."

Eddie made a gesture of disgust, then stalked off ahead of John. *What's wrong, Pop? What the hell's got you so bent out of shape?* Eddie's temper was erratic, his judgment dubious at best. The strong father figure of John's youth was being replaced by an increasingly frail old man, and it was all happening faster than it should.

Eddie kept up a brisk pace as they walked to the diner. John could have caught up with him in a few strides, but he hung back, letting his father lead the way. He wasn't much in the mood for conversation and he doubted if Eddie was either. He'd seen the look of fear in his father's eyes. Eddie suspected something was wrong, same as John, but both Gallagher men were pros when it came to avoiding the truth.

His old man had claimed a counter seat by the time John caught up with him. He refused to make eye contact with his son. The Gallagher men also knew how to hold a grudge.

Dee peeked out from the kitchen. Her long dark red hair was pulled back in a ponytail that was already beginning to droop. She didn't look old enough to be the mother of a seventeen-year-old boy. "You guys are early today. The grill's not even hot yet."

"You got coffee?" John asked as he sat down two stools away from his father.

"We've always got coffee," Dee said, looking from John to Eddie. Her eyes lingered on the pajamas. "Everything okay?"

Eddie cocked a thumb in John's direction. "He's a horse's ass."

"Tell me something I don't know." She disappeared into the kitchen to get their coffee.

"Now that," said Eddie, "is what we used to call a good woman." He sounded like his old opinionated self.

"You won't get an argument from me."

"Your damn stupid brother should've married her when he had the chance."

"No argument about that either." Except for the fact that Eddie was sitting there in his pajamas, it was your regular morning at the Starlight. The tight ball of tension inside his gut began to unravel. Maybe Dr. Benino was right, and this was all just some weird sleepwalking thing his father was going through. Scary as that might be, it wasn't half as scary as some of the alternatives John had been dwelling on lately.

"You ever think about maybe giving her a call?"

John shot his father a look. "Dee's a friend. You don't date friends."

"*You* don't date at all."

"Don't go there, Pop. It's none of your business."

"You can't mourn Libby and the kids forever, Johnny. Sooner or later you've got to get on with your life."

Wrong again, Pop. He could mourn forever. Libby and his sons had been everything to him, the reason he got up in the morning, the reason he had set out each day, looking to conquer the world. People said men didn't give a damn about family, that you could plug in a new wife and kid where the old wife and kid had been, and the bastards wouldn't know the difference, but they were wrong. Three years had passed, and the ache inside his heart was as strong as ever. He hoped it never left him, because that ache was all he had left of his family.

ALEXANDRA PULLED INTO THE DINER'S parking lot at 6:33 A.M. Except for a blue Chevy parked around back, there wasn't another car in sight. She angled to a stop in front of a line of newspaper vending machines and breathed a sigh of relief. She wasn't too late. The ''Help Wanted'' sign was still in the window. Now all she had to do was walk in there and convince the owner that she was the answer to the Starlight's prayers.

You can do it, she told herself. *Just walk up the steps, open the door, and make your case.* She'd made endless lists of why actual waitressing experience wasn't the most important qualification for the job. A few times she'd almost convinced herself that it might be a detriment. She had her arguments all worked out, and she'd even practiced confident smiles in her bathroom mirror.

She squared her shoulders, then started up the half-dozen stone steps to the front door. She was about to march inside when she noticed two men seated at the counter, and every ounce of Dutch courage she'd managed to muster up vanished. She turned and fled.

Maybe moving to Sea Gate hadn't been such a clever idea after all, she thought as she backed out of the lot and drove away as fast as her twenty-year-old VW wagon could manage. The car was the first thing she'd bought after coming back home to the States. The salesman had tried his best to steer her toward something with a little less mileage, but she'd stuck to her guns. The VW was battered and bruised, but it was a survivor. And, as she was discovering, so was she.

The day she left Griffin she'd headed straight for Gatwick, and ten hours later she was seated in the back of
a yellow cab while a hostile New York City taxi driver
explained how foreigners were ruining the country for
real Americans. When she'd explained that she wasn't
English but a native New Yorker herself, he'd shifted
the direction of his venom to encompass liberal lawyers,
Supreme Court judges, and O. J. Simpson.

For one terrible moment she'd wondered if she'd
made the worst mistake of her life, but then she caught
sight of her bruised and swollen face in the rearview
mirror, and her backbone stiffened with resolve. If she
was going to make a success of her new life, she would
have to learn how to cope, and that was as good a time
as any to start.

From there on, it was as if a guardian angel guided
her every move. She found a clean room in a mid-priced
hotel on the West Side, then set out for Sotheby's. Three
days later she had managed to sell all of her jewelry,
save for one diamond bracelet and matching earrings
that she withheld as a savings account against the prob-
able tough times ahead.

The only thing she was sure of was that she wanted
a home she could call her own—four walls and a roof
that nobody could take away from her, no matter what
life had in store. She had no intention of staying in New
York City; the cost of living was exorbitant, and it
would be the first place Griffin looked for her. Assuming
he looked for her at all, which was doubtful.

She went to a huge bookstore near Columbus Circle
and gathered up as many out-of-state newspapers as she
could find, then sat down with a cup of good old American coffee and began studying the real estate ads. A
giddy sense of excitement had filled her as she considered the merits of Iowa versus Oregon, South Carolina

versus Maine. The more she read, the more confused she got. Places that had been nothing more than names on a map suddenly became real as she closed her eyes and tried to imagine living her life in Albuquerque or Atlanta, El Cajon or Effingham.

She wanted to live by the water, so that eliminated the Midwest. She loved each of the four seasons, so that eliminated the South and California. Deserts did nothing for her, which meant the Southwest wasn't a good bet. That left the Northeast. She flipped open a copy of the *Star Ledger* to the real estate section. People snickered about New Jersey, but one of her few happy memories of her parents had to do with the much-maligned Garden State.

Her father had rented himself a yacht the summer she turned sixteen. He'd decided they would sail from Maine down to the Chesapeake Bay, stopping wherever they felt like stopping, staying however long they felt like staying. Of course, Dan Curry had used the vacation trip more as a way to do business with the yacht-and-country-club types than to spend time with his daughter, but Alex remembered it as a golden time. A time when she'd felt part of a family, not an encumbrance to be packed off to boarding school.

In early August, sailing up from the Chesapeake, her father had run into problems with the boat, and he docked at a marina on the Jersey Shore for repairs. They stayed in a tiny B&B on Ocean Avenue. Alex pretended they lived there, that those streets were her streets, that the teenagers scarfing pizza at Lou's Subs were her friends.

She ran her index finger down the listing of houses for sale in New Jersey, looking for the name of the town she remembered. Beach Haven. Brigantine. Sea Bright. Sea Gate. Sea Girt—wait a minute. *Sea Gate*.

NEW LISTING!
COTTAGE FOR SALE. FOUR ROOMS. AS IS CONDITION.
FULLY FURNISHED. 1/4 ACRE.

Best of all, she could afford it. She drove down the
Shore the next day, looked at the cottage, and fell in
love. Five weeks after she left her husband's house for
the last time, she moved into a home of her own.

She had done all of that with no help from anybody.
She'd found strength when she needed it and taken control of her life. So what was she doing now, running
away from the diner like some kind of coward? Great
waitress she'd make—put a customer in the place, and
she fell apart. The second she saw the two men sitting
at the counter, her knees had begun to knock and her
resolve vanished.

She'd noticed the "Help Wanted" sign in the window
yesterday when she stopped at the grocery store for supplies. It was the only "Help Wanted" sign in a town
littered with "Going Out of Business" and "For Sale"
notices. She remembered Sea Gate as a quaint seaside
village where working fishermen added a Springsteen-
esque atmosphere to a postcard-pretty place. Of course,
she'd been sixteen then, a sheltered sixteen easily impressed by the sight of broad-shouldered young men
working shirtless on the dock.

She wasn't sixteen anymore, and Sea Gate was no
longer quaint, both of which suited her fine. The town's
bad luck had been her good fortune. Sagging property
values had made it possible for her to buy the Winslow
house with cash. No matter what happened, the house
belonged to her.

My house. The words sent a thrill of excitement up
her spine. *My home.*

She parked around the corner from the diner and
drummed the steering wheel with her thumbs. Light rain

splashed against the windows and danced across the hood. She debated turning off her windshield wipers but she wasn't entirely convinced she'd be able to turn them back on if she did. The VW had more than its share of quirks, but that was okay. She'd learn how to deal with them, same as she'd learned how to deal with everything else. It seemed as if she'd done one impossible thing after another in the past month—asking for a job should be a piece of cake.

Besides, it wasn't as if she had a choice in the matter. Last night she'd sat down at the kitchen table and taken a good look at her finances. She'd prepaid a year's worth of property taxes, but there were utility bills to worry about and food and gas and God knows what else. She had one thousand eight hundred seventy-three dollars and sixty-seven cents, a pair of diamond earrings, and a platinum-and-diamond bracelet that would have to last the rest of her life unless she found a source of income fast.

She took a deep breath, then looked at her reflection in the rearview mirror. Maybe there had been something to all of those ridiculous lessons in charm and deportment they'd foisted on her at boarding school. Her expression was cool and untroubled, her brow unfurrowed by lines of worry or stress. Her panic didn't show.

Now, if she could just figure out what to say. "Hi. I'm Alexandra Curry. I'm here about the job." *Too boring.* "Hi, I'm Alex. Your search is over." *Too obnoxious.* "I'm Alex Curry and I've never worked a day in my life." *Too honest.* The truth made her sound like a twenty-eight-year-old deadbeat. Other women her age had degrees from fancy universities and resumes they could be proud of. Alex had an indentation where her wedding ring used to be and the determination that she would never depend on anyone else again as long as she lived.

• • •

"HEY, MURRAY!" JOHN BELLOWED. "WHERE'S the damn coffee?"

The swinging door opened, and Dee appeared, carrying two outsized white cups and a plate of toasted bagels. She deposited everything on the counter in front of John and Eddie, then fixed them with a look. "So how do you want your eggs?"

"Over easy," said Eddie.

"In the shell," said John. "I don't want eggs."

"No eggs?" Dee asked.

"No eggs."

"You've got to eat," she observed, her brown eyes soft with affection. "How about a short stack?"

His stomach growled in response. "You convinced me."

"Hate to tell you this, Johnny, but you're easy."

Eddie snorted with laughter as Dee hustled back into the kitchen to relay the order to Will, the Starlight's cook. A blast of cold air accompanied the squeak of the front door as Dave O'Hurley and Rich Ippolito stepped inside.

"Gonna be a cold mother of a winter," Dave said, brushing droplets of rain from his graying hair. "If it's this cold before Thanksgiving, what the hell is it gonna be by Christmas?"

"You worry too much," Rich said, hanging his plaid lumber jacket on a hook by the door. "Save your worrying for something you can change."

The two old-timers bickered their way over to the counter, where Eddie joined the fray. John hunkered down over his cup of coffee and let the conversation ebb and flow around him as the other regulars began to file in. Marty Crosswell, Vince Troisi, Jake Amundson, Sally Whitton—it seemed as though half the population of Sea Gate had crowded into the Starlight by the time John's short stack of pancakes was ready.

"You need help," Vince said as Dee took their orders. "When's Nick gonna spring for another waitress? That sign's been in the window so long I started to think the name of the place was 'Help Wanted.' "

"Don't look at me," Sally, owner of the local bait shop, said. "I like my worms on a hook, not trying to wiggle out of leaving a tip."

The diner erupted in raucous laughter.

"Anyone tried that, you'd tackle him before he made it to the door," Jake Amundson said.

"Damn right I would," said Sally, "and don't any of you deadbeats forget it." The fact that Sally was eighty-five if she was a day didn't fool anyone. She was as tough as they came and twice as feisty.

Eddie looked up from his eggs. "That sign's been in the window since the Fourth of July. If you ask me, people today are scared shitless of real work."

"Damn straight," said Vince, nodding his head. "Rather sit on their fat asses and let the government work for them."

"Big talkers," Dee said, wiping down the counter in front of John. "Why don't one of you hotshots apply for the job? You're here all day anyway. Might as well get paid for it."

"Don't want to work as hard as you do, Dee Dee." Eddie's voice was warm with affection. "We'd rather sit here and watch you do it."

"What's so hard about coffee and eggs?" Vince asked. "Now, when I was on the docks, we . . ."

Vince was off and running. It was familiar territory and good for at least twenty minutes. John hunkered down lower over his pancakes. Let the old guys reminisce about sixty-hour workweeks and unions more powerful than God—he'd rather listen to them debate the job situation than his lack of a social life any day.

He polished off his stack and was draining his third cup of coffee when Sally dropped the bombshell. "Did you hear the news? Somebody bought the Winslow place."

"That dump?" Jake tilted the sugar canister over his coffee cup. "I didn't know Marge's kids had put it up for sale."

"Some woman saw an ad in the *Star-Ledger* the first day they ran the listing and bought it, cash price."

"Cash price?" John looked up from the remains of his pancakes. "Who the hell pays cash for a house?"

"Nobody from around here, that's for damn sure." Eddie motioned for a refill on his coffee.

"Carol at Gold Key Realty says she's foreign," Sally informed them.

"Who's foreign?" Dee asked.

"The woman who bought the Winslow place."

Dee's mouth opened. "Somebody bought the Winslow place? I didn't even know it was on the market."

"Carol says she's English," Sally continued, "but nobody knows for sure."

"Right," John said, draining his cup of coffee. "She's probably Princess Di looking for a place to hide out from the paparazzi."

"English people like the ocean," Vince said.

"English people like Florida," Marty said, shaking his head in disgust. "Not New Jersey."

"What the hell's wrong with New Jersey?" Vince's voice rose in irritation.

"Nothing's wrong with New Jersey," Marty shot back, "but you're not gonna bump into Princess Di on the Turnpike."

Dee leaned against the counter. "So when does she move in?"

"She did already," Sally said, obviously enjoying her

moment in the spotlight. "Frank the mailman saw her standing in the doorway yesterday afternoon."

"Gotta admit it was a good buy," Eddie said. "If I had any dough, I would've bought it myself."

"The place is a termite trap," John said bluntly. "The Winslows didn't give a damn if it collapsed on poor old Marge."

"They fixed it up," Dee said. "My brother Charlie worked on the renovation."

"They fixed it up after Marge died." John wasn't about to back down on this. "And only enough so they could sell it. The roof's ready to cave."

"So what's it to you?" Dee asked, her tone huffy. "I never saw you offering poor old Marge any free legal advice."

He met her eyes. "I'm not a lawyer anymore, Dee."

She started to say something, then turned away. There was a lifetime of history between them, and he didn't have to hear the words to know what they were. A long time ago Dee had wanted to go to law school, too, but a teenage pregnancy and bad marriage had derailed those early dreams. The fact that John had tossed away his own career was something she'd never understand. Hell, why should Dee be any different? Everyone in town thought he was certifiable, and maybe they were right. You did what you had to do to survive, even if there were times when you didn't know why.

"I don't know about the rest of you," Sally said, "but you wouldn't catch me living alone down by the marina. Not with all that vandalism going on."

"Any woman who'd pay cash for the Winslow place isn't about to be scared away by some rowdy kids," Jake pointed out. "She's probably tough as nails."

"A real Tugboat Annie," Rich agreed, laughing. "Could probably arm wrestle the lot of us to the ground without even trying."

"You're all terrible," Dee said, barely restraining her own laughter. "You haven't even met the poor woman yet."

"I know the type," Rich said, "and you can keep her."

"I thought we were dealing with another Princess Di," John said. "Now we're talking about Tugboat Annie."

Jake nudged Eddie in the ribs. "Maybe she'll be your dream girl."

"You talk too damn much," Eddie said good-naturedly. "Maybe—" He stopped dead, staring over Jake's shoulder toward the front door.

John swiveled around to have a look. A woman stood near the cash register. She wore a long black raincoat that brushed against the hem of her jeans. Her honey-colored hair was pulled back severely from a face devoid of makeup. She didn't need any. She was easily the best-looking woman to cross the Starlight's threshold in at least a dozen years.

Good bones, he thought. He'd never given the matter much thought until now. Maybe there was something to the concept.

"I don't believe it," Dee muttered. "She's waiting to be seated. You'd think this was a restaurant or something." She raised her voice. "Sit anywhere, honey. I'll be there in a sec."

"Take it easy on her, Dee. I don't think she's going to be a regular around here." It was obvious the woman by the cash register was passing through on her way to somewhere else. She had an air of money and breeding about her, two things that were in short supply in Sea Gate.

Dee made a face at him, then glanced toward the register again. "Oh, great," she mumbled. "Now she's coming this way. What did I do to deserve this?"

A hush fell over the counter as the old men and Sally turned to watch.

"Wow," Rich said under his breath.

"Hubba hubba." Jake sounded downright reverent.

Eddie just stared.

It was her walk that got to John. She walked like a goddess. He could feel her rhythm in his bones.

Dee gestured toward an empty stool at the far end of the counter. "Coffee?"

The goddess smiled. "Coffee would be lovely," she said, "but what I'd really like is a job."

THREE

"THAT'S A GOOD ONE." THE woman behind the counter broke into a grin. She smelled faintly like Maxwell House and Shalimar, Alex thought; an intriguing combination. "Take a seat. I'll pour you a cup of coffee while you read the menu."

Alex wanted to pull her raincoat over her head and disappear. *You can't run away, Alex. You need the money.* She straightened her spine and summoned up a phony but confident smile.

"Has the position been filled?" she asked.

"You want to wait tables?" The waitress made it sound as if Alex had announced a hostile takeover of the diner.

The room was so quiet she was sure they could all hear her heart pounding. "That's the position being offered, isn't it?"

" 'Position'? I'm not even sure it's a job."

"Lighten up, Dee." The man in the fisherman's sweater looked up from his cup of coffee. "You've been waiting six months for someone to walk through that door and ask for the job. At least give her a chance.''

Alex met his eyes. They were dark blue with thick straight lashes. His chestnut brown hair was in need of a trim, and a night's growth of beard shadowed his strong jaw. His fisherman's sweater had obviously seen better days, as had his sweatpants. To her surprise, his feet were bare. They were strong feet, long and tanned despite the fact that it was November. She felt a flutter of recognition in the pit of her stomach, but that was utterly ridiculous. She'd never known his type of man in her entire life. They didn't exist in her old world. ''Thank you very much.''

He inclined his head. ''No problem.''

''Don't say I didn't warn you,'' the waitress named Dee said. ''Leave your phone number, and I'll give it to the owner.''

Alex's cheeks reddened. ''Actually, I don't have a phone yet.''

''You don't have a phone?'' the man in blue pajamas and running shoes piped up. ''Everybody has a phone.''

''I just moved into my house yesterday,'' she said, wondering why nobody else seemed to notice his strange garb. ''The phone company won't get to me until this afternoon.''

The man in the fisherman's sweater started to laugh. ''You bought Marge Winslow's house.''

''Yes, I did,'' she said, lifting her chin. ''Do you have a problem with that?''

''Hell, no,'' he said, ''but you might the next time it rains.''

''Meaning what?''

''You need a new roof,'' he said. ''The one you've got won't make it through the winter.''

''The real estate agent said the roof was new.''

''Compared to the house it is. It's a matter of perspective.''

"You have a very peculiar sense of humor," she observed. "I wouldn't laugh if your roof—"

"Are you from England?"

The quavery female voice brought her up short, and she turned to the woman with the missing bridgework. "What?"

"You sound foreign," the woman said, studying her with the same blatant curiosity that Alex saw on every other face in the diner.

"I've lived abroad." A careful answer designed to keep her secrets. She'd always been a sponge for accents. In another few months she would sound as if she'd been born and bred on the Jersey Shore.

"I hear they have real bad toilet paper over there," the woman said.

Alex grinned despite herself. "It's dreadful."

"I'm Sally Whitton, Whitton's Bait & Tackle."

"Alex Curry." She paused a beat. "The Winslow house."

In short order she was introduced to the men seated at the counter. Rich. Jake. Two Pauls. Dave. Eddie of the blue pajamas. They were all in their middle to late sixties except the one at the end in the fisherman's sweater. His name was John, and he had the saddest, most beautiful eyes she'd ever seen.

"Are you and Eddie related?" she asked as normal conversation finally resumed around her.

"The Gallagher gave it away, did it?"

"And the fact that you look a great deal like him." The older man must have been as ruggedly handsome in his day as his son was now.

"He's my father."

"Ah." Her attention strayed toward the older man.

John Gallagher followed her gaze. "You're wondering about the pajamas."

"I am curious," she admitted.

"He sleepwalks."

"That would explain it."

"You'll be seeing a lot of Eddie if you get the job."

"I'll make sure to keep his coffee cup filled." Would she be seeing a lot of his son as well? There was something slightly unsettling about him, although she couldn't pinpoint exactly what it was. She turned to Dee. "I'll call you this afternoon with my phone number."

"I'm not making any promises," Dee said, not unkindly. "My boss is the cheapest man in town. He might decide to keep me lashed to the mast alone a few months longer."

John shot Dee a look. The woman didn't seem to notice, but Alex did, and wondered if it was a signal she should get out of there before they started asking about her job experience.

"Well," she said, beginning to inch her way toward the door, "thanks very much."

"Stay," Dee said. "Have some coffee. The breakfast rush is just about over. If you can wait a little while, we'll talk."

"No!"

Dee's eyebrows shot toward the ceiling. "No?"

Oh, God, she was making a terrible mess of things. "I mean, that's a wonderful idea, but I must run. I have a million errands . . . you know, moving in and all . . ."

"It's not even seven in the morning," Dee said, obviously puzzled by her explosive reaction. "Believe me, the diner's the only place open at this hour. Why don't you—"

"She has things to do, Dee," John Gallagher broke in. He met Alex's eyes. "Next thing you know, she'll be putting up a fence to keep the paying customers inside."

"Don't give me any ideas," Dee muttered, swatting him with a dish towel. "Call me this afternoon," she said to Alex. "Maybe I'll have an answer for you."

Alex didn't need a crystal ball to know what that answer would be.

DEE WAITED UNTIL THE DOOR closed behind the woman, then motioned for John to join her in the kitchen.

"Way to go, Johnny!" Sally waggled her painted-on eyebrows. "It's about time you and Dee got cozy."

"That's what I've been telling him," Eddie said with a loud sigh. "One of the Gallaghers has to snap her up."

John ignored the lighthearted banter as he pushed open the swinging door and stepped into the kitchen. Will, the cook, was smoking a cigarette on the back step.

"So what do you think?" Dee asked as she poured herself a glass of orange juice. "Do we hire her to wait tables or call *Vogue*?"

"You were a little rough on her out there," he said, grabbing a glass of juice for himself. "Her hands were shaking."

"Did you see those hands?" Dee countered, glancing at her own hands with obvious dismay. "I don't think they've done much more than arrange flowers."

He'd noticed. Hell, he'd noticed just about everything about Alex Curry, from her thick mane of dark blond hair to the perfectly polished loafers on her narrow feet. She belonged at the Starlight about as much as he belonged at Buckingham Palace.

He leaned against the sink and polished off his juice. "So she probably doesn't know from manual labor. Do you want to hire her or not?"

"You're the boss," she said. "You tell me."

"Keep it down, will you?" He gestured toward Will on the back porch. "Nobody else needs to know." Nick, the former owner, had skipped town two months ago, leaving a paper trail of unpaid bills that shocked even his accountant. His customers thought he was visiting relatives in Greece, but the truth was he'd vanished into the ether and wasn't coming back. The bank had wanted to foreclose on the diner, but John stepped in and took over the payments, with the proviso that his intercession be kept between him and the bank. Too many people depended on the Starlight Diner to let it go down without a fight.

Dee hopped up on the counter opposite John. "I don't think she knows the first thing about waiting tables."

"Yeah," he said slowly, "you're probably right."

She inclined her head toward the front of the diner. "Did you see the way the old guys looked at her? I'll be mopping up drool marks if she comes on board."

"Could get messy," he agreed.

"It'll probably take me weeks to get her up to speed. I'll be working twice as hard."

"Which is the last thing you need."

Her brown eyes flashed. "Damn right it's the last thing I need."

"So you don't want to hire her."

"I didn't say that."

"So what are you saying?"

"Hire her." She tossed a plastic tub of maple syrup at him. "You've always been a sucker for a hard-luck story."

"Who says she's a hard-luck story?"

Dee's familiar glower melted into a grin. "She wants to work here, doesn't she?"

"THAT'S IT." THE TELEPHONE INSTALLER crawled out from behind the sofa and slapped dust off his knees. He handed Alex a sheet of paper. "Your phone number is on there."

Alex started to laugh as she read off the ten digits.

"This is wonderful!" she said, unable to contain her excitement. "Thank you, thank you!"

"Hey, it's only a phone number, lady. No big deal."

Maybe it wasn't a big deal to him, she thought as she locked the door, but it was a *huge* deal to her. A house, a car, and a telephone. Now all she needed was a job and she might be able to hang on to them. *So what are you waiting for? Call the diner and give them your number.*

She flipped through the crisp new phone book until she found a listing for the Starlight Diner, then quickly dialed before she lost her nerve.

"Starlight, Dee speaking."

"Hello, th—this is Alex Curry. I came in this morning and spoke to you about—"

"The job," Dee interrupted. "I remember."

Alex's knees were knocking, and she sat down on the arm of the sofa. "I—um, I said I'd call you with my new phone number and—"

"You've got the job."

Alex slipped off the arm and landed on the end sofa cushion. She must be dreaming.

"Are you still there?" Dee asked.

"Did you say I've got the job?"

"That's what I said."

"Oh, my God."

"You've changed your mind?"

"No!" She sat up straight, as if phone posture counted. "Absolutely not! I'm thrilled." Not to mention shocked.

"So when do you want to start?"

"I can be there in ten minutes."

Dee started to laugh. "Honey, talk to me again this time next year. I was thinking more like Monday."

"Monday?" Alex couldn't hide her disappointment.

"It's Thanksgiving week," Dee said. "We'll be

closed Thursday, and things are usually pretty light over the holiday weekend.''

Monday. Alex suppressed a sigh. "What time?"

"We open at seven, but I try to get there by six or six-fifteen.''

"I'll be there at six.''

"Why is it I have the feeling you've never waited tables before?''

Alex's heart dropped to her feet. "Is that a rhetorical question?''

"No,'' Dee said after a moment. "Actually I wouldn't mind an answer.''

"I've never waited tables before.''

"I was afraid of that.''

"I wouldn't blame you if you change your mind about hiring me.''

"I wouldn't blame me either,'' Dee said, "but I have the feeling you need us as much as we need you.''

"So I still have the job?''

"You still have the job.''

"You won't regret this,'' Alex promised as she danced around the room. "I'll be the best waitress you ever saw.''

"Just show up on time,'' Dee said. "I'll take it from there.''

THE PHONE BLASTED JOHN AWAKE at 4:14 on Thanksgiving morning. The green numbers glared at him from his digital clock as he fumbled around on the nightstand for the receiver. Not even dawn yet, and already the day sucked for air.

"Is this John Gallagher?'' A woman's voice. That got his attention. Even his sleep-fogged brain recognized it as a damn fine woman's voice. Vaguely familiar. Definitely not a hometown voice.

"Who is this?''

"I'm looking for John Gallagher," she repeated. "If this isn't his number, I—"

"This is John Gallagher."

"Your father is here with me."

"Who the hell is this?"

"Alex," she said. "Alex Curry."

The goddess. He woke up the rest of the way. The goddess was calling him? "He can't be there. My old man's sound asleep."

"Yes, he is," she agreed. "In *my* living room."

He groaned and dragged a hand through his tangled hair. Twice in two days. What the hell was going on?

"I found him on my front porch in his pajamas," she went on. "I think he was sleepwalking and stopped here."

"You're the Winslow house, right?"

Her laugh was soft, infinitely enticing. "I'd rather think of it as the *Curry* house now."

"Whatever you do, don't let him leave," he said, reaching for the jeans he'd left draped over the closet door. "I'll be there in five minutes."

FIVE MINUTES? ALEX'S STOMACH DID a back flip. She'd found John Gallagher unsettling enough at the diner. The thought of him in her living room almost made her wish she'd left Eddie out there on the front porch. She wasn't afraid of John Gallagher—he was just so overwhelmingly male that he made her aware of herself as a woman in a way she hadn't been for a long time.

"Idiot," she murmured as she hung up the phone. He hadn't even come close to flirting with her the other day. All he'd done was tell her that her roof leaked. Still, that brief exchange had been enough to remind her how it was between men and women, that unspoken acknow-

ledgment that yes, the sexes were different, and thank
God for it.

She filled the teakettle with tap water, then set it on
the stove. The burner clicked twice but refused to light.
She waved her hand briskly to dissipate the smell of gas,
then lit a fat kitchen match and held it near the jet. The
flame was unenthusiastic but viable, and she congratulated herself on another domestic victory.

She'd bought the house in "as is" condition, with all
of the furniture and household goods included. Some of
the appliances had seen better days, but they still
worked, and that was all that was important. She was
also the proud owner of a Formica kitchen table with
four chairs, each of which was covered in a different
shade of Day-Glo vinyl fabric, a sofa and matching chair
that had been past its prime when *I Love Lucy* was cut-
ting-edge television, a dark pine coffee table, two standing lamps with built-in mosaic tile ashtrays, and an oak
bedroom suite that she'd actually grown quite fond of.
The kitchen boasted a double sink, a window that over-
looked the backyard, and everything she could possibly
need in the way of chipped dishes and well-worn pots
and pans.

And it was all hers. Every rusty nail, warped floor-
board, leaky ceiling. If John Gallagher didn't show up,
then she'd claim the old pajama-clad man asleep in front
of her television, too.

Outside the wind picked up and rattled the windows
in their frames. The sound was eerie, like keening almost. In her old life, she'd been insulated—both from
the weather and from sounds like rattling windows and
creaking floors. She didn't want to be insulated any
longer. She wanted to feel the rain on her face, taste the
tang of sea air on her tongue, fall asleep to the sound of
the ocean crashing against the marina.

A draft ruffled the back-door curtains and made the

flame under the teakettle waver, as if it were deciding whether or not to give up the ghost.

"Don't you dare," she warned the burner, shielding it from the breeze with her body. The poor man was half frozen out there. She'd covered him with a granny square afghan and a crazy quilt she'd found in the attic crawl space, but he needed to be warmed up from the inside out.

Besides, Eddie Gallagher was her first guest, and that alone was cause for celebration.

IT WAS GETTING SO JOHN could do it in his sleep. He yanked on his jeans and sweatshirt, then stumbled out of the house with Bailey hard on his heels. She was young and energetic, and sometimes her enthusiasm made him feel a hundred years old. A bitter blast of wind knocked him back, but it only invigorated Bailey. She let out a series of three quick barks, then pawed at the door of his truck, leaving muddy paw prints everywhere she touched.

The old-timers called this good sleeping weather, the kind of weather that made you burrow deeper under the covers and snuggle closer to the one you loved. It figured they'd like it; most of them still had someone to sleep with. Lately the only one willing to sleep with John was Bailey.

He wondered who Alex Curry spent her nights with. He'd noticed the white mark where a wedding ring used to be. Dee was convinced she was a divorcée on the run. "Prima facie evidence," she'd said about the missing ring. When John suggested she might have left her ring on the kitchen counter, Dee had told him that her cat Newt had a better romantic imagination than John had, and Newt had been fixed three years ago.

She was right. He had no romantic imagination. If he had he would be wondering about the sad look in Alex

Curry's eyes or the way she carried herself like a queen without a country. And he sure as hell would be wondering how it would be to wake up with a woman like that in his arms.

But Dee knew what she was talking about. His romantic imagination had died three years ago with Libby and the boys.

He turned the key in the ignition, but nothing happened. He tried again and was rewarded with an ominous grinding sound. "God damn it," he muttered. He thought about his brother Brian with the weekday Saab and weekend Porsche. The SOB probably hired someone to start them on winter mornings.

"Don't count on me to be there," Brian had said the last time they talked about Eddie. "I can't be running down the Shore every time he's got a problem. I've got a life, baby brother. You might want to try it sometime."

Tried it, John thought as the engine finally turned over. Tried it and ruined three lives.

EDDIE WOKE UP TO FIND a strange woman standing over him. She wore a floor-length white gown with lacy trim at the neck and sleeves, and her hair flowed over her shoulders and down her back like Rita Hayworth's did in *Gilda*. Okay, so Rita was a redhead, and this woman had hair the color of gold coins. Eddie never worried much about details. This woman was gorgeous same as Rita and she was smiling down at him like they were old friends.

He should be so lucky.

"Am I dead?" Eddie asked.

"Dead?" She started to laugh. "Why would you think that?"

"I don't wake up with angels very often."

She sat down on the arm of the sofa opposite him.

"Oh, I think you kissed the Blarney stone a time or two in your day, Mr. Gallagher."

She had a sense of humor, Eddie thought. That meant he probably wasn't dead. He'd never read anything about angels having a sense of humor.

She extended a white mug of something hot. "I thought you might like a cup of tea. I put milk and sugar in it. If you don't like it, I can make you a cup of coffee."

Eddie wrapped his fingers around the mug. His hands had been aching a lot lately, and the warmth felt good. "Much obliged, miss."

"Call me Alex," she said, sitting down on the sofa opposite him. "Alexandra, really, but I prefer Alex."

"Call me Eddie."

"Did you have a good nap?"

"Fair to middling," he said. "Sorry to barge in on you like this."

"You didn't barge in on me at all," she said, taking a sip of her own tea. "You were sitting on my front porch, and I came out and asked if you were cold."

"I was on your front porch?"

"That you were."

She didn't seem upset, and he supposed that was a good sign. How bad off could he be if a woman like this still smiled at him? He looked down to see what he was wearing. "Jesus, Mary, and Joseph," he muttered. "I'm in my damn pajamas." At least they were his good blue ones and not the red plaid with the frayed seams and missing button.

She patted his forearm, and the gentle gesture brought tears to his eyes. No one had touched him that way since his wife died, and he missed it. "I think you were sleep-walking."

He drew his fist across his eyes and hoped she didn't

notice. ''That's what Johnny and Doc Benino say, but I don't believe them.''

''Why don't you believe them?'' she asked. ''Your son wouldn't lie about something like that.''

What she said made sense, but there was a part of Eddie that couldn't let go of the suspicion that there was something else going on.

''This place looks familiar,'' he said, glancing around at the prints in their supermarket frames and the threadbare furniture.

''The Winslow house,'' she said, a wide smile spreading across her face. ''I moved in on Saturday.''

He jumped as a drop of rainwater landed in the middle of his bald spot. ''The Winslow house?'' He shook his head sadly. ''You got your work cut out for you.''

''I know,'' she said happily. ''Isn't it wonderful?''

Bits and pieces of conversation came back to him, but he couldn't quite grab hold of their meaning. ''How did you know Johnny was my son?'' Hell, how did she know his name was Gallagher? He didn't walk around with ID pinned to his pajamas, although if he kept on sleepwalking like this he might have to start.

''We met at the diner the other day, Mr. Gallagher.'' She paused for a moment. ''When I came in to apply for the waitress job.''

He forced a hearty laugh. ''Must be getting old,'' he said, smacking his head with the heel of his hand. ''Never used to forget meeting a pretty girl.''

''Don't worry about it,'' she said, smiling easily. ''I'm not all that memorable.''

And I'm not that old, he thought as he sipped the hot tea. Not old enough to explain what was happening to him.

LIGHTS BLAZED FROM EVERY WINDOW AT the Winslow place as John turned into the driveway. The wind-driven rain whipped the bare trees into grotesque shapes that made the bungalow look more like a miniature haunted house than usual. It didn't help that it was set off by itself at the end of the block, closer to the marina than to any of its neighbors. When he was a kid, he was convinced ghosts lived there with Marge, huge malevolent ghosts that gobbled up troublemaking little boys like popcorn.

John pulled into the dirt driveway behind a VW that looked more like a toasted marshmallow than a car. It had to be at least twenty years old. The car probably had more mileage on it than the space shuttle. Everything about Alex Curry screamed money and privilege, but here she was living in Marge Winslow's firetrap and driving a VW wagon a high school sophomore would sneer at.

Bailey yelped with excitement as John turned off the engine. "Sorry, girl," he said, scratching the dog under her chin. "You stay here." There was a limit to how many uninvited Gallaghers you could expect a woman to put up with.

He skidded his way across a path of wet leaves and mud to the front door. If the thermometer dipped any lower, the front yard would be a skating pond. Marge used to keep a sack of halite on her top step. He had the feeling Alex Curry didn't know about things like rock salt and calcium chloride. She'd better learn, he thought, or her homeowner's insurance would get a hell of a workout before the winter was over.

He rapped on the front door, but he knew they probably couldn't hear him over the blare of the television. Leave it to his old man to make himself at home. He rapped again, waited, then tried the doorknob. It was unlocked. Didn't she know that dead bolt was there for a reason? He pushed the door open and stepped across the threshold.

The sight in front of him was straight out of a Fellini movie. Alex Curry was standing on his old man's back like a performer in a circus act, a very weird circus act where the star performer wore a white nightgown instead of sequins and tights. She was doing something to the exposed ceiling beam with a flashlight and a bright blue plastic bucket.

He was about to ask what the hell was going on when he heard a noise behind him. Bailey bounded through the door and headed straight for Eddie.

"Bailey!" he roared, grabbing for the sixty-pound guided missile. "No!"

Too late. Bailey slammed into Eddie.

Eddie tipped over.

And Alex Curry came tumbling down.

FOUR

ALEX WASN'T SURE HOW HE managed it, but John Gallagher caught her just before she hit the ground. One second she was falling through the air and the next she was pressed up against his chest like a wet T-shirt.

His enormous hands gripped her by the hips, and she was acutely aware of the fact that her cotton nightgown was all that kept those hands from encountering her naked body. The thought was so electrifying that she had to remind herself to breathe or she was sure she'd die right there on the spot. He smelled like the storm outside, an unforgettable mix of the sea and the rain and a thousand dark fantasies. The wild urge to plunge her fingers into his wet, curling hair came over her, and it took all of her willpower to keep from giving in to it. She didn't do things like that. She didn't even *think* things like that.

She cleared her throat. "You can put me down now."

He had a crescent-shaped scar at the outer corner of his left eye. She wanted to trace the pale line with her tongue. A terrible, wonderful heat blossomed between

her legs, and a slow smile spread across his face, as if
he knew what she was thinking.

"Put me down," she said again, more softly. If he
didn't put her down soon she might spontaneously com-
bust.

Another man might have slid her down the length of
his body and enjoyed the ride. She couldn't have
stopped him if he had tried. John Gallagher, however,
was a better man than that. His grip moved from her
hips to her waist, and he lowered her to the ground with
a minimum of body contact.

"Are you okay?" he asked.

Her nightgown settled around her ankles where it belonged. "I should be asking you that. I don't know how
you managed to catch me, but thank you."

"My pleasure," he said. He didn't leer or put a sexual
spin on the words, but the sense of awareness, of appre-
ciation, was there just the same.

Another wave of warmth spiraled its way across her
midsection. She barely knew John Gallagher, and yet
already he had touched her with more real affection than
her husband had shown her in the last five years of their
marriage.

He gestured toward his father. "Thanks for bringing
him inside. Not everyone would have bothered."

"Does this sort of thing happen often?"

"Let's just say it's been a hell of a bad week."

He looked so tired and worried that her heart went
out to him. "Let me make you some coffee." She turned
toward the kitchen and saw Eddie sitting on the floor,
cleaning muddy paws with a roll of paper toweling.
"There's a dog in here!"

"That's Bailey," John said. "I told her to stay in the
car but—"

"Is she yours?"

"Muddy paws and all. If she wrecked anything, the bill's mine."

She waved away his words. "I love dogs. She's welcome here any time." What a stupid, idiotic thing to say. As if the dog would come calling without the owner.

"Don't let Bailey hear that. She'll take you at your word."

"Hey, Bailey." She held out her hand to the dog, then grinned at Eddie. "Guess my idea wasn't so terrific after all."

"What idea?" John asked.

"It's like somebody opened a faucet up there," Eddie said. "Alex was going to hang a bucket from the beam. I told her it wouldn't work, but she wanted to try."

"It worked in theory," Alex said as John took in the array of pans positioned strategically across the living-room floor. "I figured if I could stem the major leak I could finesse my way around the smaller ones."

"Is there anyplace that isn't leaking?"

"Every house has problems." She felt like a new mother defending her ugly child. "I'll take care of it."

He followed the trail of pans, pots, and bowls to the middle of the room. "So where's your ceiling?"

"What a ridiculous question. It's where a ceiling is supposed to be."

"The hell it is."

"The broker told me exposed beams are an asset." An architectural extra she should be pleased to have.

"Yeah, but that doesn't mean ceilings are optional, Alex."

She liked hearing him say her name. She would have liked a ceiling more, but still it was something. "I guess I should have brought in someone to check things out but I couldn't afford it."

"I'm surprised the bank didn't send an engineer over."

"There was no bank," she said. "I paid cash."

He looked at her as if she'd announced she was here on a mission to find Elvis.

"You paid cash?"

"Is that really such an alien concept?" she countered.

"Around here it sure as hell is. Most people have trouble swinging a down payment." He looked at her with open curiosity. "The crew at the diner said you paid cash, but I didn't believe them. The Sea Gate grapevine is better than I thought."

"I'll have to keep that in mind."

He grinned at her. "You're not going to tell me how you managed it, are you?"

She smiled back. "Not on your life."

"Secrets don't stay secret long around here."

"I'm not worried about it," she said. Which wasn't entirely true. The fact that the whole town knew she'd paid cash for the Winslow house was highly unnerving. She opted to change the subject. "I promised you a cup of coffee. Why don't I put on a pot for all of us?"

JOHN WANTED TO FOLLOW ALEX into the kitchen, but the guarded look in her eyes held him back. It wasn't a warning exactly—she was too sophisticated for that. He had the sensation that for a few moments her defenses had been lowered and she needed time to get them back in place. He didn't blame her for that. He'd built himself a pretty good defense mechanism over the last four years, only to find it was suddenly in danger of crumbling.

Something had happened between them, something unexpected and powerful, and now he knew that she'd felt it, too. Her smell, the heat of her skin through the thin fabric of the nightgown, the gentle silhouette of her legs—he felt as if he'd been branded. It hadn't been that way with Libby. The buildup with his late wife had been slow and gentle; the gradual shift from friendship to love had seemed as natural as breathing.

Bailey nudged his leg, and he scratched her head absently. He'd been without a woman too damn long, that's what the problem was. He'd forgotten how it felt when the hormones kicked in and the brain shut down. For all he knew Alex Curry was a married woman with a husband and three kids asleep in the other room.

Not even that thought was enough to cool his heat.

His old man would have a field day with this. Eddie had been trying to push him in Dee's direction, but some friendships weren't meant to be anything else. Alex, however, was another story entirely. He turned, expecting to field some major razzing, but Eddie was asleep in the chair facing the television. His father's breathing was slow and regular, and John tried not to notice how fragile Eddie looked in his blue pajamas and worn slippers.

I'm not ready to lose you yet, Pop, he thought, then brushed the notion aside as too ridiculous to contemplate. There was nothing wrong with Eddie Gallagher that a good night's sleep wouldn't cure.

John paced the room, his gaze sliding over old-fashioned lamps with pull chains and frilly shades, frayed avocado green curtains, and enough weird knick-knacks to fill Giants Stadium. A trio of pictures clipped from a magazine hung on the wall behind the couch. The frames were obviously garage sale rejects.

He'd stake his life on the fact that everything in the room had belonged to Marge Winslow. He didn't claim to be an expert on women or interior decorating, but he'd thought most women couldn't wait to put their own touch on a place. China pitchers in the shape of Elsie the Cow didn't exactly seem Alex's style. No, he'd bet his last dime that she was Wedgwood and Steuben all the way.

There were no family photos propped up on the end tables. No kids' toys sticking out from under the couch. No men's shoes or jockstraps draped over the back of a chair. Not even a magazine or book left open on the coffee table. If she had a personal life of any kind, you'd never know it by her home.

Maybe he wasn't being fair. She'd only been there a couple of days. Hell, when he and Libby moved into their first house, they'd lived out of boxes for weeks while they tried to figure out what went where. That would explain it. As soon as she unpacked, she'd replace Marge's eclectic mix with her own things. He glanced around again. He even went so far as to peer into the narrow hallway that led to the bedrooms. So where were the boxes? Where were the floor-to-ceiling stacks of stuff waiting to be unpacked? All he saw were two very expensive leather suitcases propped up in front of one of the bedroom doors.

The pieces didn't fit. She carried herself like a woman who'd never wanted for anything in her life. The kind of woman who'd known only the best life had to offer. A woman who'd rather die than live in Marge Winslow's old house or wait tables at the Starlight.

He told himself it was none of his business, that people were entitled to their secrets, but he was lying. When it came to Alex Curry, he wanted to know everything.

IF ALEX HID OUT IN the kitchen much longer, John Gallagher would think she'd gone to Seattle for the coffee.

She placed the cups and sugar bowl and milk pitcher on a metal tray, then frowned. The array looked a little skimpy, so she opened a box of cookies and arranged them as best she could on a dinner plate. She used to love arranging tea for Griffin and their guests, taking time to make sure each aspect of the ritual was as perfect as she could possibly make it. For a moment she missed her silver tea service, the china plates so translucent you could see your hand reflected through them, the linen napkins imported from Ireland. Those things were wonderful, but they belonged to her old life and she was better off without them.

She'd thought that escaping to the kitchen would help her regain her equilibrium, but she felt as dizzy and disoriented as she had in Gallagher's arms. *Get over it,* she told herself sternly. This was her problem, not his. She wasn't blind. She'd picked up on the chemistry between him and Dee at the diner. For all she knew they were having a torrid affair. Maybe they were even married to each other. Anything was possible. These people were strangers to her. She didn't know the first thing about them, and they didn't know the first thing about her, which was exactly the way she wanted it.

She took the plate of cookies off the tray, then carried the coffee into the living room.

"Sorry I took so long," she said, placing the tray on the table in front of the sofa. "I'm still not used to that stove."

"What's wrong with it?" John asked. He was standing by the window.

"It's a little fluky but—"

"I'll take a look at it." He started toward the kitchen.

"No!" The word sounded angry, but she wasn't angry at all. She simply didn't want anyone getting any closer. Especially not him. She tried to soften her outburst with a smile. "I mean, that's not necessary. I'm sure the stove and I will reach an accommodation."

"Johnny's good with his hands," Eddie said from the chair in front of the TV. "He can fix anything."

Another wave of heat flooded her chest as she remembered exactly how good those hands had felt as they'd held her. "Really," she said. "I'm not going to impose on either one of you. If I need something done, I'll hire a professional."

"Tell her, Johnny," Eddie persisted. "He rebuilt the carburetor on—"

"Drop it, Pop," John broke in. "You heard her. She said she'll take care of it."

"That's right," she said, vaguely annoyed. "It's my responsibility."

"I think we'd better shove off," John said to his father. He was acting as if she weren't even there.

"I could use that cup of coffee," Eddie said.

"Pop." John aimed a thumb toward the door. "Let's go."

"What's the rush?" his father complained. "I've never seen you turn down a cup of joe."

"Feel free to leave," Alex said to John in a sharp tone of voice. This was her home. Nobody was going to make her feel invisible within her own four walls. "I'll make sure Mr. Gallagher gets home safely."

John looked at Eddie. Eddie looked at Bailey. Bailey looked at the pot of coffee. At least someone appreciated her effort.

"You know what?" Alex bent down and picked up a mug. "I don't care if either one of you drinks my coffee." She took a long sip. "It's delicious, by the way." The two men were staring at her as if she'd lost her mind. Let them stare, she thought. She could do what she wanted in her own home.

Eddie hesitated, then grabbed a mug for himself. "You're right," he said to Alex. "This is damn fine coffee."

His son shrugged and claimed the last cup. He took a sip, then nodded. "Not bad."

She inclined her head. "Thank you. Maybe I can take

over coffee-making duties at the Starlight.''

"You got the job?" Eddie asked her.

She nodded, her good spirits returning as quickly as they had vanished. "I got the job."

"How the hell did Dee get hold of Nick so fast?" Eddie wondered out loud. "I thought he was away on some kind of vacation."

John looked uncomfortable. "Hey, Pop, let Dee worry about running the diner."

"You don't think it's a mistake, do you?" Alex asked, suddenly struck with the terrible notion that she might not have the job after all. "Maybe I misunderstood."

"You spoke to Dee?" John asked her.

She nodded.

"And she said you had the job?"

She nodded again.

"So don't worry about it."

"But what about the owner? What if she didn't ask him and he comes back and fires me?"

"That's not going to happen."

"How do you know it's not going to happen? I don't have any—" She almost bit off the tip of her tongue in her haste to stop her words.

"Experience?" he asked.

Color flooded her cheeks. "I didn't say that."

"You didn't have to. It's obvious."

"What do you mean, it's obvious? You don't know the first thing about me."

"I have eyes," he said.

"And what is that supposed to mean?"

"Waitresses don't pay cash for their houses or wear Burberry raincoats and Ferragamo loafers."

She opened her mouth to say something witty and cutting, but no words came out. She'd blurted out the truth to Dee. Why was it so much harder to tell him?

A funny little grin lifted the left side of his mouth. A funny little flutter rippled through her belly.

Next to her, Eddie cleared his throat. She'd forgotten his presence entirely. "Bailey needs to get a good foot under her," he said, edging toward the door while the dog danced at his feet. "We'll meet you back home, Johnny."

"You're going to let him walk home in his pajamas?" Alex asked as Eddie closed the door behind him.

"It's not like this is the first time."

"It's raining," she said, horrified. "He'll catch his death."

"He's not going anywhere," John said. "He's sitting in the truck smoking a cigarette."

"But he said he was going to walk home."

The look in his eyes almost melted her on the spot. "My old man says a lot of things, Alex. Believe me, he's in the truck."

She parted the living-room curtains and looked outside. "You're right," she said. "He's in the truck." She turned back to John. "You were right about something else, too: I've never waited tables before."

"Does Dee know?"

"I told her."

He whistled low. "You're either the most honest woman on the planet or the craziest."

"Crazy," she said. "Definitely crazy." She started to laugh, softly at first, so soft he wasn't sure it was really happening. That serious face of hers suddenly broke apart like the sparkling pieces of a kaleidoscope, then came together in a brilliant smile.

"Poor Dee," she said. "I hope she doesn't regret it. I don't know the first thing about waiting tables."

He couldn't take his eyes off her. If she'd been beautiful before, she was otherworldly now. He'd never seen a woman so transformed by something as simple as a smile. "That English accent of yours will have the crowd at the Starlight eating out of your hand in no time."

Her smile wavered. "What English accent?"

"Tomato, to-mah-to—your accent."

"I was born in New York City." She looked uncomfortable somehow, as if she hated to give up even that much of herself, but maybe that was his nonexistent romantic imagination kicking in, creating mysteries where there weren't any.

"Back at the diner you said you'd lived abroad."

She looked away as the kaleidoscope shifted one more time, and her smile disappeared. *You're pushing, Gallagher. It's none of your business.*

"Forget I said anything." He crossed the living room to the front door. "Thanks for the coffee."

"No problem."

"And for taking Eddie in."

"I enjoyed his company."

"See you at the Starlight," he said.

"Yes," she said. "See you at the Starlight."

If he was looking for something more, she wasn't about to oblige. He turned to leave. The rain had turned icy while he was inside. He had a vision of himself tumbling down the three brick steps to the ground, but he managed to keep his footing and slid his way toward the truck. Behind him he heard the sound of the front door squeaking shut, followed by the thud of the dead bolt sliding into place. At least she remembered to lock up this time.

"Took you long enough," Eddie said as John motioned for Bailey to jump into the rear of the truck.

"I thought you were walking home."

"In this weather?" Eddie snorted. "I may be old, but I'm not crazy."

"You're the one in pajamas." John stuck the key in the ignition.

"Did you ask her out?"

"Don't start," John warned as he waited for the engine to turn over.

"It's Thanksgiving. You gonna have her eat alone?"

"Maybe she's not going to be alone, Pop. She might have a husband and six kids."

"And maybe she doesn't have anyone." Eddie swung open the passenger door.

"Where the hell are you going now?"

"Where do you think?" Eddie countered. "I'm going to ask her out."

ALEX QUICKLY LET THE CURTAINS drop back into place as Eddie started up the pathway to the front door. She hoped they hadn't seen her peeking out the window at them. She told herself she'd wanted to make sure John made it to his truck without slipping on the ice, and there was a kernel of truth in that. Unfortunately that kernel of truth was overwhelmed by the real reason: She couldn't take her eyes off John Gallagher.

She opened the door at the first knock and gave Eddie her best smile. "Did you forget something?"

"Sure did," he said as she motioned him in from the cold. "What are you doing for dinner today?"

"Dinner?" She tried to visualize the contents of her refrigerator and cupboards. "Probably soup and a salad."

His frown threw the lines on his weathered face into even sharper relief. "For Thanksgiving?"

His words took her by surprise. "It can't possibly be Thanksgiving yet."

"Fourth Thursday in November," Eddie said, "regular as clockwork."

"You're right," she said. "I can't believe I forgot."

"Why don't you have Thanksgiving dinner with us?"

She was so touched by his offer that tears welled in her eyes. "Oh, I couldn't do that, Eddie."

"You got someplace else to go?"

"No, but—"

"So it's settled. Three o'clock. Number 10 Lighthouse Way."

A family Thanksgiving, she thought. Her first in more years than she could count. "I really shouldn't," she said. God help her, she sounded like a woman in need of convincing.

"Why not?" Eddie asked. "You're not a vegetarian, are you?"

She laughed again, the second time in less than an hour. "I'm not a vegetarian." She met his eyes, looking for the slightest hint of uncertainty. "Will your family mind?"

"The more the merrier, they always say."

"Then I'd love to join you."

Eddie beamed his approval. "Now you're talking. 10 Lighthouse Way. Three o'clock."

"I'll be there."

"One more thing," Eddie said. "Are you married?"

How could such a simple question be so hard to answer? She glanced down at her left hand. "No," she said after a moment. The truth fell somewhere in between. "Not anymore."

Eddie nodded as if he'd known it all along. "Perfect," he said, his bright blue eyes twinkling with delight. "Neither is Johnny." He turned and left without another word.

Alex stood in the doorway and watched as Eddie climbed into the truck. The two men exchanged words, then John looked toward her. Their eyes met. She felt the way she'd felt when he held her in his arms, dazed and yielding; all the things she didn't want to feel.

So turn away, she told herself. All she had to do was go back into the house and close the door behind her. It was an easy enough thing to do.

But she stood there on the top step, in the wind and the rain and the cold, and she watched until the truck turned onto Soundview and disappeared.

FIVE

NO GROWN WOMAN SHOULD GREET the dawn with her arm wedged up to the elbow inside a turkey.

Dee was a firm believer in the importance of holiday rituals and traditions, but there was something about dealing with twenty-five pounds of naked poultry before your first cup of coffee that made her think it was time to adopt a few new family traditions. Like vegetarianism. She yanked out the bag of giblets, then tossed it into the trash without remorse. Call her a renegade, but she drew the line at gizzards and neck bones.

Vegetarians didn't have to go through any of this, she thought wistfully as she ran cold water through the carcass. All across the land, vegetarians were cuddled under their eiderdown quilts, secure in the knowledge that there wasn't a vegetable on earth that needed six hours in a 325-degree oven. Vegetarians could sleep until noon if they wanted to and not feel a moment's remorse.

"Next year," she muttered as she patted the turkey dry with paper towels, then set it down in the gargantuan roasting pan that came out at Thanksgiving and Christmas. Next year it would be a festival of vegetables, and she'd personally strangle the first person who uttered a complaint.

She worked swiftly, spooning stuffing into the bird, then stitching up the cavity with a wide-eyed needle and butcher's twine. She quartered onions to place around the turkey the way her mother had taught her to do. Her mother had also taught her how to make a gravy so dark it was sinful, and the best pumpkin pie in New Jersey. Maggie Murray was ten years dead, but she was never closer than when Dee was in the kitchen. She rummaged in the junk drawer for the meat thermometer, then plunged it deep into the turkey's breast as she stifled a yawn. Turkey. Stuffing. Onions. Thermometer. That about covered it. She grasped the pan and slid it into the preheated oven.

A new speed record, she thought, glancing at the clock over the sink. Gizzard patrol was over, and it wasn't even seven-thirty yet. "You'd be proud of me, Mom," she said out loud. "Looks like I've finally gotten the hang of it."

"Talking to yourself again?"

She whirled around to see Mark, her sixteen-year-old son, yawning in the doorway. He wore a Hootie & the Blowfish T-shirt, a pair of threadbare gray sweatpants, and thick white socks that looked as if he'd used them to track grizzlies. A lump formed in her throat as she smiled at him. Whoever said love hurt must have been the parent of a teenager. You tuck him in one night and he's a little boy with a teddy bear, and you wake up the next morning to find he's turned into six feet of raging hormones.

"Did you get taller overnight?" she asked as he sat down at the kitchen table.

"You're getting shorter," he said around another yawn. "Happens to all of you old people."

"I'm not old," she snapped. "I wasn't much older than you when—"

"—you had me. Heard it before, Ma." He sniffed the air. "When's breakfast?"

"You know how to pour yourself some cornflakes, Mark."

"Yeah, but I was hoping for waffles."

She pointed toward the mound of waxy turnips piled on the counter. "You start peeling them, and I'll make you waffles."

He made a face. "Geez, I hate doing that crap."

"Surprise, Mark, sometimes so do I. Get to it."

She flung open the pantry door and pulled out a red box of Aunt Jemima, then grabbed eggs and milk from the fridge. Mark was searching through the dishwasher for a clean knife, and she had to bite her tongue to keep from sliding open the utensil drawer and handing him one. *You can't do everything for him,* she told herself as she cracked eggs into a metal bowl. *You have to let him find his own way.* Another two years and he'd be in college, and she wouldn't be able to help him at all.

"You want these things cut, too?" he asked.

"Quartered," she said as she measured pancake mix. "Be careful with that knife, Mark. I don't want you to get hurt."

"Ma, I'm sixteen. I know how to handle a knife."

"Accidents happen," she said, hearing her own mother's voice echoing inside her head. "The kitchen's a dangerous place."

"Yeah, right," he said.

She opened her mouth to deliver a lecture on culinary safety, but her son was saved by the telephone.

"A little early, isn't it, Johnny?" She cradled the phone between her shoulder and ear and whisked the batter.

"How would you feel about one more for dinner?"

She started to say what she always said, that one more at the table hardly made a difference, but she caught herself. "Depends on who the one more is."

"Alex Curry."

She laughed out loud. "Great," she said, pouring batter into the sizzling-hot waffle iron. "Why don't you ask Princess Di to come, too?"

"Eddie asked her. I had nothing to do with it."

"I can't have that woman in my house," Dee said.

"Why the hell not?"

"Because I don't have time to redecorate, that's why."

"The woman bought Marge Winslow's place, didn't she? That isn't exactly House Beautiful."

"Give her six weeks," Dee said darkly. "She'll turn it into a showplace."

She hung up the phone and glared at the waffle iron. Her house needed a paint job badly. Her sofa was covered in cat fur, dog barf, and pizza stains. She'd had to borrow folding chairs from her brother, her next-door neighbor, and Sally Whitton in order to seat everybody for dinner. She wondered if she'd be able to find a throne for Alex Curry on such short notice, then felt guilty as hell for even thinking that. *You're becoming a bitch, Dee.* Just because the woman was beautiful and classy, she had her pegged as a snob. Snobs didn't wait tables at the Starlight or move into the scuzziest house on the water. And you could be classy without being rich—at least that's what her mother always used to tell her.

No, it was her own insecurity rearing its ugly head. She'd seen the look on John's face when he first saw Alex. Hell, she'd seen that same look on the face of every man in the diner the other morning. Worshipful. Awestruck. Amazed. No one had ever looked at her that way, and she had the feeling no one ever would. She didn't inspire awe in anyone but her banker, and that was only because she managed to do so much with so damn little.

"Finished," Mark said.

She pointed toward the basket of brussels sprouts next to the sink. "Wash them and cut an X in the bottom."

"Of each one?" He sounded horrified.

"Life's tough," she said.

Her son grumbled but got back to work. Although it wasn't much of a victory, she'd take it.

All in all, things could be worse. Alex Curry was coming for dinner, but Brian Gallagher wasn't. At least she had that much to be thankful for.

BRIAN THOMAS GALLAGHER MOTORED DOWN the window of his bright red Porsche and tossed a pair of coins into the toll basket. He waited, engine revved and ready, until the signal turned green, then roared back onto the Garden State Parkway. Traffic had thinned out after Toms River, and he could move at a pretty damn good clip now. Of course, he always had to keep one eye out for the fuzz. Red sports cars seemed to bring out the worst in the breed, and he'd learned a long time ago to throttle back and fake humility when necessary in order to avoid a ticket.

A woman in a white Lexus pulled alongside and kept pace for a few miles. She was okay-looking, albeit in an obvious way. The makeup was too heavy, and the hair too overdone in a Jersey Shore kind of way, but she had enough going for her that he entertained motioning her over to the shoulder and asking her to dinner. Fortunately his brain got the better of his dick before he followed through.

Hell, he was a married man. Married men weren't supposed to pick up women on the Garden State. Of course, married men weren't supposed to be alone on Thanksgiving Day either, but that hadn't occurred to him or Margo when they'd said good-bye at the airport.

"Are you sure you can't join us, darling?" she'd asked just before boarding the flight to Aspen. "Mother and Daddy will be terribly disappointed."

His two daughters were tugging on his pants legs like a pair of golden retriever puppies. "I have a deposition to take on Friday," he said, looking appropriately crestfallen. "No way I could be back in time." He bent down and hugged Caitlyn and Allison. By tacit agreement he didn't hug his wife. Margo had been brought up to believe public displays of affection were hopelessly middle class.

"The Roswells are having people in for a buffet tomorrow," Margo said as they called her flight. "You're welcome to attend."

"Not without you, darling," he said smoothly. The truth was he couldn't stomach the Roswells and wouldn't go near their buffet on a bet.

Margo smiled. "Cook is off for the holiday," she said. "Where will you go?"

"This is New York City. I think I can find someplace."

So why the hell was he heading down the Shore? He should have stayed in town and grabbed himself a bite to eat at one of those trendy Columbus Avenue places that offered free-range turkey with fat-free dressing and organically grown sweet potatoes—food with about as much soul as his life. But who needed soul? he thought, gripping the wheel tightly. He had money, and that was supposed to be enough.

It was raining like hell, a steady downpour that was giving his wipers a workout. People drove like assholes in the rain, especially on New Jersey highways. All he needed was for some idiot in a Geo to hydroplane across six lanes of traffic and crash head-on into his Porsche.

If he had half the brain he liked to tell people he had, he'd be home drinking Scotch.

Who in hell would have figured the pull of his old hometown would be too strong to resist?

Brian had spent most of his life trying to put as much distance between himself and Sea Gate as humanly possible, but lately the only time he felt like a success was when he roared down Ocean Avenue in his Porsche, the local kid who'd made good. They all bought into the illusion of fancy cars and hand-tailored suits and haircuts that cost more than the Starlight Diner probably cleared on a good morning. They didn't like him, but they all wanted their kids to follow in his footsteps, to go off to the big city and swim with the urban sharks.

Not that Dee was impressed by any of it. When she bothered to acknowledge him at all, it was only to shoot him a withering glance that made him feel as if he were the one waiting tables at a third-class hash house. *I'm the one who got away, Dee,* he wanted to say to her. *I'm the only one who managed to pull it off.* She'd married and moved to Florida seventeen years ago, but when her teenage marriage collapsed a few years later, she came back to Sea Gate. His old man had never even tried to get away. Eddie Gallagher seemed to think everything he needed could be found within the town's limits.

Not even his little brother Johnny had managed to escape permanently. He'd tried life in the big city but turned tail and run back home. When Libby died, John's last chance to be a success had died with her. He'd fallen into a grief so dark and black that he lost sight of what was important. The powers that be at Samuel, Roberts, and Margolin had been patient, but after a while their patience had run thin. They'd told John to shape up or lose his position, and John had told them to shove their corner office up their corporate ass. Baby brother would live and die in Sea Gate and never know there was a whole wide world out there.

He slowed down the Porsche as he approached another toll plaza. He hated the Garden State. How the hell were you supposed to make time when you had to stop every few miles and toss coins in a basket? As far as he was concerned, they could drop a bomb on the Jersey Shore, and he'd never miss the damn place. Hurricanes, floods, brown tide—how many hints did Mother Nature have to drop before the light dawned? The old Jersey Shore was gone. The days of ramshackle bungalows and town-square picnics were over. People expected more from a summer vacation place than four walls and a roof. They wanted to be catered to; they wanted a certain amount of luxury. The working class wanted to aspire toward the middle, while the middle wanted to emulate the rich. Places like Sea Gate were yesterday's dream, and the sooner they realized it, the better off they'd be.

The world was changing faster than the speed of light, and you had to change with it or be left a few centuries behind. The last time he saw John, he had tried to explain some of his ideas, but his little brother had the foresight of a sea urchin. "The marina's dead," he'd tried to tell John. "Hell, the whole town's dead. Get out before it takes you under with it." He'd had a developer lined up who was willing to take it off his brother's hands at a profit, but John wouldn't budge. John gave him a load of crap about the local fishermen, what it would do to their livelihood, but Brian wasn't buying any of it. His brother was a fucking pussy who didn't have the balls to grab opportunity when it came along.

But it wasn't over. Brian had an arsenal of weapons at his command, and he wasn't afraid to use them. Change was coming to Sea Gate whether or not his brother wanted it. Brian had put together a group of like-minded businessmen who were looking to grab a piece of the Jersey Shore for their own. Sea Gate was close enough to Atlantic City to cash in on the money being made in that gambling mecca. He'd taken a look at the specs and liked what he saw. They'd raze the town from the docks west to Barnegat Road, which led to the highway. The marina, houses, down-on-their-luck businesses—they'd all go under the wrecking ball if Brian had his way. The town center would become a mega-mall-sized parking lot. A new upscale marina would be erected, stretching from the south end of Sea Gate's shoreline to the north. There would be restaurants, a small hotel, and berths for thirty dinner yachts that would ply the waters between Sea Gate and the Atlantic City marina.

They'd tried to ace him out of what was rightfully his, but one day soon Brian would have the last laugh.

The Sea Gate exit loomed a mile ahead. Another thirty minutes and he'd pull up in front of Dee's house. The driveway would be clogged with cars, most of them aging clunkers with bad exhaust systems and enough rust damage from salt air to choke a horse. His garaged Porsche would stand out like a victory flag.

They'd never been behind him. Right from the start, they'd made it clear whose side they were on, and it wasn't his. They'd wanted him to give up his future and settle down right there with Dee, but he couldn't do it. He'd wanted her, but he hadn't wanted the complications that came along with her. He would have lost his scholarship—hell, his entire future would have gone down the toilet.

So he made his choices and now he was trying his damnedest to live with them. He had the cushy job in a prestigious law firm. He had the apartment and the cars and the two little girls and the trophy wife who had never quite managed to creep inside his heart.

Only one woman had ever done that, and he'd lost her a long time ago.

SIX

LAST THANKSGIVING ALEX AND GRIFFIN had attended an intimate supper at the home of a British lord who happened to be married to a homesick American woman. Fifteen couples, none of whom knew each other well at all, gathered around an ornate cherrywood table to celebrate a holiday that had absolutely no meaning for most of the people in the room. Instead of turkey, they served squab. Wild rice replaced sweet potatoes with marshmallow topping. And, to Alex's utter disbelief, there wasn't a pie in sight.

She had wanted to bake an all-American apple pie and bring it with them as a Thanksgiving offering, but Griffin had been horrified at the thought.

"Leave the cooking to the help, darling," he'd said, dismissing her the way one would a backward child. "A magnum of Dom and flowers is more the thing."

She never argued points of etiquette with Griffin. He was older and more sophisticated and knew how to navigate the shark-infested waters of London society. An apple pie wasn't much in the scheme of things, but it had represented a basic difference between herself and Griffin, in the way they looked at the world. She'd thought about that miserable Thanksgiving many times in the twelve months since and wished she'd had the guts to listen to her own instincts.

What a difference a year made.

The timer dinged, and she jumped up from the kitchen table to take a pair of apple pies from the oven. The latticework top crusts were baked to a perfect golden brown and the juices bubbled merrily in the cinnamon-sugar syrup. Her two years of gourmet cooking classes hadn't been wasted, she thought as she admired her handiwork. She might not be turning out tournedos of beef in a morel sauce, but she'd bet her spatula these pies could hold their own anywhere.

She'd also bet her VW that the Gallagher men wouldn't have anything like this on their Thanksgiving table—not unless there were some Gallagher women on the premises. No one had mentioned any Gallagher women. Eddie had the rudderless look older men often got when their wives were no longer around to guide them. And John—there was an almost visible barrier around him, as if he'd been hurt once and wasn't about to let it happen again. The two men probably lived alone in a house that was even more in need of repair than her own, eating frozen dinners and forgetting to take out the trash.

She sank down onto a kitchen chair and rested her chin in her hands. She didn't even know these people, and she was trying to analyze them like some sleazy pop psychologist.

Get a life, Alex, she thought as she stared at her perfect pies. *Preferably one of your own.*

ALEX TOLD HERSELF SHE WAS changing her clothes to celebrate the occasion, not because she was going anywhere. It was Thanksgiving Day, after all, and the holiday deserved some respect. She peeled off her jeans and T-shirt, took a quick shower, then dressed in dark charcoal gray trousers, a cream-colored silk shirt, and a cardigan in a heathery shade of pink. She brushed her hair until it shone, then carefully French-braided it until it swung between her shoulder blades like a heavy golden rope.

A woman owed it to herself to look her best, even if there was no one around to see her. It was part of maintaining discipline. Which was all well and good, but it didn't explain why she redid her eye makeup twice or changed her shoes three times, struggling to find the perfect pair of flats to go with the straight-leg trousers. Her naked lobes begged for adornment, but all she had was the pair of earrings she'd tucked away for a rainy day. She glanced out the window at the soggy landscape. It *was* raining. And it wasn't as if she was planning to go anywhere. Besides, even if she did and someone happened to notice her earrings, who would believe they were real.

She puttered around the kitchen, wiping down the sink, dusting off the top of the fridge, staring at the pies. What a shame for two such perfect specimens to go to waste. Maybe she would drop them off at John and Eddie's house.

The broker had given her a small map of the village that showed all the inlets and cross streets. She rummaged around in the shoe box she used as a·makeshift filing cabinet. There it was, tucked under the stack of legal documents that said she was the proud owner of the Winslow place. Her house was highlighted in yellow. Ocean Avenue, the marina, the triple inlets just beyond— there it was. Lighthouse Way. How strange, she thought. It wasn't even near the water. Lighthouse Way was at the far end of town, tucked in the middle of what looked to be a small residential housing development.

It shouldn't take her more than fifteen minutes round-trip to zip over there, wish the Gallagher men a happy Thanksgiving, then drive home.

NUMBER 10 LIGHTHOUSE WAY WAS a small Cape Cod with raised dormers, a chain link fence around the backyard, and a bright red mailbox decorated with sham-rocks. The shamrocks puzzled her. Try as she might, she couldn't quite imagine either John or his father painting shamrocks on their mailbox. Maybe there was a Mrs. Eddie after all.

John's truck was parked in the driveway, surrounded by a half-dozen vehicles in varying states of disrepair. Either he was running a freelance used-car lot, or she was just one of many guests invited to share turkey and cranberry sauce chez Gallagher. Good, she thought as she turned off the ignition and gathered up her things. This way there would be no hard feelings when she told Eddie she wasn't staying.

She dashed through the rain to the front door, juggling two pies, one umbrella, and a slim black clutch bag. "First and ten . . ." she heard a TV announcer say from inside the house. "Ball on the forty-yard line." A chorus of loud male commentary erupted in response. She pushed the bell with her elbow, then waited. Maybe they couldn't hear her over the blare of football and male laughter. She pushed the bell again, two short blasts this time. She knew an omen when she saw one. If someone didn't open the door by the time she counted to three, she and her pies were going home.

She was about to leave when the door swung open.

"Dee!" The waitress at the Starlight was the last per-son she'd expected to see. She quickly recovered her composure. "Happy Thanksgiving."

"Happy Thanksgiving to you, too," Dee said. "Hang

your coat in the closet and make yourself at home.''

Make herself at home? She might as well have told Alex to click her heels three times and fly off to Oz. ''I brought pies,'' she said, limiting herself to words of one syllable. ''I thought I would just drop them off and—''

''Great.'' Dee pushed her heavy red hair off her face with a quick gesture. ''The more the merrier. The way this crowd eats, there won't be any leftovers.'' She cocked her head. ''The phone. I'll be right back.'' She darted down the hallway.

Alex didn't know whether to laugh or cry as she peered into the coat closet. Eddie said John wasn't married, but that didn't mean he wasn't living with someone. Plastic storage boxes were lined up on the top shelf, neatly marked *Hats*, *Gloves*, and *Scarves*. No man on the face of the earth would even think of doing such a thing. And there was more. The scent of Shalimar rose above the mingled smells of cherry pipe tobacco and Old Spice. She didn't have to ask who wore the Shalimar.

She started toward the rear of the house, where she assumed the kitchen was located. The hallway was papered in a pale blue shell pattern and lit by a pair of electric sconces hung on either side of an oval mirror. Someone cared a great deal about how this small house looked, and that someone probably was missing the Y chromosome.

''Need some help?'' John Gallagher popped up at her elbow.

''Where on earth did you come from?'' She'd been so busy analyzing the wallpaper she hadn't heard footsteps. In truth, she was surprised she hadn't sensed his presence.

He aimed a thumb over his right shoulder. She peered into a dimly lit room that was shrouded in a thick haze of cigar smoke.

''It's halftime,'' he said. ''I'm on a beer run.''

"I see."

He took the pies from her arms. "Did you bake these yourself?"

"Absolutely." She tried to be modest, but it was impossible to keep the pride from her voice.

He peered under the aluminum foil. "I'm impressed. My mother used to make them like that, with that crisscross stuff on top."

"Latticework," she said.

"It looks hard to do."

"Actually it's pretty easy."

"You should be telling me it's the hardest thing since splitting the atom."

She met his eyes. "It's the hardest thing since splitting the atom."

He grinned. "That's what I thought."

They found Dee perched on top of the kitchen counter, her entire body curled around the telephone. She looked about sixteen.

"Sam?" John mouthed.

Dee shot him a fierce look, turned bright red, then turned away.

"Sam," John said as he put the pies down on the already crowded kitchen table.

"Who's Sam?" Alex asked.

"The guy she pretends she isn't going with."

"Oh." She looked over at Dee, then back at John. "And you're okay with that?"

"Sam's a great guy," John said. "Hell of a lot better than Tony."

"Tony?"

"Her ex-husband."

Alex's head was spinning as she followed John back out of the room. "Are you two related?" she asked.

"Tony and me?"

"No," she said, growing more puzzled by the second. "You and Dee."

"Where'd you get that idea?"

"I—what I mean is, you all live here together, and I just thought—"

"This isn't my house."

"You and Eddie don't live with Dee?"

"Dee lives with Mark."

"Who's Mark?"

"Her son." They paused in the doorway to the family room. "This is their house. He's the one sitting on the floor near Eddie."

The boy's face was illuminated by the television's glow. There was no mistaking the resemblance. He had a thick head of dark red hair like his mother and the same proud set to his jaw, but the rest of him was pure Gallagher. His eyes were dark and deep-set over chiseled cheekbones. His mouth was wide and well-shaped. He looked exactly the way she imagined John had looked sixteen or seventeen years ago.

John, however, betrayed nothing. If he recognized the weirdness of the situation he didn't let on. "Shove over and make room for Alex, Pop."

Eddie's smile warmed her heart. "Take a load off your feet, Alex, and watch the game with us."

She recognized a number of the men in the room from the diner. They greeted her warmly, and some of her nervousness ebbed. Dee's son looked up at her with a combination of curiosity and annoyance.

"Alex bought the Winslow place," Eddie told the boy by way of explanation.

The boy shrugged and turned back to the football game. She didn't blame him. When she was a girl, there had been nothing more deadly dull than her parents' friends. Even if the friend wasn't all that much older than she was.

"Where's the Michelob?" one of the men demanded of John. "You weren't supposed to come back empty-handed."

"He didn't come back empty-handed, Davey," Eddie said with a broad wink to the room at large. "He brought back Alex."

"Holy shit," Davey said, pointing toward the television screen. "Did you see that interception?"

To a man they forgot she was standing there, and she used the opportunity to escape to the kitchen. Dee was off the phone and had turned her attention to a large ceramic bowl piled high with flour.

Alex hesitated in the doorway. Why hadn't she just walked out the front door? She didn't belong here at all.

"You're still wearing your coat," Dee said, looking over at her.

"I'm not staying," Alex said. "Would you tell John and Eddie I said good-bye?"

"Why don't you tell him yourself?"

"They're watching football. I don't want to interrupt."

"Interrupt," Dee said. "They'll be watching football nonstop until the Super Bowl."

Alex smiled to hide her unease. "Really," she said. "All I wanted to do was drop off the pies and wish everyone a happy Thanksgiving."

"I don't suppose you know anything about making biscuits." Dee scratched her nose with the back of her arm, leaving a floury streak along the side of her face.

She felt her resolve weakening. "I make a mean croissant."

Dee rolled her eyes comically. "This crowd wouldn't know a croissant from a crescent wrench, honey. I'm talking plain, ordinary biscuits."

Alex slipped out of her coat and draped it over the

back of a chair. "I can do plain and ordinary with the best of them."

"Sure you can," Dee said. "That's why you look the way you do and I look the way I do."

"You look great," Alex said.

Dee wore a long kelly green sweater over tight black leggings. An enormous Maltese cross hung from a black velvet ribbon and dangling gypsy gold earrings jingled with every movement. There was nothing subtle about the outfit, but then there was nothing subtle about the woman who wore it.

Alex began measuring flour into a large mixing bowl. "I think I owe you an apology."

"I knew it. You're the one who broke my Ming vase."

"There's that," Alex said, "and the fact that you probably had no idea I was coming to dinner."

"Actually John called me this morning and told me Eddie invited you."

"I thought I was going to their house," she said. "I never would have said yes if I'd known."

"Now, I'm real hard to offend, honey, but you're coming close."

"I don't go where I'm not wanted," Alex said simply. "And I don't go where I'm not invited. Eddie should have told me."

"And he should stop wandering around town in his pajamas." Dee shrugged. "He meant well."

"I hope I'm not putting you out."

"The way I look at it, you're helping me even the odds. The testosterone level around here can get pretty overwhelming."

She thought about the boy with John Gallagher's eyes but said nothing. It was, after all, none of her business.

"SO HOW'D YOU MANAGE IT, Johnny?" Vince Troisi tossed a peanut in his direction. "She's in town two days, and you've got her coming over for Thanksgiving dinner.''

''Don't know what you're talking about,'' John said with studied blandness.

''The princess,'' Vince elaborated. ''Last person I thought I'd see here at Dee's.''

''You're giving the younger generation too damn much credit,'' Eddie said, draining his bottle of beer. ''I'm the one who asked Alex.''

The room erupted in laughter.

''Tell them, Johnny.'' Eddie nudged his son with his foot. ''You were gonna let her spend the day by herself, weren't you?''

''Yep,'' said John. A Big Mac beneath the Golden Arches was starting to sound good. ''That's exactly what I was going to do.''

''I'm telling you, youth is wasted on the young,'' Davey said with a shake of his graying head. ''In my day, I'd never let a pretty girl spend a holiday alone.''

''She's not a girl,'' John said before he had a chance to stop himself. ''She's a woman.''

Vince let out a long, low whistle. ''So that's how it is,'' he said with a knowing wink. ''Looks like Johnny's finally found someone he likes.''

John looked over at Dee's son Mark. ''Don't get old, kid. It rots the brain cells.''

Mark snorted with laughter. ''I already figured that out.''

''What the hell's his problem?'' Vince said to Eddie. He gestured toward John. ''It's not like he's married or anything.''

John unfolded himself from the recliner. ''Don't you bozos have anything better to do?''

''No,'' said Vince. ''If we didn't have you to talk about, we'd have to start watching *Oprah*.''

Mark leaned over and gave John a conspiratorial look

that would have had more impact if he were old enough to shave. "I think she's a babe."

"You're all pathetic," John said. "Why aren't you home with your wives?"

"Because they won't let us watch football," Vince and Davey said in unison.

Everyone laughed but John.

"They'll be here in time for dinner," Rich explained, not taking his gaze away from the TV screen. "The women's club is helping out over at St. John's." St. John's was the local hospital that served Sea Gate and the adjacent town.

"Johnny's forgotten everything he ever knew about being married," Vince said, popping a handful of salted nuts in his mouth.

"Hell, he wasn't married long enough to get it all figured out," Davey said. "Takes a good twenty or—" Davey stopped mid-sentence. The rest of the men in the room were looking down at the floor. "Jesus, Johnny. I'm sorry."

John nodded. There was nothing he could say to make Davey feel better, nothing he wanted to say. Libby and the boys had only been dead three years. Three Thanksgivings. A man couldn't forget his family in just three Thanksgivings.

"Where you going?" Vince called out. "Dallas is about to score."

"Let him go," he heard Eddie say as he bolted from the room. "You goddamn fools, just let him go."

"WHAT AN IDIOT," DEE SAID with a groan. "I left the sweet potatoes in the trunk of the car."

Alex placed the last biscuit on the baking sheet and stepped back to admire her handiwork. "Why don't I go out to the car and get them?"

"What about the biscuits?" Dee asked.

"Finished," Alex said. "All you'll have to do is pop them into the oven." She was trying to make it clear that she wouldn't be joining them for dinner, but Dee didn't seem to notice.

Dee tossed another peeled shrimp onto the pile. "You twisted my arm. The car keys are hanging on the peg by the door. Go get the sweet potatoes."

Alex slipped into her coat. "Back in a second." She popped out the back door, then walked around the side of the house toward the driveway. Dee's chocolate brown Toyota was parked in front of the garage door. It was old, Alex noticed, but not nearly as old as her VW. She took perverse satisfaction from that fact.

As it turned out, Dee had left not only the sweet potatoes in the trunk, but two cans of cranberry sauce and a huge turkey baster. The turkey baster had wedged itself under the spare tire, and it took Alex a minute to pry it loose.

She put the baster in the grocery bag and was about to dash back into the house when she heard a sound. She stilled her breath for a moment and listened harder. There it was again. Curious, she put the grocery bag down on top of the trunk and looked around. A gull swooped low, then darted upward again, emitting a keening cry as it rose into the sky.

Mystery solved, she thought. Was there anything as mournful as the cry of a gull? But then her eye was drawn to the cars in the driveway, and from there to John's truck . . . and from there to John. His arms were braced on the steering wheel, forehead resting against his hands. She heard the sound again, a low, guttural sound of loss that seemed to pierce her chest like a knife as she made her way down the muddy driveway.

He was a stranger, she told herself. His problems were no concern of hers. She had more than enough problems of her own to keep her occupied for a long time to come.

Still she kept moving toward him. Was he crying? *Please God don't let him be crying.* She couldn't imagine what terrible event could bring so powerful a man to tears.

He drew his right arm across his eyes, then looked up, and she froze. For one crazy second she considered ducking behind the old blue Chevy next to her, but she couldn't move. Not while he was looking at her like that, as if a world of understanding suddenly existed between them.

HOW LONG HAD SHE BEEN standing there, watching him with those sad dark eyes?

She was looking at him as if she knew what he was feeling, as if she felt it herself. He knew it was impossible, that they were strangers and nothing more, but the sense of connection seemed to pulse between them just the same.

"You're not leaving?" he asked. "You haven't had dinner yet."

She shook her head. "Dee left the sweet potatoes in the trunk of her car."

"We're lucky she didn't leave the turkey in the trunk."

She smiled, but the look of concern lingered. "Sorry if I startled you."

"No problem. I came out for a smoke."

If they gave awards for asshole remarks, he'd win hands down with that one. The family room was so smoky it looked like an opium den. You could set your lungs back five years without even lighting up. They wouldn't have noticed if he'd smoked an entire carton inside.

"Well, I won't bother you," she said, edging away. Her face was wet with rain. Droplets beaded the tips of her lashes and shimmered across her cheekbones. *Beau-*

tiful, he thought. So goddamn beautiful she made him ache with loneliness.

"You didn't," he said.

Her expression grew shadowed. "Didn't what?"

"Bother me," he said.

"I'm glad." She backed away. "I'd better get those sweet potatoes inside."

"Wait," he said, opening the truck door. "I'll give you a hand."

She picked up the grocery bag. "I can manage."

"That looks heavy."

"It isn't."

"I insist." He reached for the bag, but she clutched it against her chest.

"I'm not helpless." There was an edge to her voice, a sharpness he might not have noticed another time.

"Nobody said you were."

"In fact, I'm a great deal more capable than you might think."

Where the hell had that come from? "Nobody's going to argue that, Alex. You're the one who paid cash for your house. The rest of us have mortgages."

She softened visibly, as if just thinking about the run-down Winslow house was enough to make her happy.

"Humor me," he said. "Sister Mary Bernadette used to rap my knuckles if I didn't carry Mitzy Donohue's book bag."

A smile tugged at her mouth. "You don't expect me to believe that, do you?"

He placed a hand over his heart and stared at her in mock indignation. "Eight years at St. Aloysius leaves its mark on a man."

"Here." She handed him the grocery bag. "Since it means that much to you." She smiled when she said it, and this time the smile reached her eyes.

"Thanks," he said, tucking it under his right arm.

''You can relax now. You've done your good deed for the day.''

''I'm glad to hear that.'' She had the most amazing face he'd ever seen, filled with enough shadow and light to keep a man interested for the rest of his life. ''I've been neglecting my good deeds lately.''

''And thanks for not asking.''

She inclined her head. ''We're all entitled to our secrets.''

''Yeah,'' he said, thinking about Libby and the boys and how quickly your life can fade to black, ''but sometimes I can't remember why.''

SEVEN

❧

"GREAT TURKEY, DEE DEE," RICH Ippolito called from his seat at the far end of the table. "Even if you forgot to save a drumstick for me."

"Will you look at that?" His wife, Jen, shot him a fierce look. "Seventy-two years old, and he still talks with his mouth full. Don't they ever learn?"

"At least he keeps his teeth in." Sally Whitton looked up from her mountain of candied sweet potatoes. "Last year's boyfriend only popped his choppers in when he wanted to kiss me."

"You're a cruel woman, Sal," Dee said as she put a big bowl of mashed potatoes on the table. That made three bowls of mashed potatoes, two of candied sweets, and more biscuits than she could count. "At least you have a boyfriend."

"Hey, Dee." Eddie nudged her with his elbow. "You know I'm available."

Dee grinned and kissed him on his bald spot. "You'd be the death of me, Eddie, and we both know it."

Everyone laughed, just the way she'd meant for them

to do. She'd done the right thing, not asking Sam Weitz to join them. The crowd at the table would have read more into the gesture than was actually there, and poor Sam would have faced a level of good-natured teasing that could make a grown man weep. But she missed him. That had to be a good sign.

She reclaimed her seat at the head of the table, feeling more pleased with herself than she had in ages. Every now and then she managed to get it right, and this was one of those wonderful times. The table was set with her best linen and china. Her mother's silverware gleamed in the candlelight. The house was filled with the wonderful aromas of roasted turkey and tangy cranberries and the sounds of friendship and laughter.

"More creamed onions?" Alex Curry asked. She even managed to sound sophisticated as she passed vegetables around the table.

Dee sighed. "My stomach says yes, my hips say no."

"Listen to your stomach. You can't be more than a size eight."

"God bless your failing eyesight," Dee said. "I'm into double digits."

Alex lowered her voice. "Your secret will die with me."

I like you, Dee thought as she sipped her wine. Who would have figured it? She was glad she'd forced the issue and ordered Alex to stay for dinner. When Alex had walked into the diner the other day, Dee had been ready to write her off as a rich bitch, the kind she wouldn't give two cents for. Her mother used to say that Dee had been born with a sixth sense about people, and when she took a dislike to someone, there was a good reason.

She supposed jealousy was a pretty good reason. Alex was younger and prettier, and half the men at the dinner table were already more than a little bit in love with her;

the other half were head over heels. She smiled her thanks as John refilled her wineglass. *Even you, old friend.* Oh, he thought he was being discreet, but anyone with eyes could see he was smitten with the new kid in school.

New kid in school. When was the last time she'd heard that expression? If only things could be as simple as they had been in the old days. Back then all you needed was the right outfit and a working knowledge of teen slang, and romantic happiness was guaranteed. Nobody told you that happy endings happened only in books or that Prince Charming didn't always live up to his press.

Of course, she probably wouldn't have believed them if they had.

And she wouldn't have Mark.

Her son was seated between Sally and Theresa Ippolito, Rich and Jen's daughter. He was slumped in his chair, shoulders rounded, head bowed, the poster boy for teen angst. She actually felt sorry for the poor kid, but not sorry enough to grant him a reprieve. It was Thanksgiving, and part of the Thanksgiving ritual was making those near and dear to you totally miserable.

Besides, how many more Thanksgivings would they have together? In two years Mark would go off to college, and once he got a taste of freedom, who knew how often he'd come back home.

"Are you okay?" Alex leaned close so only Dee could hear the question.

"Just feeling old," Dee said with a sigh. "He's growing up, and I can't seem to figure out a way to stop him."

Alex looked down the table at Mark, and an odd expression drifted across her face.

"Do you have any kids?" Dee asked.

Alex shook her head. "No kids."

Dee wanted to ask if she'd ever been married, but

woman's intuition told her not to go there. Besides, all she had to do was glance at the ring finger of Alex's left hand to know the story. That white band of skin was a dead giveaway. She'd had one of those herself thirteen years ago. "Nobody ever tells you how hard it's going to be," she said as much to herself as to Alex.

"Would you have believed them if they had?"

She chuckled softly. "Probably not. Back then I thought I knew all the answers." She took a sip of wine and forced a wide smile. "Maybe I didn't know all the answers, but at least I knew what was important."

Which was more than she could say for Mark's father.

"ANOTHER BEER?"

Brian Gallagher looked up at the bartender. "No," he said, tossing down a ten-dollar bill. "I'm fine." Two Coors were enough. Beer was one of those things he'd left behind when he moved to Manhattan years ago. Beer and flashy clothes and bad haircuts that marked you as Jersey Shore before you opened your mouth.

"If the Shore's good enough for that Bruce Springsteen guy, it's good enough for you." His old man was New Jersey–born-and-bred and proud of it. Which was great if you were a rocker with an attitude and a truckload of black leather, but it wouldn't wash in the world Brian was part of, the homogenized world of old money and WASP connections where kids were enrolled at tony preschools in utero. Over the years he'd managed to airbrush away the crucifixes and rosary beads dangling from the rearview mirror, the stink of fish and beer and salt air, but his past was always there in the background, waiting to trip him up.

So what the hell was he doing here, not five miles from his father's house? There was nothing for him here. His mother was dead. His brother was a loser. He was the only one in the fucking family who'd managed to make something of his life. So what if it was Thanksgiving and his wife and kids had fled to Aspen? All he had to do was get back in the Porsche and point it north, and two hours later he could be nursing a single malt Scotch while the city lights twinkled beyond his window.

But the minutes passed, and he continued to sit there in South Jersey, thinking of all the reasons why he shouldn't bother and the one reason why he had no choice.

ONE OF THE THINGS ALEX had learned during her marriage to Griffin was that you could learn a great deal about people simply by listening. She chatted a little with Dee and John but mostly she sipped her wine and listened to the conversations as they ebbed and flowed around her. She quickly learned which of the marriages were thriving, which were on hiatus, which were nothing more than a forty-year-old habit. She also learned that Eddie was a widower, Sally had never married, and Dee had been divorced since 1984.

The one person she'd learned absolutely nothing about was John Gallagher, which was quite a feat considering the fact that he was part of every conversation at the table. She found herself studying his face and then Mark's, trying to determine if the resemblance was only in her mind. When she first saw Mark she'd been certain that the name "Gallagher" was stamped across his forehead. Now she wasn't so sure. Mark's actions certainly didn't give her anything to go on. He ignored John the same way he ignored everyone else at the table. No, she had to look elsewhere for clues.

The unmistakable affection between John and Dee might be a good place to start.

The two of them were laughing about something Eddie had said, some remark about Vince's boat, *The*

Lady Gee. Laughing together in a way that was foreign
to her. She'd been married to Griffin for almost eleven
years, and they'd never once laughed like that. They'd
had their private jokes, same as most married couples,
but they'd never been able to go any deeper. Looking
back, she wasn't sure they'd wanted to.

Maybe it had something to do with the fact that John
and Dee had grown up together. They'd shared the same
experiences, had the same frame of reference. They
spoke to each other in a verbal shorthand that seemed
more intimate to Alex than a kiss or caress. The moment
of understanding she'd shared with John this afternoon
paled by comparison. A vivid image of Dee Murray in
John Gallagher's arms exploded behind her eyes, and
she tried to blink it away. Dee's fiery red hair . . . John's
brooding good looks—

If she didn't know better, she'd think she was jealous.
To her surprise, that notion held some appeal. She'd
spent so much of her life swallowing her emotions in
favor of maintaining the status quo that white-hot jealousy might feel good. At least then she'd know she was
finally plugged into the real world.

A car roared down the quiet street, all engine and
radio.

"Where's the fire?" Eddie grumbled. "Don't those
damn kids know this is a residential neighborhood? You
don't go driving around like a bat out of hell."

"How do you know it's kids?" John asked, a half-
smile on his face. "You had your share of speeding
tickets before they took your license away."

"Looks like he's making a U-turn out there," Rich
said as a flash of headlights danced past the windows.
The faintest hint of exhaust fumes tickled Alex's nos-
trils.

"Will you listen to that engine?" Vince asked. "That
ain't your average V-6."

Dee and John exchanged looks, and Alex watched as a deep red flush rose up the woman's throat and stained her cheeks. A moment later the doorbell rang.

"Someone's at the door, Dee," Sally called from the other end of the table.

Dee frowned and caught her son's eye. "You're not going out with Todd Franklin, are you?"

"No way," he said through a mouthful of candied sweet potatoes. "Todd's a loser."

The doorbell sounded again.

"You want me to answer it?" Sally asked. "I'm closest."

Dee shook her head. "Probably Jehovah's Witnesses," she said. "They'll go away."

It rang a third time.

"You've got to answer it," John said. "There are ten cars in the driveway, Dee. It's pretty obvious someone's home."

Dee didn't say anything. She also didn't get up from her chair. *She's afraid of something,* Alex thought. *Or someone.*

"I've got my hunting rifle in the car," Vince said sotto voce.

His wife socked him in the arm. "You idiot. What good's that going to do when—"

"Greetings, everyone." A handsome dark-haired man strode confidently into the dining room like the baronial master in a historical romance novel. The phrase "droit du seigneur" sprang to mind. "Glad I didn't miss dinner."

"Brian!" Eddie leaped to his feet and embraced the newcomer. "You're a sight for these sore eyes."

John's brother?

"Good to see you, Pop." Brian Gallagher said the right thing, but Alex noticed that he didn't return his father's hug. He broke away from Eddie and aimed his klieg-light smile at the table. He worked the room as if he were at a Shriners convention, kissing the women, shaking hands with the men. He had something special to say to every one of them. "Look at you," he said to Mark. "You must be pushing six-one by now."

The boy grunted something, but Alex couldn't make out the words. His mother, however, had no trouble.

"Mark." Dee's voice held a warning.

"He's a teenager, Dee Dee," Brian said with a false laugh. "He doesn't want to waste time talking to us old folks."

Dee turned toward Brian Gallagher. "You take care of your kids," she snapped, "and I'll take care of mine."

Mark pushed back his chair. "I'm outta here," he said, then took off for the front door.

"You want me to get him?" John asked. His voice was low, pitched for Dee's ears only, but Alex's hearing was almost as acute as her curiosity.

Dee shook her head. "Let him go. I don't blame him. If I weren't the adult, I'd run, too."

Brian was either oblivious to the undercurrents at the table, or he just didn't give a damn. He flattered Sally outrageously on her bright red hair and matching blouse, then kissed her hand. In many ways his studied charm reminded Alex of Griffin, and she found herself shrinking down into her chair, praying he'd overlook her.

"We know each other, don't we?" He towered over her and knew how to press the advantage.

She settled her expression into studied lines of composure. "I don't believe so." She offered him her hand. "I'm Alex Curry."

His grip was just shy of familiarity. "Brian Gallagher."

"John's brother?"

His smile widened. "Eddie's son."

She slid a quick glance in John's direction. The anger in his eyes was unmistakable.

"Are you sure we haven't met?"

"Positive," she said.

John stood up and faced his brother. "What are you doing here?"

"No 'Happy Thanksgiving,' little brother?"

He ignored the gibe. "Where are Margo and the kids?"

Brian met Alex's eyes, and she could see the wheels turning inside his head. "Aspen," he said, his attentions clearly divided. "With her parents."

"And you weren't invited?"

They're hanging on every word, she thought as she glanced around the table. From Eddie to Vince's wife, they were all paying close attention to the byplay between John and his brother.

"It's a holiday, Johnny." Brian made to pat his brother on the shoulder, but John took a large step back. "Why the third degree?"

Next to Alex, Dee stood up. "Are you hungry?" she asked Brian. There were no words of welcome or greeting. "If you are, I'll fix you a plate."

Brian met Dee's eyes, and Alex's breath caught. *So that's the way it is,* she thought. Dee Murray and Brian Gallagher. The teenage marriage that didn't work out.

"I'd like that, Dee Dee."

Dee's expression softened, and Alex's heart ached for her. *Don't look at him that way, Dee. Don't give him that power over you.* She seemed so young and vulnerable, not nearly old enough to be the mother of a sixteen-year-old boy.

"You can sit there." Dee motioned toward Mark's empty seat. "I think it's safe to say we won't be seeing him any time soon." She headed for the kitchen.

Alex stood up. "I'll see if Dee needs some help."

"Stay here," Brian said. "She likes to work alone."

"No," she said firmly, "I'm going to give her a hand." She wasn't about to sit there while he tried to figure out where he knew her from.

Dee was standing by the back door, smoking a cigarette.

"I thought you could use an extra pair of hands," Alex said as she approached.

Dee exhaled. Smoke wreathed her head like fog. "Only if the extra hands are willing to strangle him."

Be careful, Alex warned herself. *You don't know anything about the situation.* The only thing she did know was that—right or wrong—she'd disliked Brian Gallagher on sight.

"I'm not up for attempted murder," she said, "but I'd be happy to nuke the gravy for you."

Dee took a drag on her cigarette. "Some friend you are."

"I take it he wasn't invited."

"He was invited, all right," Dee said with a laugh. "It just took him almost twenty years to show up."

Alex couldn't think of a single thing to say that would be of any value. Any advice she might offer would be based solely on conjecture, as Dee hadn't offered any clues about her relationship with Brian Gallagher. "Why don't I fix the plate for him?" she offered.

Dee took a drag on her cigarette, then tossed it out into the rain-soaked backyard. "I'd appreciate that," she said. "I might add a side of hemlock just for the hell of it."

Alex took a microwavable plate from the cupboard and set about arranging turkey and all the accoutrements in the pinwheel fashion she'd learned in one of her cooking classes. She left a spot for the cranberry sauce. "What do you think?" she asked Dee. "A thirty-second nuking should cover it."

"You're really good at this," Dee said, admiring Alex's handiwork.

Alex grinned and popped the plate into the microwave. "You have to be good at something."

BRIAN EXCUSED HIMSELF TO GET something from his car. John followed him out to the driveway.

"So what the hell are you doing here?" he asked as Brian unlocked the car door.

"It's Thanksgiving," Brian said. "We're family. Families spend Thanksgiving together."

What a crock of shit. Brian had an angle, and John was going to find out what it was. "Then why are your wife and kids in Aspen?"

Brian leaned across the front seat and grabbed a large bottle. "A magnum of Dom," he said, locking the door again. "Think Dee Dee will like it?"

"She might have liked a phone call before you showed up at her door." Or something she could actually use. Brian was still more into impressing people than making them happy.

"Sounding a little possessive there, Johnny. Have you and Dee Dee finally—"

John's fist met his brother's chin in mid-sentence. Brian staggered back against the Porsche, and John caught the champagne bottle just before it crashed to the driveway.

"Say something like that again," John warned, "and you'll be picking your teeth out of the asphalt."

Brian rubbed his chin gingerly. "I'd sue your fucking ass, but the paperwork would cost more than the settlement I could get out of you."

"Did Margo finally have enough of your shit and move out?" His sister-in-law was too upwardly mobile for his tastes, but she'd always been pleasant enough to him. Sometimes more pleasant than he deserved.

"Her parents opened the ski lodge a week early. She took the kids out to celebrate the holiday with them."

John couldn't contain the smirk. "And they didn't roll out the red carpet for the aging Boy Wonder of Bailey, Banning, and Horowitz?"

"Go to hell." Brian tried to push past John, but John wouldn't move. "I'm taking a depo tomorrow in White Plains. If I went to Aspen, I'd never get back in time."

"Leave Dee alone," John said through clenched teeth.

"Fuck off."

Work before family. Brian's priorities had been set in the cradle, and nothing would ever change them. A long time ago he'd said he would be a full partner by his fortieth birthday and so far he was on track to his goal. Most of the fight seeped out of John, and he turned away.

"You're not going back to the house?" Brian asked.

"What's it to you?"

"I wouldn't mind having a chance to talk to the new face without you shooting me dirty looks."

"Are you talking about Alex?" His hands were curling into fists again.

"There's something familiar about her," Brian said, "but I can't quite get a handle on her yet."

"You're pathetic. You've got a wife and kids, you bastard. Do you have to try to score with every woman you bump into?"

"Who said anything about scoring?" Brian's outrage didn't quite ring true. "I'm saying I think I know her from somewhere."

"She doesn't know you."

"Maybe she does and she's not saying."

John made a face of utter disgust. "Who'd blame her?"

Brian ignored the slam. "So where'd you meet her?"

He hesitated, but he wasn't sure why. After all, it was a matter of public record. "She bought the Winslow house."

"What?"

"The Winslow house," John repeated.

"It wasn't supposed to be on the market until the New Year."

"How the hell would you know when the Winslow house was going on the market?"

Brian's face closed in on itself. "Let's call it a lucky guess."

EIGHT

BRIAN GALLAGHER'S PRESENCE AT THE dinner table changed everything, Alex thought as she served dessert. Where the conversations had been free-flowing and lively before, they were careful and formal now. Except for John, who wasn't talking at all; he just stabbed at his apple pie as if it were a rattlesnake on the attack. She wouldn't say the other dinner guests disliked Eddie's elder son, but it was painfully clear they were very uncomfortable around him.

She didn't blame them one bit. Every time she looked up, she found him looking at her with a curious expression in his eyes that made her uneasy.

"Looks good, Dee Dee," Brian said as Dee dropped his dinner plate in front of him. "How about some more stuffing?"

"All out," she said.

"Cranberry sauce?"

"None left."

"You wouldn't happen to have a—"

"The cupboard's bare, Brian," Dee said, taking her

seat at the head of the table. She picked up her dessert fork. "You're lucky you have that much."

"Lucky and grateful," he said, sweeping a smile from one end of the table to the other.

"Sweet Jesus," Eddie erupted, "this isn't one of your candy-ass New York dinners, Brian. Can't you just shut up and eat like everyone else?"

A ripple of laughter moved its way down the table. Even Dee grinned as she poked at her pumpkin pie. John was obviously too angry to find any humor in the situation, but Brian, to Alex's surprise, took the gibe with good grace.

"You're right, Pop," he said, spearing a sweet potato with the tines of his fork. He popped it in his mouth, chewed, then swallowed. "Good food, Dee."

The woman's face flushed dark red. "Enjoy," she said, not meeting his eyes.

"Hear a nor'easter's working its way up the coast," Eddie said as he polished off his apple pie à la mode. "Should hit after midnight."

"You better batten down your hatches, missy." Sally wagged a fork in Alex's direction. "Poor old Marge had herself the devil of a time whenever a storm blew in."

"You'll have to do something about that roof," John said, breaking his silence, "and soon."

"Better start with a ceiling," Eddie chimed in, "or you'll need a rowboat to get from the living room to the kitchen."

That remark got everyone's attention, including Brian's.

"Marge Winslow's house?" he asked.

"Yes," Alex said.

"John told me, but I didn't believe him."

"I don't know why you wouldn't believe him," she said, careful to maintain an even tone of voice. "People buy houses all the time."

"The Winslow place is a dump," Brian said. "What idiot steered you to it?"

"I steered myself," she said, then mentioned the newspaper ad in the *Star-Ledger.*

"That's where you made your mistake," Brian said. "You should have used the *Times.*"

John started to say something, but she beat him to it.

"I did try the *Times,*" she said, aware that she and Brian were the focus of everyone's attention. "I'm afraid their offerings were too rich for my blood."

"Come on," Brian said with a laugh. "Those earrings you're wearing probably cost double what you paid for the house."

Sally almost choked on her coffee. Dee's fork clattered to her plate. John looked ready to go for his brother's throat. Everyone else stared at her ears as if the crown jewels were hanging from her lobes.

"I hope you bring an expert with you when you buy jewelry for your wife," she said, "because these are cubic zirconium."

"CZ and platinum?"

How on earth could he tell platinum from across the table? "Wrong again," she said. "Sterling silver. I bought them from QVC. I'm sure I have the order number filed away someplace if you'd like it."

"I couldn't live without my QVC," Sally piped up. "I got a four-carat Diamonique band that could fool Mr. Tiffany."

God bless you, Sally Whitton, Alex thought gratefully, and God bless the fact that she'd watched the popular home shopping channel more than a few times herself. She chatted with Sally and the other women about the different show hosts, uncomfortably aware of the fact that Brian was evaluating every word she uttered.

For that matter, so was John, and yet his scrutiny didn't give her the uneasy feeling that she was about to walk straight into the jaws of a trap. John's attention made her feel alive.

BRIAN MANAGED TO CORNER ALEX as she came out of the bathroom an hour later.

"Oh!" She jumped back in surprise. "I didn't know you were waiting out here."

"No problem," he said, that same bland smile on his face that she knew so well from Griffin.

She flattened herself against the wall, expecting him to walk by and cross the threshold into the bathroom. He didn't, and her anxiety level escalated.

"I'm sorry if I made you uncomfortable out there," he said.

"Uncomfortable?" She hated to think that she could be so transparent to a stranger.

"All that talk about your house. It was insensitive."

"Yes," she said, "it was."

"It's probably a great fixer-upper."

"I hope so."

"I imagine you'll keep half of Sea Gate employed."

"How would I do that?"

"Fixing up the house."

"I'd figured to do it myself."

"You don't look like the kind of woman who likes to get her hands dirty."

"Is there a point to this conversation?" she asked bluntly. "Because if there isn't, I'm going to rejoin the crowd in the family room."

"Only that you don't see too many pairs of Ferragamos in Sea Gate."

"I'm a good shopper."

"Or an even better liar."

"You've never heard of thrift shops?"

"I've seen you before," he said, and she knew from

his tone of voice that he believed it. "I can't figure out where but I will."

"This is quite amusing," she said. "Please make sure you let me know what you find out."

"I will, Alex Curry," he said as she pushed past him. "You can bank on it."

"HE DID SOMETHING TO UPSET her," Dee said to John after Alex left. They'd gone to the kitchen to get more coffee for the crowd. "I don't know what but I know that son of a bitch did something."

"I asked her," John said, adding sugar to his own cup, "but she shrugged it off."

Dee was almost in tears. "It was such a nice day until he showed up. Damn him." Her voice shook with emotion. "I wish he'd—" She stopped abruptly and turned away.

John glanced at the kitchen clock. "It's after eight. How much longer is he going to stay?"

"Until the rest of you leave." Dee turned back to face him. "Don't you know what he's doing, Johnny? He's here for me."

"You gotta be kidding."

"I wish I was."

"What do you mean, he's here for you?" She'd made it sound like something from an old horror movie.

She gave him a pitying look. "What planet are you from, Johnny? His wife's away, and he's had too much to drink. Classic," she said. "Pathetic and classic. It's not like it hasn't happened before."

He grabbed her by the arms. "Happened before? What the hell does that mean?"

She pulled away from him. "He wants to fuck me. Is that clear enough for you?"

"Jesus." His stomach twisted with anger. "You're not—"

"I'm a fool," she said, "but not that big a fool. At least not yet."

"You've been there, Dee, and it didn't work."

"Like I need to be reminded? All I have to do is look at Mark."

"Want me to set him straight?"

"You already socked him in the jaw. That's enough for one holiday, don't you think?"

"Why don't I—"

"You don't need my problems," she said. "You have enough of your own." She took his hand. "Like Eddie."

"Eddie?" He pulled his hand away. "Nothing's wrong with Eddie."

"You know something's wrong, honey, and you're going to have to deal with it sooner or later."

"So he walks in his sleep. Since when is that a crime?"

"You're kidding yourself, Johnny, and it's not being fair to your father."

"Good try, Dee," he said. "Now, why don't we talk about being fair to your son."

Her eyes welled with tears. "You bastard."

"Yeah," he said, turning away. "I guess it runs in the family."

"DAMN!" ACROSS TOWN ALEX SLAPPED the steering wheel of her VW in frustration. "Start, car, *start*!"

She turned the key again and was rewarded once more with the sound of utter silence. How could a car break down at a stop sign? The salesman had promised her she'd get at least another year out of the battery, and she'd believed him.

Talk about a clean sweep. Her house had more leaks than the Clinton White House, and her car was a candidate for Dr. Kevorkian. What was next, a visit from space aliens?

Dark sheets of rain fell across the windshield, making it impossible for her to see beyond her own fender. She'd been stuck in the intersection for ten minutes, and not one single car had driven by. She had the feeling she could sit there another ten with the same result.

To make matters worse, she'd left her umbrella in the brass stand in Dee's foyer. She'd been in such a rush to leave that it was a wonder she'd remembered her coat and car keys.

"Stay a little longer," Dee had urged. "I usually make sandwiches around eleven."

"Sounds wonderful," Alex had said, "but I couldn't eat another bite."

"I could shoot Brian," Dee said fiercely. "I'm sorry if he made you uncomfortable."

Alex had said nothing. Brian had made her uncomfortable, but that wasn't why she was leaving. His relentless probing unnerved her, but not half as much as simply being in the same room with his brother. John made her feel things she'd only read about, a mix of heat and longing so fierce it shattered her fondest illusions about herself. About the kind of woman she was. Sex had never been an important part of her life. She'd craved the tenderness and closeness that came afterward when Griffin held her in his arms, but she'd never known how it felt to burn with desire for a man's touch.

She knew now. She could still feel his powerful grip as he'd held her last night to keep her from falling. The shameless way she'd wanted to press herself against him and brand herself with his heat. Now it was even worse. Now she wanted to know his secrets.

Wind rocked the small car like a cradle. It was obvious a traveling auto mechanic wasn't going to materialize, and she certainly couldn't spend the night here.

She didn't have a choice. She'd leave the car where it was and worry about it first thing in the morning.

She ran through the rain-soaked streets, dodging puddles and potholes with varying degrees of success. Five minutes later she let herself into her house, just in time to empty the pans and buckets she'd left beneath the leaks in the living room before they overflowed. She knew that sooner rather than later she would have to find a more permanent remedy, but ceiling or no ceiling, she was glad to be home.

And it really did feel like home. She wouldn't have believed a person could put down roots in less than a week, but that's exactly what had happened. Within these four walls, she was more herself than she had ever been in her life.

JOHN DID HIS BEST TO outlast his brother, but Eddie's hiatus hernia started acting up, and they called it a night around ten o'clock.

"Want me to come back?" he said quietly to Dee as she saw them to the door.

"I'm a big girl, Johnny," she said. "I can take care of myself."

John glanced toward the living room, where Brian—together with a bottle of Scotch—was holding court. "He's drunk, Dee. What if—"

"Don't worry," she said, kissing his cheek. Her breath smelled like wine and cinnamon. "I've called for a very expensive limousine to drive him home." She grabbed his wrist and checked his watch. "In one hour he'll be on his way to Manhattan and a major hangover."

She wasn't his wife or sister. He didn't have any right to tell her how to live her life. "I hope you know what you're doing."

"Of course I know what I'm doing," she said, her

tone heavy with sarcasm. "That's why I'm divorced and waiting tables at the Starlight."

The drive home took ten minutes. Eddie slept for nine of them.

"Getting old stinks," he said, climbing out of the truck. "I used to be able to kick butt until the sun came up." He groaned and rubbed a spot at the top of his chest. "Now I can't even eat two pieces of pumpkin pie without catching hell."

John laughed. "I'll take care of Bailey. You go pour yourself a Pepto cocktail."

Grumbling, his old man let himself into the house. A second later Bailey exploded through the front door and aimed herself straight at John. "Glad to see you, too, girl." He scratched her behind the ear. "In case you haven't noticed, we're having a nor'easter. How about getting down to business?"

Bailey didn't care about the weather. A full-blown tornado wouldn't have stopped her. She ran laps through the muddy front yard, paws sliding in all directions. Every now and then she threw a look in John's direction as if to reassure herself that he was still there. It felt good. Nobody else seemed to want him around.

He leaned against the truck, letting the wind and rain pummel him. He didn't much like thinking about Dee being alone with Brian. His brother was a sly son of a bitch. Some men practiced law to help right society's wrongs; Brian practiced law to see how far he could push the envelope. Unfortunately that was the same way he treated women. Dee was a lot more vulnerable than she cared to admit, and John was afraid a little sweet talk at the right moment would be enough to persuade her to take a horizontal walk down memory lane.

"Not your business, Gallagher," he said out loud. She had made it clear to him, and it was time he listened. Bailey stopped in her tracks and cast him a quizzical look. You were in sorry shape when your dog wondered about your sanity. He called Bailey to his side and scratched her under her chin, but she wasn't buying it. He didn't blame her. He felt restless and agitated, as if the storm had centered itself in the middle of his chest and was looking for a way out.

He'd felt that way since Alex Curry walked into the Starlight and asked for a job. The sound of her voice, that strangely elegant accent, filled him with delight. There was an air of sadness about her, a look of loneliness in her tawny gold eyes that he understood. She was the stranger at Dee's Thanksgiving Day dinner table, and yet he felt closer to Alex than to anyone else in the room. Looking at her beautiful face, he'd felt a sense of longing so deep it scared him.

He'd thought those feelings were three years dead, buried with his wife and children. Buried with what remained of his heart.

Bailey finally got tired of running around in the mud and galloped up to the front door, barking to be let inside.

"Come on in, girl." Eddie opened the door wide. "Who'd want to be out on a night like this?"

Bailey licked his hand and disappeared into the house.

It struck John that that was the last place he wanted to be.

"You gonna stand there all night?" Eddie asked. "Dog's got more sense than you."

"You take your Pepto?"

"Couldn't," Eddie said. "I'm all out."

John jingled his car keys in his pocket. "I'll go get you some."

"Don't be a schmuck. There's no place open."

"There's an all-night CVS near the mall."

"I'll live," his father said.

"That's not what you said back at Dee's."

"Yeah, so maybe I exaggerated."

"You either hurt or you don't." Lately it seemed like Eddie could change his mind mid-sentence.

"What's it to you?" Eddie countered. "I'm not asking you to play nursemaid."

"Dee wanted us to stay."

"You can't run interference between those two for the rest of your life, Johnny. Sooner or later it's going to happen, and there's nothing you can do to stop it."

"Lock up," John said, turning away. "I'm going out."

"Hey," Eddie called after him. "You're not taking the truck?"

He ignored his father.

"You're running in this weather? You really are crazy."

You're right, Pop, he thought as he broke into a run. *Crazy about covers it.*

ALEX COULDN'T SLEEP. EVERY TIME she closed her eyes she saw John the way he had been that afternoon, with his great head bent over the steering wheel of his truck. No matter how hard she tried, she couldn't forget the terrible sounds of anguish that had torn from his throat. She'd felt like an intruder, the worst kind of voyeur, peering into the secret part of his heart.

The old Alex would never have stood there with her own heart on her sleeve, fighting the urge to hold him in her arms and ease his pain. She would have turned away the instant she saw him, pushing the images of his raw pain from her mind as if she'd never seen them at all. That was what polite people did. They averted their eyes from unpleasant sights. They closed their ears to things they didn't want to hear. They pretended the world was a perfectly wonderful place until it exploded and left them wondering what had been wrong in paradise.

She should have asked Dee about him. People asked questions about other people all the time. Is he married? Does he have kids? Who does he love? Whole industries had sprung up around the need to know the most intimate details of other people's lives. But every time she'd tried to form the words, her throat had closed up, and she was left with the certainty that he deserved better than her curiosity.

She kicked off the covers and sat up against the headboard. Rain beat steadily against the roof, and she tried not to think about the leaks or the missing ceiling—or how much money it would cost her to repair them. She'd never thought about things like that when she was Griffin's wife. There hadn't been a reason to. Money—or the lack of it—had never been an issue. She spent money how and where she wanted to, and somehow the bills got paid. It hadn't occurred to her to ask how.

Brian had zeroed in on her earrings immediately, and while she'd done a good job of deflecting attention away from them, her facile lies had left a bad taste in her mouth. She didn't want to begin her new life on a foundation of lies and half-truths. She would be better off selling the earrings so she could resurrect her dead car and make sure what remained of her roof didn't drop down and crush her one night while she slept.

Maybe next week she'd take the train up to New York and—

There was a knock at the front door, and her breath caught. They'd warned her about the vandalism going on at the marina next door. Did vandals knock before they trashed your house?

"Alex." A man's voice, smoky and dark. A *familiar* voice. "Alex, are you in there?"

She climbed from bed and padded to the window.

Rain sluiced down the panes of glass, obscuring her vision. She could just make out a male figure by the front door.

John, she thought as heat began to build inside her body. It was John.

His voice resonated inside her chest. "If you're in there, let me know you're okay. I found your car and—"

She dashed from the bedroom and through the hallway, then swung open the front door a few seconds later. "I'm fine," she said as the rain whipped her nightgown around her legs. "I stalled the engine at the stop sign. I think the battery's dead."

"I saw the VW in the intersection." He wore a battered leather jacket and a look of such stunning tenderness on his face that she thought she would die of it. No one had ever looked at her that way before. "I pushed it over to the curb so you won't get a ticket."

"Thank you." She wrapped her arms around her chest, suddenly aware of her body in a way she hadn't been a few moments before. "I'm sorry I left it there. I didn't mean to—"

"I didn't come here for an apology, Alex. I came to see if you're all right."

Her mouth trembled slightly as she smiled. She was conscious of every movement of her body, each breath, every beat of her heart. "I'm fine."

"Good," he said. "That's all I wanted to know. Go back inside. It's cold out here."

He turned to leave. It was the one thing she couldn't let him do. "You're soaked to the skin. Come in and let me make you some coffee."

He met her eyes. "That's not a good idea."

She chose to misunderstand his look. "Coffee is always a good idea."

She stepped back and ushered him into the house.

Droplets of water fell from his hair and shoulders as he moved past her. One landed, like a teardrop, on her cheek.

"I hope you don't mind waiting," she said cheerily as he followed her into the kitchen. "I don't have one of those coffee machines that work at the speed of light. Believe it or not, I actually have to boil water on the stove."

"Primitive," he remarked, lingering in the doorway. "Next you'll tell me you don't have a dishwasher."

She frowned and thrust her hands behind her back. "No fair," she said. "You saw the dishpanned evidence."

He didn't laugh or smile, just watched her as she filled the whistling teakettle with water from the sink, then set it on the stove. "Come on," she murmured, holding a lighted kitchen match near the right front burner. "I know you can do it."

His footsteps squeaked against the linoleum. "What's wrong?"

"Nothing," she said as her entire body registered his approach. "The stove likes a little encouragement, that's all."

"Marge used to complain about the pilot light." He stopped no more than two feet away from where she stood. Close enough that she could smell the rain on his leather jacket. "Why don't you let me have a look."

"That's not necessary."

"You don't fool around with the pilot light." He reached for the match. "Let me—"

His hand closed around hers. Her head shot up, and their eyes met as the match flared, then died.

"Let me," he said again, his voice low and tender. "Let me, Alex."

There was no mistaking his words. No mistaking their meaning. It was where they had been headed since they'd first met. Since the first moment. He waited. *This is your choice,* his look said. *Your decision.*

Her pulse beat wildly at the base of her throat. *I barely know you,* she thought. *All I know is how you make me feel.* Alive and wild and strangely, wondrously safe. It was so little—and yet somehow it was enough.

NINE

❦

YOU'RE GOOD AT EXITS, JOHN told himself. He knew how to walk away with the best of them. Put one foot in front of the other and don't look back. He'd done it before. He could do it again. What difference did it make that she was looking at him with such open need, such powerful sweetness, that he felt himself stirring in both body and soul?

Loneliness did terrible things to a man. It made him want things he shouldn't have.

And he wanted Alex.

Her hand was cocooned in his, the match and stove forgotten. The connection between them seemed to grow stronger with each second that passed. She didn't know what she was doing; there was no way for her to know. A better man would have warned her away, told her that she should find someone else, that he didn't have anything to give but a few hours of pleasure, but it was too late.

She was already in his arms, and he was lost.

• • •

ALEX HAD NEVER BEEN HELD this way before. She fit against his body as if they'd been made for each other. He held her as if he meant it, as if holding her was an end in itself. She pressed her face against the side of his neck, and the smell of his skin made her almost dizzy with longing. Her palms rested against the front of his jacket, and the silky feel of rain and leather struck her as almost unbearably erotic.

They stood in the middle of the kitchen, with the rain falling and the wind howling and their hearts pounding like thunder inside their chests.

"Is this really happening?" she whispered, looking up into his eyes. "Are you really here?"

He traced the contours of her face with his thumbs, and his touch sent a current of electricity coiling straight to the center of her being. "You can still change your mind, Alex. If you don't want this, tell me now."

"I don't want to change my mind." She lifted her face toward his. "I don't want promises. I don't want a commitment." She touched the corner of his mouth with the tip of her finger. "All I want is tonight."

He kissed her then, a deliciously wet and sensual kiss that made her tingle from head to toe. She opened her mouth for him on a sigh of pure pleasure. *Yes,* she thought. *Oh, God, yes!* She craved his touch, a skin hunger that went soul deep.

He swept her up into his arms and cradled her against his chest. She laughed softly, equal parts delight and anticipation, as he carried her into the small bedroom at the end of the hall.

"Lights?" he asked, stopping in the doorway.

"No," she whispered. "No lights." She wanted nothing but his touch and the velvety blackness of night. They fell to the bed together, a tangle of arms and legs and hungry mouths and eager hands and a ferocious need that was pushing them close to madness and beyond. She'd never known anything like this before, never known the touch of a man's hand could make her feel so shatteringly, wildly alive.

She tugged his jacket from his body.

He slid a hand beneath the hem of her nightgown.

She worked at the zipper on his jeans.

He found the nest of curls between her thighs.

A low moan formed in her throat as he caressed her with his fingers.

"So soft," he murmured against the skin of her breasts. "Like wet silk."

So hard, she thought, cupping him with her hand. Like the purest, hottest steel.

He rocked against her, and her hips arched to meet his. She could feel herself blossoming, opening for him, wanting everything he had to give and more. It had been so different with Griffin toward the end. Dry and joyless and so without tenderness that it hurt her to remember.

"Alex?" His voice curled inside her ear. "Is something wrong?"

"Yes," she said, willing the past away. "This isn't enough."

He stripped her of her nightgown, then ripped off his own clothes. He leaned over the bed, a fierce god ready for battle. She slid to the edge of the mattress and pressed her lips against his flat belly, then traced his coarse mat of curls with the tip of her tongue. A guttural moan sounded from deep within his chest, and it was all she could do to keep from crying out in triumph. His erection was long and full, a hot and throbbing presence between them. She rubbed it against her cheek, stroking its length with curious, but not gentle, fingers. He smelled like sex, a dark and vibrant smell that made her want to mark him as her own.

She cupped his buttocks with her hands as she attempted to learn the secrets of his body. Her breasts rubbing against his bare flesh, she took him in her mouth and savored the weight and length and taste of him. It was all so new, so dangerous, so wonderful—she felt as if she had awakened from a long sleep to discover that the world was more amazing than she'd ever dreamed.

JOHN'S MUSCLES BURNED WITH THE effort to restrain himself. He'd been with other women, but it had never been like this. She held him in her mouth as if he were a carnal sacrament, something both holy and profane, moving her lips up and down his shaft, tracing the sensitive ridge of flesh with her tongue, making him see God in the curve of a woman's sweet naked back.

She was urging him on, begging him to come by the way she cupped his testicles in her hand, with the catlike sounds she made in the back of her throat. It would be easy to let it happen. All he had to do was lower his guard for a second and let sensation take over and he'd explode inside her mouth.

But that wouldn't be enough. He wanted more from her, more than he'd ever wanted before . . . maybe more than she had to give. He gripped her by the shoulders.

"Your turn," he said, then knelt down between her open thighs and took her hot and swollen nub into his mouth. She cried out, and for a moment he was afraid he'd hurt her; but then her hips began to move to that age-old rhythm, and he smiled as her honey flowed. He couldn't get enough of her, piercing her with his tongue, moving against the slick, rippling walls of her sheath, imagining how it would feel when he buried himself inside her, when she wrapped her legs around his hips and drew him deeper and deeper. Until she brought him home.

SHE WASN'T SURE WHEN PURE pleasure had stopped being enough, but again she found herself wanting more.

There was an emptiness inside her, a yearning emptiness
that only he could fill, and miraculously he seemed to
realize that almost before she did. He kissed her thighs
and her belly, her breasts and the base of her throat, then
eased himself between her legs.

She trembled with wanting him, a delicious tension
that hummed through her body and made her want to
cry out with joy. He cradled her face between his hands
and kissed her, lightly at first, his lips barely grazing
hers, then more deeply, easing her lips open with his
tongue, sweeping past her teeth, drawing her own tongue
into battle. She wrapped her legs around his waist, and
he found her with his hand and then he found her again,
easing himself into her body with wondrously maddening
slowness, each simple move designed to take her
one step closer to the edge.

SHE MATCHED HIS RHYTHM, HER hips bucking sweetly
against him, urging him closer, deeper, harder. He felt himself climbing higher and higher, sailing across the sky like
a white-hot comet. She pleased him in ways he'd never
known before, ways he'd never known existed. The sweet
musky woman scent of her body enflamed him, and he
hungered for her, body and soul.

Something amazing was happening between them,
something that went beyond physical pleasure. He
wanted to know her secrets. He wanted to know what
made her cry. He wanted—Jesus, he didn't know what
he wanted. All he knew was that he was so damn tired
of being alone.

THEY MADE LOVE FIERCELY, WILDLY, hearts colliding as they came together in a climax that left them
dazed and grateful.

They didn't speak when it was over. Words were a
poor substitute for magic. And it *was* magic. They both

were old enough to know that what they'd found together in that narrow bed was worth celebrating.

The second time they made love was different. They
knew each other's bodies now. Where to touch. When to
stop. How to coax and urge and satisfy. Nothing was off-
limits. No pleasure too forbidden to enjoy. The buildup
was slow and voluptuous, the payoff cataclysmic.

Outside the cold rain splashed against the windows
and beat down on the roof. Inside her home, it was warm
and safe. He gathered her close and drew the covers up
over them. She curled against him, burrowing her nose
between his arm and chest, and drew in a long breath.
His smell—was it possible to fall in love with the way
a man smelled? Could a woman get drunk just by
breathing in a man's scent?

She could hear his heart beating inside his chest. It
was the last sound she heard before she fell asleep in
his arms.

WHEN JOHN DREAMED, HE DREAMED that he wasn't
alone. He dreamed of the sweetly familiar weight of a
woman's body pressed close to his. The erotic mix of
rumpled sheets and sex. A deep sense of joy where sadness used to be.

He woke up before dawn to find out he wasn't dreaming. Alex Curry was nestled in the spoon-shaped curve
of his body, her bare rump pressed up against his groin,
his erection hard between them. His right arm rested
across her body. His hand gently cupped her breast.

The dim gray light of morning was beginning to seep
through the curtains. In another hour Sea Gate would
begin to stir. Rain or shine, a group of lawyers from
Atlantic County chartered a boat every Friday morning.
They didn't catch many fish, but John was damn glad
for the income. One thing he didn't want was for them—
or anyone else—to see him leaving Alex's house.

Quietly he climbed from her bed, shivering as the chill November air hit his naked body. The last thing he wanted to do was leave her, but he had no choice.

She stirred, and the blanket slipped down. Her soft dark gold hair spilled over the bare skin of her shoulder like a mantle as she opened her eyes. "You're not leaving?" Her voice was husky with sleep and very sexy.

"I'm leaving." He bent over her and kissed her full on the mouth. "Sea Gate's a small town, Alex. People talk."

"I don't care if they talk."

He smoothed her hair back from her forehead. "Go back to sleep. I'll call you later."

She sat up and tucked the covers neatly under her arms like a makeshift nightgown. "You don't have to call," she said, lifting her chin a fraction. "I said no strings and I meant it."

The mattress dipped as he sat down next to her. "I know I don't have to call," he said. "I want to."

She considered him for what seemed like forever. In the cover of darkness he'd felt as if he knew everything there was to know about her, but he'd been wrong. He didn't know anything at all. She was as much a mystery to him now as she'd been when he first saw her walk into the Starlight a few days ago.

"Call if you want," she said at last, "but I probably won't be home."

"Where are you going?"

"John." Her tone was unmistakable. "What difference could that possibly make to you?"

"You're right," he said, pulling back. "No difference."

She placed her hand on his forearm. "I didn't mean to hurt you."

"You didn't," he lied. He stood up and grabbed his shirt.

"John, please. You don't understand."

He slid his arms into the shirt. "Do I have to?"

"No, you don't. It's just—"

"Then save it, Alex. I have a charter group that expects to sail in an hour. I've got to go."

"A charter group? You work at the marina?"

"Does it matter?" It was a cheap shot, but cheap shots were about all he could manage at the moment.

He expected her to either slap back at him or crumple under his sarcasm. He should have known she wouldn't do either one.

"I deserved that," she said quietly. "I'm sorry for pushing you away."

"You don't owe me any explanations." He found his socks under the bed; where his shoes had ended up was anybody's guess. "No strings means no strings. It won't happen again."

She scrambled to her knees, clutching the bedcovers around her slender torso. "You don't understand."

"So what?" he countered. "Doesn't matter much either way."

"It does matter." Her amber eyes were wide and serious. "At least I hope it does."

He didn't say anything. His shoes were sticking out from under the window curtains, and he bent down to retrieve them.

"I'm afraid I'm not very good at this," she said.

He shoved his feet into his running shoes. "You made yourself pretty clear."

"That's not what I mean. I—oh, damn it, John. I've never done this before, and I'm making a real mess of it."

He made no attempt to hide his curiosity. "Done what?" She wasn't a virgin. Even during the heat of the moment, that much had been clear.

"This!" Her gesture encompassed him, herself, the entire room. "I've never had an affair."

He started to laugh, but there was something so unexpectedly innocent about her words that the laughter died in his throat. "You haven't?" He thought about the obvious wedding band mark on her left ring finger.

She shook her head. "I haven't." She met his eyes. "I don't know the rules."

What he wanted to do was gather her in his arms and kiss her senseless. What he did instead was sit back down on the edge of the bed. "There are no rules, Alex. There's just us."

US. THE WORD SENT A shiver through Alex's body. She had the feeling it meant something very different to John Gallagher than it had to her husband.

"I don't want you to think I expect anything from you," she said carefully. "Neither one of us knew this was going to happen."

"I knew."

She met his eyes. "You couldn't possibly."

"I knew the minute I saw you at the Starlight."

"I didn't." She couldn't withhold a grin. "I thought about it but I didn't know."

He ruffled her hair. "So where do we go from here?"

"I was hoping you'd tell me."

He looked at her as if he could see inside her soul. "What happens next is up to you."

"This was"—she searched for the right word—"amazing." He started to say something, but she raised her hand to stop him. "It was so wonderful, John, that it scares me. I moved here so I could learn how it felt to live my own life. If I start depending on you, I'll undermine my goal."

"Depending on me for what?"

"For—well, I'm sure you know what I'm talking about."

"No," he said, his eyes narrowing, "I don't."

The now-familiar heat spread outward from her belly. "For sex."

She waited for his reaction. If he laughed, she'd kill him with her bare hands. But once again John Gallagher surprised her.

"Don't depend on me, Alex." He sounded weary, as if he knew things she could never understand, and a wave of sadness filled her heart. "We'll both be a hell of a lot better off if you don't depend on me for anything."

It was exactly what she'd wanted to hear, but with one difference: She'd thought it would make her happy. Instead she felt as if something precious had slipped from her grasp before she'd even known it was there for the taking.

THE STREETS WERE DARK AND quiet as John made his way back home. The only sounds were the steady rumble of the ocean and the rhythmic thud of his footsteps as he ran. He couldn't outdistance his thoughts, but he could damn well give it his best shot.

You got what you wanted, he told himself as he headed south on Ocean Avenue. He'd found a woman who wanted as little from a relationship as he did. Sex with no strings, no hang-ups, no commitments. The kind of relationship most men would sell their Corvettes to find.

Her fierce independence was unmistakable in every move she made. She defended the space around her the way a medieval warrior defended his land. Her boundaries were invisible, but they were every bit as real as mortar and brick and wire. He respected those boundaries. He had a few of them himself.

The woman who didn't want anything and the man who had nothing to give. Any way you looked at it, they were the perfect match.

T E N

DEE'S SON MARK WOKE UP at five on the morning after Thanksgiving. He climbed from bed and reached for his jeans and a sweatshirt. It was still raining outside, but he didn't care. The house stunk from turkey and cigarette smoke, and he knew he had to get out of there or go frigging nuts.

He hated Thanksgiving. His mother always invited every old fart in town to have dinner with them, and, as if that wasn't bad enough, they stayed so long they practically grew roots. He didn't mind Eddie Gallagher, but the rest of them sucked. All they did was sit around and talk about getting sick and dying. As far as Mark was concerned, it couldn't be too soon. They all looked at him like it was his fault his mom worked as a waitress at the Starlight, like he'd done something to ruin her life. All he'd done was be born, and he hadn't had any choice in the matter.

He grabbed himself a quart of milk from the fridge and went out the back door. His mother's Toyota was in the driveway, and, to his disgust, that stupid SOB's red Porsche was parked right behind it, blocking the way. Gallagher had been on his way to getting plastered when Mark left. Mark figured he'd probably finished the job, and then been sent home in a cab by his mother.

At least he hoped that's what had happened.

He'd actually cracked her bedroom door and peered into the darkness to make sure she was alone. Thinking about her with Brian Gallagher made him want to puke. He knew about how she used to go out with the guy before she married his father. His father was a mean drunk who spoke with his fists. Gallagher must have been some bastard if his mother had left him for that.

He thought about it as he walked through the rain to the marina. He liked the rest of the Gallaghers just fine. John had been around a lot the last few years, since his wife and kids had bought it in a car crash. He wasn't bad, as far as adults went. In fact, Mark realized, he wouldn't mind at all if his mother fell for a guy like that instead of the string of losers she'd managed to find. If his mother hooked up with John, then Eddie would be his grandfather, and that sounded like a pretty good deal.

Eddie was cool. He'd been part of Mark's life for almost as long as he could remember. Eddie had taught him how to bait a hook, how to cast a line softly so he didn't ripple the water, and to toss back the little ones not just because the rules said so, but because it was the right thing to do. Once, when Mark was a little boy, Eddie had taken him out in an old sneakbox, a wide-beamed boat of light Jersey cedar, and shown Mark what the Shore was really about.

Mark and his mom had just come back up from Florida. New Jersey seemed like a different world after the bright white sunshine and tropical heat. He'd been scared and lonely until Eddie took him under his wing, inviting him to spend the day learning about his new home. They'd moved quietly along the shoreline, sailing atop the shallows as if they were lighter than air. There were no seats in a sneakbox. You sat on the floor with only your head sticking up, and Mark had had to stand in order to watch the bullheads and helldivers and sea pigeons.

He'd never forgotten that day, and until lately he'd always believed it was one of Eddie's fondest memories, too. One night Mark had had a fight with his mother, and he'd stormed out of the house and headed where he always headed when he was hurt or angry or scared. He'd found Eddie at the marina, bent over the *Kestrel* with a sledgehammer lying across his feet. A huge chunk of wood had been whacked from the starboard side, and Eddie's clothes were covered with splinters.

"Shit, Eddie." He'd felt stupid tears fill his eyes at the sight of his old friend sobbing as if his heart would break. "What did you do?"

Eddie had looked at Mark as if he didn't recognize him, and for a second Mark wanted to turn and run away. But he didn't. He threw the sledgehammer into the water and brushed the splinters of wood off Eddie's clothes. When the cops showed up, he even let them think he might have been the one who was responsible.

"You wanna press charges, Eddie?" Dan Corelli, one of the veteran Sea Gate cops, had asked.

Eddie had just looked at Dan as if they didn't even speak the same language.

That had happened about six months ago, and since then Eddie had taken to walking in his sleep and lots of other scary stuff. Sometimes Mark thought he never wanted to get old, that he'd rather die in a car crash or while sky-diving before his brain and his body failed him.

He pulled up the hood of his sweatshirt as he made his way along the pier. The boards were warped, rotted in places, but he knew exactly where to step and where not to step. The place stunk from fish and saltwater and motor oil, but he didn't mind. He liked everything about the marina. There was something about the place that made him feel like he belonged. He did his best thinking there at the end of the dock. He liked watching the sun come up over the Atlantic, turning the choppy gray waters to a deep greenish-blue. Sometimes he'd sit there and imagine that he had a real family, the kind you saw on television with brothers and sisters and a father who actually remembered his name. He was lucky if his old man remembered he was alive.

Six years ago Tony had stopped by to see him on his way up from Florida to New York. He'd clapped Mark on the back and muttered something stupid about line-backer's shoulders, then they'd stared at each other for fifteen minutes until Mark asked if he could go swimming with his friends. Mark had the feeling Tony had been as relieved as he was when his mom said he could go. He'd raced to his room to get his gear, but by the time he reached his door, a huge fight had broken out.

He tried to blank out the words, but some of them had crept into his head anyway and had never gone away.

"Some other guy's bastard . . ."

That night he'd asked his mother what that meant, and she'd told him some crap about how adults sometimes said things they didn't mean and how he shouldn't pay any attention to it. That had been all a ten-year-old needed to hear. His father left, his mother relaxed, and before long life went back to normal.

But lately he found himself thinking a lot about it. He knew what a bastard was, what it meant. It was bad enough thinking he was Tony Franco's son, but it was worse thinking he was nobody's son at all.

"Hey, Mark." John Gallagher's hand rested on his shoulder. "How's it going?"

"Okay, I guess."

"You seemed a little pissed when you walked out last night." John leaned against the mooring next to him.

"Yeah," he said, shrugging. "So?"

"So maybe you feel like talking about it. Your mom was pretty upset."

"It's got nothing to do with her."

"You know that, but I'm not so sure she does."

Mark watched as a gull circled twice, then landed on a piling. He kept his eyes riveted on that bird. "Why the hell did he have to show up and ruin everything?"

"You're talking about Brian?"

He nodded. An ugly lump of anger formed in his throat, and he didn't know exactly why. Or worse, maybe he really did. "Yeah," he managed. "Nobody asked him to show up. Why didn't he just stay the hell away?"

"I've been asking myself the same thing."

He glanced over at John. "You don't like him much, do you?"

"Not a hell of a lot."

"What about when you were my age? Did you like him then?"

"I tried." John lit a cigarette, took a drag, then tossed it. The butt made a hissing sound as it hit the water. "He didn't make it easy, I'll tell you that."

"He and my mom used to date each other when they were my age, didn't they?"

"Yeah, they did," John said, watching him. "That's not news, sport. You've known that since you were in diapers."

Sure he'd always known it, but he never really understood until he saw them together yesterday.

"The bad news is Brian's a pain in the ass," John said. "The good news is, he doesn't live here anymore."

• • • •

LIVING IN A SMALL TOWN had its advantages, Alex thought as she dialed the telephone. She didn't have any trouble picking a towing service. Sea Gate only had one to choose.

She explained the situation to the man who answered the phone. He sounded a trifle confused.

"It's really very simple," she said, switching the receiver to her other ear. "My car stalled out at the corner of Margate and Barnegat. I need you to tow it into the shop and fix it as quickly as possible."

"A VW wagon, right?"

"Yes, but how—"

"It'll be ready this afternoon."

"You know that just by what I told you?"

There was a brief silence. "Your car's here, lady."

"That's not possible. You must have my car confused with somebody else's."

"Believe me, I haven't seen one of these babies in at least ten years."

She sank down onto a kitchen chair. "Did the police tow it into the shop?" God only knew what kind of fines she'd be facing if they had.

"Hold on a minute." She heard him cover the phone, then yell a question at someone. "John Gallagher called in the order."

"What?" There had to be some mistake.

"I'm looking at the order sheet right now. Johnny Gallagher called in around six-thirty. Said it was an emergency."

She gritted her teeth. "When did you say I can pick it up?"

"We'll drop it off when it's done."

"Did Mr. Gallagher tell you to do that?"

"He sure did." The poor man had no idea he was speaking to a woman on the verge of an explosion. "Everything's paid for, too."

That did it. She managed to thank the man for his trouble, then slammed down the receiver. Who did John Gallagher think he was? She grabbed her jacket from the coat closet and stormed out the front door.

"LAST CHANCE," JOHN SAID TO Mark. "Once we push off, you're in for the long haul."

"I'm ready," Mark said.

John had been twelve the first time he went out on the *Kestrel* with his old man. He'd heard all the stories about party boats and figured some of the fun had to filter down to the crew.

He'd figured wrong. Not only didn't the fun filter down, but also the crew had to work their asses off trying to keep the beer-swilling great unwashed from falling overboard.

The kid was definitely in for a surprise.

"Vince will throw you the line," he told Mark. "You remember what to do with it?"

Mark nodded.

"Okay," John said. "Let's get going before we have a mutiny." The six Atlantic County lawyers on board were starting to get a little restless, and restless lawyers were ugly lawyers. John knew. He used to be one of them.

He motioned for Mark to follow him around the stern.

"Where the hell is Vince?" he asked, scanning the dock. He cupped his hands around his mouth. "Yo, Vince! We're ready."

Vince popped out of the office. "You better come down here, Johnny."

"Whatever it is can wait until we get back. Toss the line up."

"You're not listening," Vince hollered back. "You'd better get down here pronto, and I mean pronto."

Eddie, John thought. What else could it be?

He turned to Mark. "Keep your eye on the lawyers," he said. "I'll be right back."

Mark looked as if he was being left alone in a shark tank. "What if they try to trash the boat?"

"If they try that, hose 'em down."

He vaulted the rail and headed for the marina office.

"This had better be good, Vince," he said as he pushed open the door. "I've got half a dozen lawyers on board, and they'll sue my ass from here to Cape May if I don't—" He stopped cold. "Alex."

She was sitting in his desk chair, looking up at him. He'd seen killer bees who weren't half as angry.

Vince looked from Alex to John. "I think I'll leave you two kids alone," he said, then let himself out the front door.

"How dare you," she said, her voice shaking with outrage. "You had no right."

What had happened between them had been consensual. At least it had seemed that way to him at the time.

He'd started to frame a defense when she reached into the pocket of her raincoat and pulled out her wallet. He watched, in shock, as she withdrew two crisp hundred-dollar bills.

"There," she said, pushing them into his hand. "That should cover it."

"What the hell are you talking about?" he demanded.

"Must you swear all the time?" she countered. "Your language seems unnecessarily salty."

"It comes with the territory." He tossed the money back at her. "If I charged, I'd ask for a hell of a lot more than that."

Her cheeks reddened. "What on earth are you talking about?"

"Payment for services rendered."

"You arrogant—" She stopped mid-sentence.

"Go ahead. Say it."

Her amber eyes flashed fire. "The money was for my car."

"Your car?"

"The repairs," she said, speaking slowly as if English wasn't his first language. "You shouldn't have done it."

He waved away the money. "A thank-you would be enough."

"I'm not thanking you," she said. "It's my car, my problem."

"You're new in town. I figured you wouldn't know who to call."

"Not a difficult thing to do," she said. "Take a look at the yellow pages, John. There's only one choice in town."

His impulsive gesture was turning into a disaster. "Look," he said, "I wasn't trying to upset you. I gave in to impulse. " He shrugged. "So sue me."

"You think I'm overreacting, don't you?"

"I didn't say that."

"It's written all over your face. And I resent it."

"You're right," he said. "You are overreacting. It was a gesture of affection, not domination."

"You could have sent flowers, you know."

"You didn't need flowers. You needed your car."

"It's not up to you to give me what I need."

That had to be one of the more loaded statements he'd heard in his time. "So what are you saying, Alex?"

He could almost see her spine stiffen. "I'm saying that it's my life. I'll make my own decisions."

He met her eyes. "Fine," he said. "You've got it." He turned and stalked toward the door. "See you around, Alex."

"John, wait."

He paused in the doorway. "I've got a boatload of lawyers looking to catch Jaws."

"You won't let me reimburse you?"

"Let it go, Alex."

She took a deep breath. "If you won't take the money, then come to my house for dinner."

"Real warm invitation," he said, arching a brow. "You act like there's a score to settle."

"There is." The expression on her face softened noticeably. He took it as a good sign. "What I mean is, I don't like being in someone's debt."

"You're not in my debt."

"I'm two hundred dollars in your debt."

"That's a lot of dinners."

"I know," she said. "That's why we should get started."

It was tough, but he managed to maintain a neutral expression. Splitting the atom would have been easier. She was the most difficult, most confusing, most desirable woman he'd ever met. "Can I bring flowers?"

"Yes," she said, a soft smile lighting up her serious face. "Flowers are fine."

Her smile slid inside his heart and began to grow. "I'll be bringing the boat back in around six."

"Then you can come over at eight."

He glanced outside. There was nobody around. "Come here," he said.

"You come here."

He did. He swept her into his arms, bent her backward like the pose on the cover of one of those romance novels he saw at the grocery store, and kissed her.

"Oh!" Her eyes glowed with delight. He took that as a personal triumph.

"I'll be there by seven," he said. There were times when a man had to put his foot down.

She touched the corner of his mouth with her fingertip. "I'll be ready by six."

•   •   •

THE BUZZER WOKE BRIAN UP a little before eleven. He stumbled from bed, his head throbbing as if it was ready to burst, and made his way through the long narrow hallway to the intercom. He pressed the button and managed a shaky "Yes?"

"Delivery for you, Mr. Gallagher."

"Sign for me, Ray. I'll pick it up later."

"I don't think I can sign for this one, Mr. G. It's your Porsche."

"My car? What the—" He looked down and saw he was wearing the same clothes he'd been wearing the day before. His mouth tasted like a landfill and his head— Jesus, his head. Classic hangover, he thought. Probably Scotch. "Give me ten minutes."

He made his way toward the master bathroom. Every step he took sent aftershocks rocketing through his body. Dead would be better, he thought. A hell of a lot better.

He stripped off his clothes, then turned on the shower full blast. The sound of the water splashing against the tiles made him wince. A man was in bad shape when water hurt.

Good thing he'd been lying about the depo in White Plains. If any of his clients saw him like this, he'd be chasing ambulances in Queens.

Twenty minutes later he strode across the marble lobby as though nothing had happened.

Ray the doorman was talking to a young guy in jeans and an Aerosmith sweatshirt. Brian's Porsche was double-parked in front of the building, surrounded by UPS trucks and kamikaze cabs and messengers on bikes from hell.

"Morning, Mr. Gallagher." Ray tipped his hat. "I'll leave you two to settle up."

The young guy in the Aerosmith sweatshirt jingled Brian's car keys in his hand. "That'd be three hundred forty-five dollars."

"Who the hell are you?" Brian demanded. "I don't remember hiring anyone to tow my car."

"Sea Gate Towing and Repairs." The guy pulled an order sheet from his pocket. "Somebody named John Gallagher called in the order this morning. Said you'd take care of the bill."

"You take plastic?"

"You name it, we take it."

He tossed an American Express card at the guy. "You fill out the paper while I park the Porsche." New York City streets were notoriously unkind to fancy sports cars. It was a miracle it hadn't been totaled already.

"You can't take the car until I get a signature," the guy protested.

"So sue me." He grabbed the keys from the guy and headed for the Porsche.

Some of the details were starting to come back to him, and he was less than thrilled. Would it have killed Dee to let him sleep it off on her living-room couch and leave in the morning? He was sure he could've persuaded her. This whole thing had his brother's fingerprints all over it.

Nice try, Johnny, he thought as he steered the car around the corner to the garage entrance. *You're going to pay for it, but it was a nice try.* His little brother was trapped in the past, trying to hang on to things that didn't exist anymore—if they'd ever existed at all.

You could level Sea Gate, and nobody would miss it. The houses, the stores, the marina, every goddamn thing. The days of catering to the B&B crowd were over, and they weren't coming back. Brian and his partners were going to make sure of that. Sometimes it amazed him how blind people could be when they wanted to. Half the businesses on Ocean Avenue were shuttered, and not just because the owners had cut great deals for themselves. Mortgages got sold, notes were called in, fortunes

changed. Sometimes a man fell on hard times he didn't
expect, and the only thing he could do was cave. It was
Brian's job to be there when it happened.

Nothing lived forever. Not people. Not towns. Not
even families. He should have fought his mother's will.
She'd had no fucking business cutting him out the way
she had, trying to punish him from the grave for wanting
more than Sea Gate had to offer. Truth was, she'd never
forgiven him for not marrying Dee. Rosie Gallagher had
left her half of the marina to John, and she'd done it to
spite Brian.

But he still had Eddie's power of attorney. If something happened to his father, he—

The thought hit him hard.

Christ, what was happening to him? Eddie was his
father. You didn't wish things like that on your own
father. *Live long and prosper, Pop,* he thought. Four
score and ten and more.

Maybe it was those stories Dave had told him yesterday about his old man that had put ideas in his head. He
hadn't seen Eddie in a year, and the changes in him had
caught Brian by surprise. Eddie's hair was thinner, his
wit slower, but you expected those changes in a man
who was pushing seventy.

No, it was the other things Dave had told him that
lingered with Brian. Eddie had been sleepwalking, wandering through town in his pajamas, showing up at the
docks at all hours, then not remembering why he'd gone
there in the first place.

Which didn't make Eddie Gallagher the kind of man
you wanted making decisions that could affect an entire
town.

It was something worth thinking about.

EDDIE USED TO LOVE THE day after Thanksgiving. The
only traffic at the marina was the occasional visit from

a Coast Guard cruiser or a weekend sailor trying to squeeze in one last outing before winter finally took hold. He would open up around seven in the morning, then be home to stay by noon.

"Will you look at them?" his wife Rosie used to say as they watched news reports of shoppers clogging the malls to get a head start on Christmas. "Wouldn't catch me there on a bet."

Rosie would make turkey sandwiches for lunch, and they'd eat them together at the kitchen table, then spend the afternoon playing gin rummy for pennies. It hadn't taken a lot to make them happy back then. All it had taken was each other.

Gone, he thought. Those days were gone, and they were never coming back.

Dee had given him some sliced white meat and a drumstick to take home. She'd wrapped it neatly in tin-foil and given him strict orders not to share it with John. "This is for you, Eddie," she'd said, then kissed him on the cheek in a way that made him want to weep for what he'd lost. He sat alone in the kitchen, picking at the meat right from the unfolded square of foil like an old man eating from a garbage pail.

Bailey placed her head against his nose and looked up at him with sad brown eyes.

"As if I could be refusing you, girl." He chucked her under the chin, then tossed a few healthy slices of meat in her dish. Maybe he would even—

"EDDIE!" HE HEARD HIS NAME clear as a bell. "What are you doing out here without a coat?"

The objects in front of him tumbled like the pieces of a giant's jigsaw puzzle. Big blue. Yellow. Green. Brown rough tall. What were they? He looked at the man who'd called out his name. The man was smiling at him. The

man knew what those things were, so why didn't Eddie?
Were they a secret?

"Hop in," the man called out. "It's cold as a witch's
tit out here. Lemme give you a ride home."

The man wanted Eddie to do something, but he didn't
know what it was. He tried to take a step toward the
man. He told his feet to move, but they weren't listening.
A terrible fear overtook him. *Think, you old jackass,* he
told himself angrily. It couldn't be that hard to do.
Everyone around him was managing just fine.

"Damn it, Eddie, will you move your ass? I told Cora
I'd be home in time for *Oprah.*"

Where was Bailey? He'd been about to feed her a
slice of turkey just a second ago.

"Why the hell are you ignoring me?" Vince Troisi
was looking at him through the open window of his
powder blue Caddy. He wore a windbreaker with the
bright yellow scarf his granddaughter had made for his
birthday. "If you don't want a lift home, just say so. I
gotta get my ass back or else."

Oh, Jesus—oh, sweet Jesus. He wasn't home in his
kitchen, sharing lunch with Bailey. He was standing in
front of the 7-Eleven on the other side of town, right
near the big dark green pine tree the Knights of Columbus decorated every Christmas.

"Hey, pally, I can't wait all day," Vince hollered to
him. "Come on already."

"I c-can't."

"What?" Vince cupped his hands around his mouth.
"I can't hear you."

"Can't m-move . . . c-can't move . . . can't m-move
. . . can't—" *Can't remember how . . . can't remember
why.*

"Eddie?" Vince threw open his car door and climbed
out. "What's wrong? You don't look so good."

C-can't move . . . can't m-move . . . can't—

Vince put his arm around Eddie's shoulders. "I'm here, pally. I'm with you. I'll get you home."

"Rosie will help me," he said. "She always knows what to do."

Vince looked at him as if his heart was breaking. "Rosie's gone, Eddie. Don't you remember? She died a long time ago."

In the instant it took Vince to say the words, Eddie remembered everything. He remembered his wife and how she'd looked at the end, when the cancer had destroyed everything but her beautiful soul. He remembered the empty house . . . the empty bed. And he remembered that something terrible was happening to him, something so awful that it was slowly stripping him of the one thing he had left: his memories.

"Don't forget the seat belt," Vince said as Eddie settled in the passenger seat. "You'll be home before you know it."

Eddie fastened the seat belt the way Vince told him to do, and then he turned toward the window and began to cry.

ELEVEN

ALEX QUICKLY DISCOVERED THE SECRET great chefs hid from the masses. It was relatively easy to turn out fabulous food when money was no object. When you could load your shopping cart with radicchio and oakleaf lettuce and balsamic vinegar and perfectly aged beef tenderloins, odds were the end result would be delicious.

But hand the same chef a cart filled with on-sale chicken, red onions, and iceberg lettuce and you separated the women from the girls. What began as a tongue-in-cheek method of paying off a debt quickly evolved into a contest between Alex and her ego.

"We could bring in a pizza," John said after two weeks of gourmet meals on a shoestring.

Alex looked up from her slice of pound cake with strawberries. "You didn't like the coq au vin?" She'd been particularly proud of that dish—as much because of its $4.76 price tag as because of its taste.

"I ate two helpings, didn't I?" He poured himself another cup of coffee. "You're knocking yourself out, Alex. We can order in."

"The way I see it, I owe you another eleven meals before I'm paid up." She thought a moment. "I could always make you a beautiful focaccia with oven-dried tomatoes and basil."

"I was thinking more like a pepperoni and anchovy from Carlo's."

"If that's what you prefer. . . ."

"I'm not trying to hurt your feelings," he said, reaching across the table for her hand. "You're putting in long hours at the diner. I figured you could use a night off."

"Whatever," she said, feigning disinterest.

"I didn't mean to hurt your feelings."

"You didn't hurt my feelings."

"You're sulking."

"I never sulk."

"Come here," he said.

She ignored him, turning her full concentration to devouring her piece of pound cake.

"You're a tough woman, Alex Curry."

"No I'm not," she said, "but I'm learning how to be."

"Come here," he said again.

She laid down her fork on the side of her plate, then touched the corner of her paper napkin to her mouth. Slowly she pushed back her chair and stood up.

His chair crashed to the floor as he stood up opposite her. His eagerness thrilled her. It almost matched her own. She wanted him to come to her, to bridge the distance between them. She wanted to be needed in some way, even if it was only for the pleasure they found together in bed.

The seconds ticked by slowly, and their gazes held. She wondered how her life would have been if she'd met John first, if it had been John she'd turned to when her world fell apart after her parents' deaths—

But those were dangerous thoughts. She couldn't change the past any more than she could control the future. This moment was all they had. . . . Maybe it was all they would ever have. He had his secrets, and God knew she had hers. If she let this moment escape, she'd regret it for the rest of her life.

He took a step toward her. It was all she needed from him. She was in his arms before he took his next breath.

He swept his arm across the kitchen table. Plates and glasses crashed to the floor. The sound made her want to throw back her head and shout with joy. He bent her back on the table, pinning her down with the weight of his body.

He helped her wriggle out of her pajama bottoms. She freed him from the confines of his jeans. No preliminaries, no anticipation, nothing but a hunger so powerful it should have scared them. But they were beyond reason.

He was hot and hard as iron. She was soft and wet and yielding.

All the things they couldn't say with words they said with their hands and lips and bodies. All the secrets they couldn't share any other way.

ALEX DEPOSITED THE PLATE IN front of the sullen-faced teenaged girl. It was the next afternoon. "Enjoy your lunch," she said with her best waitress smile.

"I didn't order this." The girl gave Alex an aggrieved look as she poked at the scrambled eggs with the tines of her fork. "This isn't mine."

Alex checked her order pad. "Scrambled egg, wet, with dry toast. I have it written down right here."

"I ordered tuna salad on rye."

Alex flipped back a page. "Oh, God," she said, offering the girl a sheepish smile. "I'm so sorry. I confused you with booth number twelve."

"I gotta get back to school," the girl said. "Where's my sandwich?"

"Give me two seconds. You'll have your sandwich, I promise you."

She burst into the kitchen. The swinging doors banged against the walls.

As usual Will was standing by the back door, smoking a cigarette. "What now?" he asked. He didn't sound particularly friendly, but then he never did. Their relationship had gone from not-so-good to terrible in the time she'd been working at the Starlight.

"I need a tuna salad on rye and scrambled eggs, wet, with dry toast and I need them fast."

"Didn't I just give you that?"

That familiar sinking feeling returned to the pit of her stomach. "I made a mistake, Will. I need you to help bail me out."

"What's your problem?" he asked, tossing the cigarette into the snow-covered yard. He wiped his hands on his stained apron and gave her a nasty smile. "You don't *look* stupid."

She felt her face turn red at his insult. "I confused booth twelve with booth seven." Yesterday she'd served liver with bacon to a visiting vegetarian and steamed carrots and broccoli to a practicing carnivore. Both customers, she'd discovered, were capable of violence, at least of the verbal variety.

"You gotta be kidding," Will said. "My little sister worked here last year, and even she didn't do that."

"Look, I'm sorry," she said as tears threatened to complete her humiliation. "I didn't do it on purpose."

He cracked eggs into a bowl. "I don't get paid extra for this, you know." He grabbed a fork. "And I sure as hell don't get any tips."

Neither do I, she thought as she packaged the rejected

food for the women's shelter. Not when she made such a mess of things.

"You're making my life difficult," Will went on. The beaten eggs sizzled as they hit the griddle. "Where the hell is Dee?"

"You know as much as I do, Will. She said she'd be in after lunch."

"She didn't pull that crap when Nick was around," he grumbled. "I can tell you that."

"I wouldn't know about that," she said. "I wasn't working here when Nick was around."

"Damn right you weren't." He pushed the eggs around with a spatula. Even from where she stood she could see that the eggs were on their way to turning into yellow blobs of rubber.

"You're overcooking those eggs," she said.

He ignored her and turned up the flame.

"Will." She crossed the kitchen to the stove. "The order was for scrambled, wet."

"You said dry."

The poor eggs were turning brown. "The toast was dry. The eggs were wet."

"That's not what you said."

She flipped open her order pad and pointed to her notes. "That's what I have here."

She'd barely uttered the words when he picked up a skillet and threw it across the kitchen where it smashed against the far wall, knocking a can of cooking oil to the floor. Then he untied his apron and threw it at Alex.

"Will." She tried to return the apron to him, but he was already reaching for his jacket. "We're having a bad day, that's all. Why don't we—"

"*You're* having a bad day, lady. At least I know what the hell I'm doing."

She drew herself up to her full height and stared down at him. "There's no need to curse."

"You think *that's* cursing?" He unleashed a torrent of verbal abuse.

"You're disgusting."

"At least I'm not stupid."

If the skillet had been within reach, she would have hit him over the head with it. "You're fired," she snapped.

Will started to laugh. "You can't fire me. You're a waitress."

"Then Dee can fire you."

"'She's a waitress, too."

"But I'm not." John loomed in the doorway like a thundercloud.

Alex stepped between the two men. "I can handle this," she said to John. "Will and I are just having a discussion."

"I heard that discussion," John said through gritted teeth. He stepped around Alex and went face-to-face with Will. "You're fired."

"You're a customer," Will said, looking at them as if they both were crazy. "Customers can't fire the help."

"They can if the customer owns the place."

"You're nuts," Will said. "Tell Dee I quit."

"Too late," John shot back. "I already fired you."

Muttering something about rubber rooms and electro-shock therapy, Will bolted for the door.

"Now you've done it," Alex said as Will backed his car out of the parking lot in a spray of snow and gravel. "I'll lose my job because of this."

John looked insufferably pleased with himself. "You're not going to lose your job."

"Dee is going to be furious."

"She'll get over it."

"What is she going to tell the owner, that one of her customers went berserk and fired the cook? I don't think he's going to be very happy about that."

"I *am* the owner, Alex."

"Very funny," she said. "The joke's over. Now help me figure out what to do."

"I'm not joking," he said. "I own the Starlight."

"You're telling me that you're my boss?"

"I'm your boss."

"Why didn't you tell me before?"

"Because I haven't told anybody, Alex. Not even Eddie knows."

"That does it." She pulled off her apron. "I can't work here anymore."

"Why can't you work here anymore?"

"Isn't it obvious?" She folded the apron and set it down on the counter. "You should have told me before I started working here, John. Now I feel like a total fool."

"Look," he said, "the original owner skipped town. They were going to shut down the Starlight. I couldn't let it happen so I bought the place. You're right. I should have told you about it."

"Why the secrecy?"

He looked at her for what seemed like a very long time. "Damned if I know," he said finally. "It seemed like a good idea at the time."

"It's Dee, isn't it? She told me she'd like to buy the diner one day. You were protecting her interest."

"It's what friends do."

"No," she said, "it's what *you* do. You tried to save my roof, my car, and my job, and now you're telling me you actually saved an entire diner. Call me crazy, but I think I see a pattern emerging here."

He turned away, but not before she caught a glimpse of pain so deep she prayed she was imagining it. But she wasn't imagining it. She knew his pain the way she knew her own. She'd seen that pain on Thanksgiving and she'd felt it when he held her in his arms. It was what had brought them together and it was what kept them apart.

He gestured toward the front of the diner with his thumb. "What are we going to do about them?"

The shift in focus startled her for a moment. "I completely forgot we had customers."

"As your boss, I'll pretend I didn't hear that."

"I guess I'll tell them to go home," she said, wiping her hands on her apron. "Without a cook, there's not much else we can do."

"Sure there is. You're a great cook. Why don't you take over for Will?"

"I'm supposed to be waiting tables."

"That chicken you made for me last night was the best I've ever had."

She dipped her head, pleased by the unexpected compliment. "Thank you, but I doubt if the Starlight is ready for chicken Florentine."

"Let me put it this way, Alex. You're a better cook than you are a waitress. Will's gone. We need somebody to replace him ASAP. Why not give it a try?"

She couldn't come up with a good reason. Actually the idea had its charm. Waiting tables had turned out to be a lot tougher than it looked. She hadn't realized how seriously people took things like eggs over easy and salad dressing on the side. Make one mistake and the wrath of God came down on your head.

"You know," she said, "you might have something there." The cook could hide out in the kitchen and let the waitress do the explaining when things went wrong. "But what are we going to do with the lunch crowd out there? I can't cook and serve, John."

"You cook," he said, grabbing an apron. "I'll take care of the rest."

•   •   •

"OKAY, DEE." DR. SCHULMAN PEELED off her plastic gloves and tossed them in the proper receptacle. "Get dressed, and we'll talk in my office."

"I'll live?" She sat up and readjusted her paper dressing gown around her chest. She hated the brittle tone her voice got whenever she was nervous.

"You'll live." Dr. Schulman turned toward the door. "I'll see you in a few minutes."

"Easy for you to say," Dee muttered as the doctor closed the door behind her. It wasn't Dr. Schulman's cellulite and spider veins that had been on display for all and sundry to see.

Was there any experience more traumatic than the yearly gynecological exam? She'd take a mammogram any day over being spread-eagled on a Star Wars table. And what was with those stirrups? What had the first gynecologist been thinking when he came up with that sadomasochistic fantasy item? She was sure it had been a male invention. No woman in her right mind would have linked horseback riding with a cold speculum.

Five minutes later she took a seat in Dr. Schulman's office.

"We'll have the Pap results back in a week or so," the doctor said, perusing her notes. "When do you want to schedule your mammogram?"

"I'll get back to you on that," Dee said, withholding a shudder. "The budget can only stand so much this month."

"You should talk to your boss about instituting an HMO plan," Dr. Schulman said. "It might make more sense for you."

There was no point reminding the doctor that she wasn't some high-priced executive at a Fortune 500 company. The thought of the Starlight ever being able to offer an HMO was downright laughable.

The doctor leaned forward, her dark eyes bright with

professional concern. "So now it's your turn, Dee. Any questions, concerns, problems you'd like to talk about with me?"

Dee wondered if the doctor used that same annoying tone of voice with her husband. "Yes, there is," she said, pushing away the thought. "I want to go back on the pill."

"Well." The doctor leaned back in her seat. "I feel obliged to remind you that while the effectiveness of the pill is undeniable, there are still some valid and pertinent reasons for the use of condoms."

"I understand," Dee said, "and I agree, but I still want to go back on the pill."

"You're in a steady relationship?"

"I'm not in a physical relationship at all," Dee said, growing annoyed. "I'm thinking ahead."

It's called wishful thinking, Doc, and I've got it down to an art form.

Brian's Thanksgiving Day visit had had an enormous impact on her, though it probably wasn't the impact he'd hoped for. He had wanted her to swoon at his feet, totally overcome by desire for him . . . totally overwhelmed by admiration for all he'd accomplished. The truth was, there had been something pathetic about him that day, a look of loneliness, of vulnerability, that she hadn't seen since they were in high school. And once again, it had drawn her to him. She'd told herself she was immune, and over the years she'd actually come to believe it. Thanksgiving had blown all of her theories to hell.

She felt like a gawky fifteen-year-old girl around Brian, the same girl who'd worshipped him like a God. The same girl who'd believed he would make all of her dreams come true.

It won't happen this time, Brian, she thought as Dr. Schulman wrote out a prescription. This time she'd fight fire with fire. The Christmas season was a dangerous time for lonely single women on the verge of middle age. Take a little mistletoe, a lot of eggnog, add a marrow-deep loneliness, and you had a recipe for disaster.

It had been three years since she'd had sex and even longer since she'd slept with a man. Really slept. Where you went to bed together and stayed there through the darkest part of the night, then woke up to find out you weren't alone.

It was what Sam wanted. He'd told her time and time again. ''I'm not going to hurt you, Dee. You don't have to be afraid.'' But she *was* afraid. Not of Sam, who was a good and decent man, but of herself. That maybe she only wanted what she couldn't have, the things and people that were bad for her.

But what frightened her most of all was the thought that the decisions she'd made as a frightened teenager would end up hurting her son.

TWELVE

JOHN WENT BACK TO THE marina around two o'clock, and by three Alex was the only one left in the diner. She rinsed dishes and stacked them in the dishwasher, wiped down the stove and countertops, then poured herself a tall glass of iced tea. It didn't matter that it was 25 degrees outside and snowing lightly. She was hot and sweaty and beyond tired.

She pushed open the swinging door that separated the kitchen from the rest of the diner and claimed the booth nearest the door for herself. She'd forgotten how wonderful silence could be. No loud jukebox music. No laughter. No spirited arguments about sex, politics, and religion. Just blissful peace and quiet.

She took a sip of iced tea, then closed her eyes to enjoy the sensation.

You did it, Alex, she congratulated herself. The world's lousiest waitress had transformed herself into a fairly decent short-order cook. Considering the fact that she'd been tossed into the deep end of the pool, she'd not only managed to stay afloat, but also she'd learned how to swim.

Sometimes her old life with Griffin seemed as if it had belonged to someone else—some sad, lonely woman who didn't have the guts to admit she deserved more from marriage than a platinum American Express card. Would it have been different if she'd showed a little backbone early on? She wondered if part of her charm for Griffin had been her malleability, or if he'd always secretly longed for someone as accomplished as Claire Brubaker.

An image of Claire, the way she had looked that afternoon at Harrods, flashed before her eyes. Her lustrous red hair pulled back in a chignon, her chic navy blue maternity dress, her stomach swollen with Griffin's child. It wasn't often a woman could point to the one moment in time when her life changed forever, but Alex could. From that moment on, the end of her marriage had been inevitable.

She didn't want to think about Claire . . . or about Griffin. They belonged to a distant past, to a world that no longer existed for her—if it had ever existed at all. He'd be ashamed of her, Griffin would. Ashamed of the beads of sweat rolling down the back of her neck, of the way her hands smelled of onion and cooking oil.

Ashamed of the fact that she had managed to survive on her own.

John wasn't ashamed of any of it. He looked at her with the same wonderful mix of desire and affection whether she was wearing her pale blue waitress uniform or nothing at all. He didn't judge her by her lack of education or accomplishment. He seemed to judge her by what was in her heart. Not even her parents had done that.

She wished with all her heart that she had met John years ago when they might have had a chance to make a life together.

"God, I'm sorry I'm so late." Dee burst through the

door like a red-haired whirlwind. "Dr. Schulman was running behind schedule, and I—"

Alex's eyes opened wide. "The doctor! Are you okay?"

"Routine maintenance." Dee slipped out of her hunter green windbreaker, then hung it from the hook near the door. "If you're looking for someone local, I'd be glad to give you her number."

"I guess." Her experiences with the medical profession in the last few years had been equal parts frustration and heartbreak.

"What do you use?"

"I beg your pardon?"

"Birth control," Dee said, sitting down opposite her. "Call me an optimist, but I just asked the doctor to put me back on the pill."

"I—well, I don't really use anything."

"Tell me you're kidding." Dee looked and sounded horrified. "You must be using condoms at the very least."

"Excuse me, Dee, but what makes you think I need them?" In point of fact, she and John hadn't been using birth control, not that it was any of Dee's business. They both had been tested, and thank God both were HIV-negative. Alex knew all too well that pregnancy would never be an issue for her.

"The guys at the counter think you and Johnny are getting married."

"Please tell me you're kidding."

"Vince thinks John will pop the question Christmas Day. Rich is betting on New Year's Eve."

"What about you?" she asked. "Are you putting fifty cents on Groundhog Day?"

"Honey, don't go getting upset. They love John and they're fond of you. They want the two of you to be happy together."

"We're not really having this conversation," Alex said. "I must be having a bad dream."

"Don't worry," Dee said. "Your secret is safe with me."

"I don't think any secret is safe in this town."

Some of Dee's sparkle dimmed. "You'd be surprised," she said after a moment. "Every now and then one manages to sneak by." She adjusted her ponytail, and her trademark grin returned. "So when did it happen?"

"That's personal, Dee."

"I'll bet it was Thanksgiving. He couldn't take his eyes off you."

Alex's face flamed. She might as well have taken out an ad in the *New York Times*.

"I promise I won't ask you all sorts of nosy questions," Dee said. "I always hate when people do that."

"Thank you."

"Of course, if there's something you'd like to tell me, I'd be more than happy to listen."

"There's nothing to tell," Alex said carefully. "We enjoy each other's company."

"I enjoy Vince Troisi's company, but I'm not sleeping with him."

"And it's a good thing you're not," Alex shot back. "I don't think Cora would be too pleased about it."

Dee tossed a packet of sweetener at her. It bounced off her shoulder and fell to the floor. "You know what I'm talking about. The sparks between the two of you could light this place for a year. I'm almost thirty-five years old, Alex. Believe me, I know when there's more than just good sex happening between a couple."

Alex put down her glass of iced tea and met Dee's challenging gaze head-on. "There isn't," she said bluntly. "No strings. No commitments. It's the way we both want it."

"Bullshit."

"Dee!" Alex wasn't sure if she should laugh or be insulted. "I think I know what's happening better than you do."

Dee refused to back down an inch. "Trust me," the woman said. "I've known Johnny all my life and I've seen him through good times and bad. The boy's in love."

"I wish you wouldn't say that."

"Why not? I'd be overjoyed if you told me a kind, handsome man was in love with me."

Instinctively Alex touched the place on her left ring finger where her wedding band used to be. Dee's sharp eyes caught the gesture before she could cover up.

"So that's the way it is," Dee said in a quiet tone of voice. "You're still carrying a torch for your ex."

The thought made Alex physically ill. She opened her mouth to say exactly that when a surprisingly sharp instinct for self-preservation sprang to life. If she let Dee believe she was nursing a broken heart over Griffin, she wouldn't have to endure endless questions about the future of her relationship with John. How could there be a future when she hadn't relinquished her past?

It would be easier this way, she told herself as the silence stretched between them. Easier for her and in some ways for John as well. He'd made his own feelings on the subject of commitment crystal clear. She imagined it would be a relief to him to know they were in total agreement.

"So call me a hopeless romantic," Dee said at last. "I was hoping—"

"I know what you were hoping," Alex said, "but that's just not in the cards for John and me." She was surprised at how hard it was to say the words.

And how deeply she regretted the fact that what there

was, was all there could ever be. She was, after all, still
another man's wife.

EDDIE LOOKED UP FROM THE sports section as John
walked into the room. "So you're going out again tonight?"

John grabbed his old leather jacket from the arm of
the couch. "I'm taking a pizza over to Alex's."

"Why don't you bring her here?" Eddie asked as
Bailey rested her head on his knee.

John let the question pass. He felt like a hormone-
crazed teenager looking for a place to be alone with his
girl.

"You're staying in tonight, aren't you?" He slid his
arms into his jacket.

"Maybe," Eddie said. "Maybe not. I might go over
to Paul D.'s for poker."

"*NYPD Blue*'s on tonight. I thought that was your
favorite."

"You take care of your life," his father said sharply,
"and I'll take care of mine."

"Hey, Pop, no offense meant. I was just reminding
you—"

"I'm not an old man." Eddie's voice went high with
anger. "I don't need my kid telling me where to go and
what to watch on TV."

Eddie had gone on one of his nocturnal rambles two
nights ago while John was piloting a two-day fishing trip
down to the Chesapeake. Alex had spotted him sitting
on the dock in his Jockey shorts, and she'd gone outside
with a blanket. She'd tried to persuade him to come
inside, but when that failed, she sat with him until the
sun came up.

John could still see the look in her eyes when she told
him about the incident. "He's not sleepwalking," she'd

said, her voice heavy with sadness. "I think Eddie has a real problem."

Bailey whimpered and nudged Eddie in the leg. She knew something was wrong, same as Alex. And, John thought ruefully, she had about as much chance as he and Alex did to make it right again.

ALEX MET HIM AT THE door wearing a pair of silky dark gold pajamas. Her hair was piled loosely on top of her head, held in place with a pair of tortoiseshell chopsticks. Her face had been scrubbed clean of makeup. Dark smudges circled her eyes, making her look tired and almost unbearably fragile.

"Pepperoni?" she asked as she closed the door behind him.

"Half pepperoni, half sausage."

"I want the pepperoni half."

He followed her into the kitchen, then placed the pizza box on the table. "Sit down," he told her. "I'll get the plates."

She opened her mouth to protest but apparently thought better of it and sat down. "The wine," she said. "I should—"

"It's on the back porch, right?"

"Yes, but—"

"I'll get it."

"I'm too tired to argue with you. "

"So that's the secret." He took down two plates from the cupboard and found a pair of wineglasses on the counter. "Get you tired enough and you'll finally let someone help you out."

She pushed back her chair and stood up. "Why don't you take that pizza and go home."

He dropped the plates and glasses on the table. "What's that supposed to mean?"

"It means I don't want you here. It means I want to be alone."

"Where the hell is this coming from?"

"Where do you think?" Her voice shook with anger. "I'm not going to be in your or anyone else's debt, John. Not for anything. If that bothers you, then maybe it's better we find out right now." And with that she burst into tears.

He stared at her in openmouthed shock. His instinct was to take her in his arms, but she'd probably have his head on a platter if he tried. He waited, expecting the tears to end as quickly as they'd started, but she surprised him again. She buried her head in her hands and sobbed as if her heart was breaking.

Finally he couldn't take it anymore and bent down to gather her into his arms. She was stiff and unyielding at first; her pain was like a third presence in the room. He stroked her hair, whispered things, foolish meaningless things, in her ear until she began to melt against him. *Who hurt you, Alex? Who did this to you?*

But he wouldn't ask her.

He knew she wouldn't tell him if he did.

ALEX PRESSED HER FACE AGAINST John's shoulder. How was she going to explain this ridiculous crying jag? He probably thought she was a total lunatic, sobbing because he wanted to set the table and pour the wine. Another woman would be down on her knees thanking God she'd found a man like him. Alex was doing her level best to drive him away.

Her conversation with Dee that afternoon had sent her emotions on a roller-coaster ride—which was the last thing she needed. Her emotions had been too close to the surface these last few days as it was. Sunsets made her heart ache. So did the way the sunshine danced across the ocean. The mournful sound of the gulls as they swooped overhead reduced her to tears. And as if that wasn't enough, Christmas was less than two weeks away. If anyone so much as whispered "God bless us, everyone," she would probably dissolve in a flood of tears.

Hearing herself say that she and John had no future together had been like hearing a door slam shut. It sounded so final, so terribly sad. But how on earth could she expect otherwise? Of course they had no future together. He couldn't have a future with a married woman. And for all she knew, he didn't want a future with anyone at all.

They told each other that the present was all that was important. In the darkness they whispered New Age platitudes about how today was all anyone really had to offer. What difference did your past or future make when it wasn't yours to give?

All of which sounded very trendy and free-thinking. Too bad it had absolutely nothing to do with the reality of their situation.

She would say she was premenstrual, but it had been so long since she'd had a normal period that she wasn't sure she'd recognize the symptoms. How long had it been? Six months. Maybe even longer. She hated feeling this way, fragile and vulnerable. After a lifetime spent feeling needy, she'd finally discovered that strong was better. But why didn't anyone ever tell you how hard it was to stay strong?

She wanted to tell John everything, spill her pathetic story on his lap like a glass of wine. She wanted to tell him about her parents. About Griffin. Even about Claire Brubaker and her enormous belly. Thank God his offhand remark about her independence had stopped her in her tracks. He'd made it clear where he stood on matters of the heart. No strings. No complications. They'd both agreed to that.

She wouldn't be the one to break the promise.

THIRTEEN

~~~

ALEX'S ROOF MANAGED TO SURVIVE a Christmas snowstorm, a New Year's ice storm, and a minor blizzard in mid-January, only to succumb to high winds on Groundhog Day. Punxsutawney Pete not only saw his shadow, but he also saw the last of her roof tiles flying into the Atlantic Ocean.

She called the roof guy that Eddie had recommended to her a few weeks ago, then called John.

"Sea Gate Roofing's going to rip you off," he said, his voice gruff. "You should have called me first. I did some roofing when I was in college."

"That's exactly why I didn't call you," she said, cradling the phone against her shoulder. "I need someone who's done roofing in this century."

There was a long silence, followed by a deep, rumbling laugh that made her grin. "In other words, back off."

"Yes," she said. "Not that I would phrase it so indelicately."

"Don't sign any contracts before you talk to me," he said. "I—"

"John." Her voice was firm. "If I like Sea Gate Roofing's bid, I'll give them the job."

"I'm not talking about the bid. I'm talking about the contract itself. They have some clauses that—"

"John," she broke in again. "I appreciate your concern, but if I have a problem with the contract, I'll take it to a lawyer."

"You don't want to end up owing the roofing contractor your firstborn."

No problem there, she thought as she hung up the phone. There would never be a firstborn.

"YOU'RE IN ONE HELL OF a bad mood today," Eddie observed as John pounded nails into the side of the *Kestrel* an hour later. "What's eating your butt?"

"Nothing," John growled, swinging the hammer with deadly force.

"You have a fight with Alex?"

"We don't fight." He landed a blow that would have shattered a lesser boat. "We don't talk. We don't fight." How could something as simple as choosing a roofing contractor turn into a battle for independence?

Eddie raised his hands, palms up. "I get the picture. Just don't turn the *Kestrel* into kindling." Eddie turned and started to walk away.

"Pop." John stopped hammering in mid-swing. "Where are you going?"

"None of your goddamn business, that's where. I'm sixty-eight years old. I don't have to answer to my kid."

"Shit." John tossed the hammer down as his old man stalked off. He couldn't keep Eddie under lock and key. You didn't strip a man of his freedom or his dignity just because he was getting forgetful. He drew his arm across his forehead. It took a lot to work up a sweat in weather like this. It took even more to work up a thirst for a cold beer. So what if it was only eleven in the morning; he'd take an early lunch and treat himself to a bottle of Sam Adams. Maybe two bottles if his mood didn't lighten up.

It wasn't as if he had anything to do, he thought as he let himself into the office. Every goddamn time he repaired the *Kestrel*, some SOB came along and bashed another hole in her side. Probably the same SOB who'd damaged the other boats. Rich men put their boats in dry dock for the winter. Poor men watched their boats destroyed by sons of bitches with nothing better to do than make life even tougher for people who were already at the end of their rope.

He pulled a bottle of beer and a sandwich from the small fridge behind his mother's old desk. Hell, he knew all about being at the end of his rope. Alex was pushing him away with both hands, and he wasn't sure he wanted to stop her. The connection he felt to her scared the living shit out of him. He didn't want to feel that for any woman, not ever again.

He'd dreamed about Libby and the boys last night. He was standing in the doorway of Eddie's house. Libby was in the foyer, struggling to get Jake into his snowsuit while Michael tried to wriggle his way out of his. She'd hated the Jersey Shore. She was a Manhattan girl, born and bred, and she couldn't understand the pull his old hometown had on John. When he told her he wanted to stay an extra day, she'd balked, and after a noisy fight he'd told her to go back home without him, that he'd take the train when he was ready.

That was the last time he'd seen his wife and children alive. Fifteen minutes later their minivan was hit head-on by a drunk driver on his way home from happy hour.

His fault. For now and for always, his fault.

In the dream he tried to talk to Libby. He tried to tell her he was wrong, that they could find a way to compromise, that she shouldn't drive off when she was angry and the snow was falling, but she couldn't hear him and he couldn't stop her and even in his dreams the ending was always the same.

He polished off the first bottle of Sam Adams and ignored the sandwich. He opened the second bottle and took a long pull. He was all sharp edges and angles. Scotch would have done a good job of rounding him off, but beer was better than nothing.

Alex made no demands, wanted no promises, asked nothing about the life he'd led before she came on the scene. Their physical relationship was fiery and intense, and if she sensed the deeper connection between them, she gave no hint. It was the perfect setup for a man who was determined to keep his heart under lock and key. Instead he felt as if something important was about to slip through his fingers and there wasn't a damn thing he could do to stop it.

There was the shadow of Libby and his sons. Of Alex, who seemed to need no one. Of Eddie and his downward spiral.

And then there was Sea Gate.

Whoever it was who wanted the town suddenly wanted it bad enough to pay a hell of a lot more for it than it was worth to get it. Since the first of the year Alex had fielded two offers to buy her place. The first one was fifty percent higher than she'd paid Marge Winslow's kids. The second was twice as high.

"What are you going to do?" he'd asked her as they lay together in her narrow bed after making love. He felt as if he were trying to hang on to quicksilver.

"I'm not going to do anything," she said, burrowing closer to him. "This is my home."

There was no reason for him not to believe her, but the image of life without her was never far from his mind.

Not everyone professed that kind of loyalty to Sea

Gate. Rich Ippolito and his wife were selling their house for twice its appraised value and were heading down to Florida come spring to live near their grandchildren. The dry cleaner was teetering on the verge of following the example of the butcher, the baker, and the barber. So far, Sally Whitton was hanging tough, but John was afraid it was only a matter of time until the bait and tackle shop closed its doors.

The marina had received its share of offers. Every two weeks, like clockwork, a pleasant-faced woman in a navy blue suit showed up at the office to make an offer, and every two weeks, also like clockwork, John turned her down flat. "My clients usually get what they want, Mr. Gallagher," she said last week with a brisk professional smile. "You may as well profit from it."

It wasn't until she was gone that John recognized the threat behind those words.

ALEX HAD NO PROBLEM GETTING the day off work. Will had come back to the Starlight not long after making his dramatic departure, and the two of them had managed to find a way to accommodate one another. She was a morning person. He was a night owl. It should have worked like a charm, except for the fact that lately she was sleeping right through the alarm clock and struggling to get to work at all.

By 9 A.M. the roofing contractor had come and gone, leaving behind a slip of paper with the bad news scrawled on it. Alex looked at it, winced, then glanced up at the sky through the enormous hole in her living-room ceiling. John had told her not to sign a contract without running it by him first, but she was determined to make her own decisions. She might make a mistake, but it would be *her* mistake.

A pair of seagulls circled lazily overhead. The sky had that thick creamy color that meant snow was on the way.

She had to make a decision and fast or she'd be shoveling out her house come morning.

What choice did she have? At the very least, she had to arrange for a temporary roof of heavy-gauge plastic to be nailed into place so she could weather the storm, but that was only a stopgap measure. If she was going to continue to live here, she needed a proper roof and ceiling, and in order to get them she'd have to sell her diamond earrings and maybe the matching bracelet as well. She'd known that day was coming, but she had hoped to postpone it a little longer. Once the last of her jewelry was gone, she'd have nothing to fall back on but her wages from the diner, and that was a frightening thought.

Well, she'd cross that particular bridge when she came to it. She didn't have time to worry about it right now; she had to call the contractor and have him send a crew out to the house. Then she'd change into her best upper-middle-class city clothes and drive up to New York and see about turning her jewelry into cash.

BRIAN LEANED BACK IN HIS office chair and listened as Clay Cantwell listed their latest acquisitions.

"Number Twelve Soundview won't budge, not even with a twenty-five-percent increase."

"Up it to thirty," Brian said, scribbling a note on his legal pad. "You might try painting a bleaker picture of the future while you're at it. Not everyone responds to the straight financial approach."

Cantwell grinned. "We let Mary handle that end of the business," he said, riffling through a stack of documents. "She has a nice subtle touch that doesn't come back to bite us in the ass."

"What about the bait shop?"

"The old broad's a tough nut to crack. She's down to less than three thousand dollars in her bank account.

Throw in a few unexpected repairs to her building, and she'll have no choice but to sell out.''

"Do it," Brian said, remembering the way Sally Whitton had shunned him when he decided to leave Dee and Sea Gate behind in favor of school. They should have known he'd have a long memory. "What about the old Winslow place?"

"Nothing," Cantwell said. "Curry actually laughed in Mary's face. She said Mary must be even crazier than she was to offer that kind of money for that dump."

"Increase the offer," Brian ordered. "Keep increasing it in ten-percent increments." One of the things he'd learned was that his brother was sleeping with the beauteous Ms. Curry, which made winning her over to his side all the more appealing.

Cantwell arched a skeptical brow. "Indefinitely?"

"I'll tell you when to stop." Except for the fact that she was sleeping with his brother, Brian knew absolutely nothing about Alex Curry. He needed something more than that in order to know where and how to apply pressure.

Cantwell removed his glasses and rubbed the bridge of his nose. "You've got to keep your emotions out of this, partner. If we spend it all now, we won't have any capital left for the overhaul."

"If we don't get the old Winslow property, there won't *be* an overhaul," Brian pointed out, annoyed at the man's presumption. He didn't need some blue-blooded asshole telling him how to do business. "Remember that old lady who blocked Macy's from building its Queens store in the sixties? They offered her millions, and she wouldn't budge, so they ended up building the store around her. That's not going to happen to us. You make the deal, I'll keep it legal."

Cantwell slid his glasses back into place. "I'm going to hold you to that." He gathered up his papers, then rose from the chair. "I'll call you this afternoon after we draw up a current map."

"Fax it to me," Brian said, standing up. "I want to see how it looks."

"Will do." The two men shook hands across Brian's desk. "Give my best to Margo."

Brian smiled broadly. "Absolutely."

The smile faded the moment his office door closed behind Clay Cantwell. He couldn't give his best or anything else to Margo—or to the girls, for that matter. Margo was still in Aspen with her parents, and had been since Thanksgiving. He supposed he should have seen it coming, but he honestly hadn't. He'd assumed their brittle, by-the-book marriage suited her down to the ground. When she called the Sunday after Thanksgiving to tell him she wasn't coming home, he'd felt as if he'd been hit with a two-by-four.

"What the hell do you mean, you're not coming home?" he'd roared into the telephone, fueled by Scotch and solitude. "The car's picking you up at JFK in two hours."

"Then perhaps you should cancel the car," she'd said in a calm voice he'd never heard before. "I need time to think, Brian, and I'd recommend that you take some time to think as well while I'm gone."

"Fuck you," he'd bellowed. Then he'd thrown the cordless across the room, where it crashed against a Chinese screen that had belonged to Margo's grandmother. When she came home, she'd see how little her absence had really meant.

The days went by. And then the weeks. She'd come home for Christmas, he told himself. She wouldn't keep the kids away from home at Christmastime.

"You're welcome to join us here," Margo had said when he asked her about her plans. "Daddy's going to take us all out caroling in a horse-drawn sleigh on

Christmas Eve. The girls are beside themselves.''

He'd locked himself up in their New York apartment and got blind stinking drunk, and the next day he had gone out and picked up a Ford model in a downtown club and fucked her brains out. It hadn't felt like much of an accomplishment.

To his surprise, he found he missed his daughters. He didn't consider himself to be a bad father, but Caitlyn and Allison had never seemed quite real to him. Maybe it was the fact that they were girls and he'd never pretended to understand anything about the opposite sex. Still, he found himself missing them more than he had expected.

He glanced at his watch. He had a four o'clock appointment with a client, but there was still plenty of time to walk over to FAO Schwarz and pick up a few things for the girls and have the toys FedExed out to Aspen. And if he was still feeling expansive, maybe he'd even pop into Tiffany and find something for Margo.

''THE MARKET IS IN FLUX,'' one of Tiffany's expert jewelers explained kindly to Alex. ''If you had come to see us three weeks ago, we could have settled on a higher number, but today I'm afraid this is the best we can do.'' He slid a folded piece of paper across the desk toward her.

Didn't anybody mention the word ''money'' these days? she wondered as she reached for the slip of paper. All of this coy posturing seemed ridiculous to her. She read the figure, looked away, then read it again. ''That's all?'' she asked, praying she needed glasses.

The jeweler nodded. ''I'm afraid that's all.''

''I'll take it.''

''Are you sure?'' the jeweler asked, obviously surprised by her decision ''If you wait another few weeks, the market may very well swing upward. It could make a substantial difference in our offer.''

She shook her head. "I can't afford to wait,'' she said bluntly.

"As you wish, Mrs. Whittaker.''

"It's Ms. Curry now.'' Unfortunately Whittaker was the name on all the paperwork for the items.

"I'm sorry. I won't make that mistake again.'' He stood up. "Please help yourself to some tea while we draw up a cashier's check for you.''

"I'd appreciate it if we could finish quickly,'' she said, glancing out the window. "The snow has started, and I have a long drive home.'' A little over two hours, and that was with no traffic.

"Of course,'' he said, then left the room.

She poured herself a cup of tea, took a sip, then put the cup back down on the table. The tea had a funny hint of jasmine to it that made her stomach close in on itself in a peculiar way. She couldn't take her eyes from the big flakes of snow swirling past the window. She'd never driven in snow, and the thought filled her with unease. Did the VW have snow tires or was that an outdated notion? She hadn't the faintest idea.

Ten minutes later the jeweler returned. "Just a few papers for you to sign and you're off,'' he said. He handed her a gold-tipped fountain pen. "If you would . . .''

She quickly signed her name three times, then handed him back the pen in exchange for the check.

"I can cash this tomorrow, right?'' she asked, slipping it into her purse.

"You can cash it now.''

"Tomorrow's fine,'' she said as he helped her into her raincoat. "Thank you.''

He escorted her down to the main level, where they

shook hands near a display of Paloma Picasso's latest designs.

"Thank you again," Alex said. "I appreciate your help."

"Our pleasure, Mrs. Whittaker," the jeweler said. "Safe trip."

She didn't bother to correct him. All she wanted to do was get home.

WHITTAKER.

Brian watched as the woman in the black Burberry raincoat exited the store. The same dark blond hair. The same loose-limbed way of walking. It had to be the woman he'd met at Dee's house. The woman his brother was sleeping with.

"Sir?" The salesclerk's voice drew him back. "These earrings are particularly lovely."

He glanced at the two chunks of gold in the palm of her hand. "Yes," he said absently. "I'll take them."

"Your wife will be quite pleased," she said, beaming up at him. "Shall I have them sent, or will you be taking them with you?"

He scribbled the Aspen address on the back of his business card. "Send them," he said, handing her the card.

"I'll be right back with your receipt."

"Just a minute," he said. "That man who just walked a customer to the door. What department does he work in?"

"Oh, that's Mr. DiCarlo. He handles estate jewelry and resales for us."

Bingo, he thought as the salesclerk hurried away. He remembered the diamond earrings Alex had been wearing at Thanksgiving. He'd pegged them for the real thing, and apparently he'd been right.

Alexandra Curry Whittaker.

He made it back to his office by three-thirty. He pow-
ered up his computer, then logged onto the Web. There
was a private and very powerful search engine that had
been set up by the executive of a Fortune 500 company.
Its sole raison d'etre was to help other executives find
each other through the labyrinthine permutations of corporate musical chairs. You could search by name, company, or social security number, and five seconds later
some poor bastard's CV from cradle to middle age was
flickering across your screen.

Scary shit, he thought as he typed in the name Whittaker. But damn useful.

There were 163 Whittakers in positions of power
worldwide, any one of whom could be the Whittaker he
was looking for. He decided to narrow the search.

SPOUSE'S NAME: ALEXANDRA

The hard drive clanked a few times, then a new
screenful of information appeared.

GRIFFIN WHITTAKER
PRESIDENT, EUROLINK VENTURES INCORPORATED
1040 FIFTH AVENUE, NY, NY
M. ALEXANDRA CURRY
NO CHILDREN
CURRENTLY BASED IN LONDON

"Yes," he said, hitting the print button.
Now he was getting somewhere.

FOURTEEN

⁓

THE DAY PASSED, AND THERE was no sign of Alex. John waited for her to show up at the marina, but by five o'clock she still hadn't made an appearance. He supposed that shouldn't surprise him. She was every bit as stubborn as he was and had probably signed a contract with Sea Gate Roofing just to spite him.

He was about to lock the office and storm over to the house to confront her when the roofer appeared in the doorway. He was covered with snow.

"She stiffed me," Bill said without preamble. "She gets me to do a temp job on the roof and disappears. What the hell kind of crap is that?"

"Disappeared?" Everything else faded away. "She disappeared?"

"What else should I call it?" Bill shot back. He shook the snow from his graying hair. "This morning she tells me she'll be back by four to pay me, and I haven't seen hide or hair of her since. What does she think—I have nothing better to do than hang around waiting for my money? I'm gonna charge her for the wait time, that's what I'm gonna do."

"What's the damage?"

Bill told him, down to the penny.

"You take a check?"

"I'll take pennies if I have to."

John wrote out a check and handed it to him. "When did you say she left?"

"Ten, ten-thirty," Bill said. Funny how money could soothe the most savage beast. "She got all dressed up. Looked pretty good too."

John barely resisted the urge to deck the son of a bitch. "Did she say where she was going?"

"Didn't ask."

Seven hours, John thought as he locked the marina office. *Where the hell could she be?*

A good three inches of snow had fallen in the last few hours, making the roads slick and dangerous. There was no sign of Alex or her beat-up VW anywhere. He checked parking lots, the local hospital, auto-repair shops. He even stopped at the police station and asked if there'd been any accidents reported. The thought of Libby and the boys was never far from his mind.

Eddie was eating supper in front of the TV when John got home. A big hero sandwich and a bottle of Bud. Bailey was lying on the floor next to him, waiting for donations.

"I thought you'd be over at Alex's," Eddie said, lowering the volume on Vanna.

"So did I." John hung his jacket on the hook by the door. "Any calls?"

"Brian called."

"What the hell did he want?"

"Beats me." Eddie raised the volume.

"Pop." John stepped in front of the screen. "He must've wanted something."

"Will you get the hell out of the way?" Eddie grumbled. "You're blocking the puzzle."

John headed for the kitchen. It was pretty clear he wasn't going to get anything more out of his father. Bailey trailed behind him, her tail wagging like a metronome. At least someone was glad to see him. He took some bread and ham from the fridge. Bailey looked up at him, her brown eyes wide and expectant.

"I think you want this more than I do, girl." He gave her a slice of ham and shoved the rest back in the refrigerator. His stomach was too tied up in knots to eat.

He glanced at the answering machine. The message light was blinking. Probably the call from Brian, he thought. His father had the habit of leaving messages on the machine for days at a time. He pressed the play button and raised the sound.

"This is Patricia Taylor from Princeton Medical Center. I'm calling for Mr. John Gallagher. Please call me at area code 609-497—" He grabbed a pencil and wrote down the number on the back of a Chinese food menu. His hand shook so hard he could barely read back the digits scribbled in the margin.

Bile rose into his throat, and he forced it back down. *Not again,* he thought as he dialed the number. *Not again.*

"This is John Gallagher," he said when Patricia Taylor answered her line. "Is it about Alex Curry?"

"Thank you for calling, Mr. Gallagher." Her voice had the high gloss of the true medical professional. Sweat broke out on the back of his neck. "Ms. Curry has been in an accident. She—"

He grunted as if someone had landed a punch to his gut, then doubled over from the waist. A cold buzz of terror filled his head.

"Mr. Gallagher." The woman's voice penetrated his fear. "Listen to me, Mr. Gallagher."

"Y-yes." His voice barely sounded human.

"Ms. Curry is not seriously injured. Her car spun off

the road, and she hit her head on the steering wheel. She's bruised, a little headachy, but that's it. We're keeping her overnight as a precautionary measure.''

"I'm on my way."

He threw the information in Eddie's general direction, then grabbed his coat and left. The roads were worse than before. He traveled the entire seventy miles between Sea Gate and Princeton in four-wheel drive and, despite that, nearly spun out twice himself.

The cold buzz inside his head grew to fill his chest as well. What the hell had she been doing in Princeton on a snowy night like this? The world was a dangerous place. In a fraction of a second, a person's life could change forever.

It was ten o'clock when he reached Princeton Medical Center. He took a parking ticket from the machine at the entrance to the covered lot, then found a spot on the second level. Two minutes later he was at the information desk in the lobby, demanding to know where Alex was.

"Room 607," a volunteer told him. She pointed to her left. "The elevator bank is right over there."

Heart pounding, he rode up to the sixth floor. The place didn't seem like a hospital. The corridor was carpeted in a soothing blue tweed, and he couldn't detect the stink of fear he associated with hospitals. A nurse sat in front of a computer, her skillful fingers skimming the keyboard as he walked by. A small kitchen had been installed between the nurses' station and another corridor. A man and woman, both dressed in street clothes, talked quietly while they sipped something from plastic foam cups. Normal everyday actions meant to keep the demons at bay.

She's fine, he told himself over and over, a mantra against the fates. *She's fine she's fine she's fine—*

The door to Room 607 was slightly ajar. The room

itself was dark, except for the dim glow of a nightlight plugged into the near wall. There hadn't been a room for Libby and the boys. Only the sterile coldness of the morgue—

"John!" She was sitting up in bed, a large bandage taped to her right temple. She wore a standard-issue hospital gown, and her skin was as pale as the white pillowcase. "The snow—you shouldn't have—"

He was at her side, kissing her face, her hands, trying to convince himself she was there and alive and not gone from him. Not gone at all.

"John." Her laugh was shaky and soft. "It looks worse than it is. . . . Poor VW took the brunt of it."

"What the hell were you doing up here in a snowstorm?" He knew he sounded angry and harsh, but he couldn't help himself. He could have lost her. "Are you nuts?"

She cupped his face with her hands. He noticed thin scratches all the way up her bare forearms. *Glass,* he thought, shuddering. *Jesus.* "I thought I could beat the snow, but I was wrong." She was looking at him as if she'd never seen him before, as if she were learning his face for the first time. He wondered if a painkiller was finally kicking in. "I want to . . . go home," she said. Her words grew slower, more halting. "They put my . . . clothes in the closet . . . by the door."

"You can't go home tonight," he said, stroking her hair back from her forehead. "They want to keep you for observation."

"You'll observe me," she said, again with that soft and loopy laugh.

He leaned back and looked at her. "How many drugs have they given you?"

"One," she said, holding up two fingers. "But it . . . was a good one."

He grinned as relief began to flood through him.

"There's no point asking you any questions tonight—you're out of it. Get some sleep, Alex." He kissed her gently on the mouth. "I'll take you home in the morning."

"No!" She struggled to climb from the bed, but he pushed her back against the pillow. "Don't leave!"

"I'm not going to," he said, pulling the blanket back up around her shivering form. She looked so slender, so fragile, in the hospital nightgown that his heart ached. "I'll sleep in the chair."

She patted the bed. "No," she said again. "Sleep here."

"Alex—"

"Sleep with me, John. . . . It's . . . one thing . . . we haven't done."

He told himself he was doing it for her sake, that she shouldn't use up her waning energy arguing with him about the sleeping arrangements, but when he positioned himself next to her in the hospital bed he saw his lie for what it was, the last-gasp attempt of a man desperate to keep from doing the one thing he feared most, the one thing that still had the power to hurt him.

Too late, he thought as he cradled her in his arms. *Too damn late.*

He loved her.

ALEX FLOATED IN AND OUT of sleep that night. Dreams drifted into reality, reality drifted back into dreams, and after a while she could no longer tell the difference between them.

Maybe there is no difference, she thought as her bruised body fitted itself against John's strength. Maybe this was how it felt to be happy. He held her as if holding her were an end in itself, as if he wanted nothing more than to feel her close to him. As if who she was

deep down, in that secret place inside her heart, pleased
him more than words could say.

"OUCH!" ALEX WINCED AS JOHN helped her into her
clothes the next morning. "Even my wrists hurt."

"You probably gripped the wheel tight when you
went into the skid, and the impact exacerbated things,"
he said, buttoning the front of her blouse for her. He
whistled low. "Not exactly work clothes."

She'd wondered if he would notice. "No," she said.
"I can't imagine frying eggs in this."

He'd started to say something when a doctor appeared
in the doorway. She was grateful for the interruption.

"Ms. Curry, I'm Dr. Bradley." He put out his right
hand.

"Be gentle," she said as she clasped his hand gingerly. "I hurt all over."

"That's to be expected. You were in a nasty accident." He turned toward John. "Are you Mr. Curry?"

John shook his head. "John Gallagher."

The doctor nodded, then turned back to Alex. "I have
a few things to discuss with you, Ms. Curry. Perhaps
you'd be more comfortable if we spoke in private."

John met her eyes. "I'll wait outside."

"No," she said, slipping into the jacket of her Armani
suit. "You don't have to do that."

He touched her cheek. "I'll get us some coffee."

The doctor waited for John to leave the room, then
sat down in the chair by the window.

Alex sat down on the edge of the bed and looked at
him. Suddenly her hands began to shake, and she
clasped them together on her lap. There was no reason
to be nervous. She knew she wasn't seriously hurt. The
only serious problem she had was how she would pay
her medical bills. For the first time in her life she un-

derstood the importance of health insurance. Too bad she couldn't afford it.

The doctor started talking about some of the tests they'd run. MRI. CT scan. Blood work and EKGs. *Oh, God,* she thought. It was worse than she thought. The bill would be in the thousands.

". . . And that brings us to the pregnancy test."

"The pregnancy test?" She laughed. "Why on earth would you run a pregnancy test?"

Dr. Bradley's expression didn't change. "There were a number of reasons for ordering the test," he said. "According to the chart, your last period was sometime last summer. You've been experiencing dizziness and nausea, and they noted some spotting while you were in the ER. We needed to understand your situation before we prescribed treatment of any kind."

"And you found out," Alex said. She couldn't count how many times she'd had a similar conversation with a doctor. "Negative."

"No," said Dr. Bradley, the slightest smile tilting the corners of his mouth. "Positive."

"That's impossible."

"Not according to the tests."

"You don't understand," she persisted, her heartbeat accelerating. "I can't get pregnant. My—my husband and I tried for ten years."

"You're pregnant now."

"There must be some mistake." She didn't believe it. She *couldn't* believe it, because it would kill her when it turned out to be a terrible cosmic joke.

"We could run the test again," the doctor said, "but I have no doubt the results will be the same."

"Please," she said, teetering on the verge of tears. "Please run another test. I know there's been some mistake."

"I'll send a technician up to draw blood. We'll call you with the results this afternoon."

THE SNOW HAD FINALLY STOPPED, but most of the roads between Princeton and Sea Gate had yet to see a plow. John swore as an eighteen-wheeler roared by.

"You're on ice, jackass. Slow down."

Next to him Alex burrowed more deeply into her raincoat.

"Sorry," he said.

"That's okay." Her voice was small and not all that steady.

"Are you sure the doctor gave you a clean bill of health?"

She looked up at him over the collar of her raincoat. "I'm battered and bruised, but it's nothing serious."

"Want some music?"

"If you do."

He didn't. What he wanted was to get her to talk to him, but apparently that wasn't in the cards. Although something was obviously bothering her, he knew Alex well enough now to know that whatever it was, she'd tell him in her own time. Or not.

They drove in silence. He focused all of his concentration on the road and tried to ignore the fact that next to him the woman he loved was crying as if her heart would break.

"YOU CAN'T STAY HERE," JOHN said as Alex let them into her house two hours later. "It's like a meat locker." He could actually see his breath.

"This is where I live," she said, turning on the lights in the living room. "Where else would I stay?"

"Stay with me."

She sidestepped a small pile of snow in the middle of the living-room carpet. "No, thank you."

"You shouldn't be alone."

"I'll be fine."

"I'd feel better if you stayed at my place."

"Listen to me, John." She met his eyes. "All I want to do right now is sleep."

"Sleep at my place," he persisted. "It's a hell of a lot warmer."

She checked the thermostat in the hall. "Mystery solved. The contractor must have turned off the heat while he was putting up the temporary roof." She turned the dial to the left, and he heard the burner click on. "See? It'll be warm in here in no time."

"Okay," he said. "You go take a nap. I'll sit out here and watch TV."

"You've been away all night. I'd feel better if you went home and checked on Eddie."

"I'll make sure he's okay." He kissed her gently. "Get some sleep. I'll bring supper back with me."

Her expression softened. "I'm counting on that."

THE PHONE RANG FIVE MINUTES after John left to check up on Eddie. Alex's hands were shaking so badly she had trouble lifting the receiver from the cradle.

"Hold please for Dr. Bradley."

She closed her eyes, wishing the buzz inside her head would stop. She was cold, so cold she doubted if she'd ever be warm again.

"Ms. Curry?"

"Yes."

"Congratulations," he said. "You're pregnant."

Her eyes filled with tears, and she sank down onto a kitchen chair. "You're sure?"

"I'm sure."

"Oh, God," she whispered. "Oh, God—"

". . . the name of your doctor, and I'll fax your records."

She forced herself to pay attention. "I'm new here," she said. "A friend mentioned someone b-but I can't remember—"

"Tomorrow will be fine," he said. "You'll want to have a complete prenatal workup. There was a slight amount of spotting, which isn't uncommon in the early stages of pregnancy, but you'll need to have it checked." He told her to get plenty of rest the next few days and to avoid alcohol, caffeine, and tobacco. "Do you have any questions?"

"Yes," she managed. "How far along am I?"

"I can't be certain," he said. "My guess is three months, give or take. Your obstetrician will be able to tell you more."

She sat alone in the kitchen for a very long time, her hands clasped protectively across her belly in that age-old female gesture. For ten years she'd prayed for a miracle, and now, when she least expected it, God had seen fit to answer her prayers. Would it be asking too much if she prayed the baby was John's?

FIFTEEN

⌘

IT TOOK A WHILE TO convince Eddie that Alex was really okay.

"It was a fender bender," he told his father. "She was more shook up than anything."

But the memory of another accident, another time, was right there in front of them, and neither man could make it go away.

"I'm going to call her," Eddie said, reaching for the phone. "I've gotta hear for myself."

"She's asleep," John said. "Why don't I have her call you later?"

Eddie wasn't thrilled with the idea, but he gave in. "Give her a kiss for me," he said. "Tell her I was worried about her."

John took a quick shower, dressed, then went out to pick up some Chinese takeout. Hot-and-sour soup. Some kung po chicken and moo shu pork. He got to Alex's around seven o'clock and let himself in the front door. She wasn't in the living room.

"Alex." He started for the kitchen. "Hunan Dragon. We deliver."

She was sitting at the kitchen table. Her freshly washed hair hung wet about her shoulders. She wore a pale pink terrycloth robe, belted at the waist. Her feet were nestled in thick white socks. She'd removed the bandage from her forehead. The two-inch cut looked angry and painful.

He put the bag of food down on the table, then nuzzled her neck. "You smell good."

She leaned into his touch. "You smell like Chinese food."

"How does some hot-and-sour soup sound? I had them add extra scallions."

Her eyes closed briefly. "I don't think I'm up to hot and sour tonight."

"Kung po chicken? Moo shu?"

"I think I'll just have some tea and toast."

"You look pale," he said, squatting down next to her so he could see her face. "Did you get some sleep?"

She nodded. "I guess the accident took more out of me than I thought."

He understood. He felt as if he'd lived one hundred years in the last twenty-four hours.

"So where's the bread?" he asked, trying to lighten the mood. "If I'm going to make that toast for you, I need to have some supplies."

"The bread's on the counter, John." She sounded amused. "Right in front of your nose."

"What about the tea bags?"

"In that canister marked 'tea bags.' "

"So I'd make a lousy short-order cook," he said, sticking two slices of white into Marge Winslow's ancient toaster.

"John," she said, "we need to talk."

He lit the burner under the teakettle. "I thought that's what we were doing."

"There's something I need to tell you."

He stopped what he was doing and looked at her. "Are you okay?"

"The doctor called," she said.

"The doctor—" His stomach catapulted into his throat.

"No, no!" She took his hand as an uncertain smile lit up her face. "It isn't bad news—at least I don't think you'll think it's bad news. It's the best possible news, John, and—"

"Damn it, Alex, spit it out."

"I'm pregnant."

His brain emptied of all rational thought. "What?"

That uncertain smile quivered and almost disappeared. "I'm pregnant, John." He could barely hear the words. All he could hear was the sound of his heart slamming against his rib cage.

"But you said—"

"I know." Her eyes shimmered with tears. "I can't believe it's true."

Neither could he. Turning, he walked out the back door.

"JOHN!" ALEX CALLED OUT FROM the doorway. "Where are you going?"

He didn't answer. He kept walking, crunching his way across the snow-covered yard toward the marina. She shoved her feet into a pair of boots, slipped her coat on over her robe, then ran after him. A full moon shone brightly overhead, reflecting off the newly fallen snow and making it easy to follow his trail.

She found him at the end of the dock. He was leaning against a piling, hands shoved into the pockets of his jeans. She should have brought his jacket; she shivered just looking at the threadbare Penn State sweatshirt. Her footsteps crunched loudly as she broke the icy top layer of snow. He must have heard her coming but he didn't turn around. His shoulders were hunched, his head down. He looked more alone than anyone she had ever seen.

She stopped a few inches away from him and placed a hand on his shoulder. "What are you thinking, John?" *Talk to me. Don't shut me out.* She could stand anything but that. She'd spent ten years of her life being shielded from real emotions, both her own and her husband's, and she wasn't going to let that happen ever again. "Tell me what you're feeling."

"Nothing." His voice sounded flat and old, and it filled her with fear. "I'm feeling nothing."

Her eyes filled with tears. "I never lied to you," she whispered, as much for herself as for him. "I didn't think this could happen. I thought a baby was a dream that couldn't possibly come true." She waited for him to say something, but his silence filled her heart with despair. "But it did, John. My dream came true. I know it's asking a lot for you to feel the way I feel about the baby. Neither one of us was looking for any kind of commitment. I'll understand if you don't—" Her voice broke on the last word, and she turned away. *Tell him about Griffin, Alex. Now is the time.*

The water was calm as black silk. The full moon was reflected in its depths. Yesterday's storm was forgotten. The scene was beautiful, so beautiful it made her heart ache even more. This was her home, and it would be her child's home as well.

I can do this, she told herself as she gathered up her courage to tell John everything. She would find a way to live without him if her truth was more than he could handle. She was strong, stronger than she'd ever imagined. She had a home of her own. She had a job. She even had friends. She couldn't imagine her life without John, but if she had to do this alone, she would.

Loving John was a miracle. So was this baby. Maybe

she'd been asking too much to think she could be so lucky, so blessed, as to have them both.

Hours passed—or maybe only minutes; she couldn't be sure. She felt as if her life were turning in on itself, blurring her perception of time and space.

"John," she said at last. Her courage was rapidly disappearing. "We need to—" She stopped at the look of anguish in his eyes. He couldn't possibly know what she was going to say.

"There's something I have to . . . tell you." His voice was etched with such terrible pain and loss she wondered that he didn't die of it.

Every instinct in her body warned her to run as fast and as far as she possibly could, but somehow she managed to stand there, waiting. "I'm here," she whispered, wrapping her arms around her chest. "Tell me."

It was a simple story. A familiar one. One of those college love stories that was supposed to have a happy ending. But she knew this one wasn't going to end happily at all. John Gallagher had met Libby Pace the first day of college when they fought over the last copy of the Western Civ text on the bookstore shelf.

From that moment on they'd been inseparable. They'd dated all through college, then married the day after graduation. Libby had worked as a receptionist at a publishing house while he attended law school. They had their lives planned out down to the last detail and had been young enough—and naive enough—to believe life would cooperate with them right down the line.

"Libby found out she was pregnant the day I passed my bar exam. We thought we were on our way."

"You don't have to do this, John." She placed her hand on his forearm. "You don't need to—"

But he did need to, and she knew it. *Let me say the right thing,* she prayed. *Let me know how to comfort him.* Because in her deepest heart, she knew how this story would end.

"We decided to have our kids close together," he said, staring at something only he could see. "We wanted them to be friends, to have each other to rely on." And they wanted to be young with their kids. For some reason that had seemed important to them.

Michael and Jake Gallagher were born right on schedule, thirteen months apart, two perfect clones of their father. They liked chocolate ice cream, blueberry pancakes, and chicken soup. They hated lima beans, tuna fish, and slimy scrambled eggs. Both boys thought pizza was the best thing since chocolate cake with icing.

"Michael was the athlete," John said, staring out at the ocean. "He could hit a ball by the time he was three. Pop used to say—" His voice broke, and he paused. "Pop used to say he'd be a major leaguer one day."

There was nothing she could say. No words that would ever ease his pain. All she could do was listen.

"Jake didn't like baseball, but he was reading by the time he started kindergarten. He questioned everything, wanted to know why and how and where—" He shook his head, a half-smile on his face. "Another Gallagher lawyer in the making."

"You must miss them so much," she said. Her baby was months away from being born, and already she understood his pain in a way she couldn't have last week.

"When the cops showed up at the door, I refused to believe them. I called them liars. I tried to throw them out." He lowered his head. "They weren't lying. They took me to the morgue—it was so fucking cold in there. . . .I'll never forget how cold—they took me to the morgue and pulled open the drawer—"

"Don't," she said, wrapping her arms around him as if she could absorb some of his pain. "You don't have to do this."

"—and they pulled down this heavy plastic, and Libby—Jesus, they said Libby was in there, and I said there was some kind of mistake, there had to be some kind of mistake, that my wife wasn't dead and then they opened two other drawers and pulled back that fucking plastic and I saw Michael and I saw Alex . . . what was left of them . . ."

Libby Gallagher was two weeks short of her thirtieth birthday when she died. Michael David Gallagher was seven years old. Jake Edward Gallagher was going on six.

John told her about the lost year after their deaths. He'd walked away from his fancy job and his fancy house, from everything but the towering guilt that tore at his gut every minute of every day.

"I drank," he said bluntly. "Whiskey, vodka, rum—whatever got me through the night." It was Eddie who pulled him back from the edge. His father dragged him out of the rathole motel he'd been living in, tossed away the booze, forced him back into the sometimes painful, sometimes wonderful world. "He was still hurting from losing my mom, but he put it all aside to make room for me. My old man saved my life."

She understood so much more now. So many pieces of the puzzle snapped into place as he spoke. You didn't hear much about the father-and-son connection. If you believed what you saw in movies and on television, you'd think a father's job was over the minute his son could field a line drive. But you couldn't tell that by Eddie Gallagher and his son John.

"That's the kind of father I wanted to be," he said, looking at her for the first time since he began telling his story. "Eddie was there for me when I needed him most."

"And now you're here for Eddie."

The look in his eyes warmed her heart. "Not everyone gets it."

"I do," she said, and she loved him for it. She thought of how different her life might have been if she'd been lucky enough to have parents who actually cared about her happiness. Her child would never doubt she or he was loved and wanted.

"I'll be a good father," John said quietly. "I've had a pretty damn good role model to follow."

Now, Alex. Tell him now.

But she couldn't do it. Not when he was looking at her like that, as if she'd handed him the keys to heaven. She couldn't tell him that the baby she carried might not be his. He had managed to survive the worst thing that could happen to a man. He deserved to be happy again and—God forgive her—her baby deserved a father who understood what being a father was all about. Her baby would be part of a family of men who understood what love was all about. Her baby would grow up knowing where he or she fit in the scheme of things. Her baby would grow up with a father who knew how to love.

He placed his hands against her belly, and a womb-deep sense of destiny filled her heart. *Yes,* she thought, pushing away the sense that she was making a terrible mistake. *This is the way it's meant to be.*

SIXTEEN

❧

SEA GATE ROOFING WANTED EIGHT thousand dollars
to repair Alex's roof and ceiling.

"This is highway robbery," Alex said to John her first
day back at the diner after the accident. It was the quiet
period between breakfast and lunch.

"You need a roof and a ceiling," John pointed out.
"That costs big bucks."

She poured herself a glass of milk and took a sip.
"He wants half of it up front. Can you imagine?"

"I can—"

"Don't say it," she warned. "It's my house. I can
manage."

"You can't live there while they're working."

She took another sip of milk. "Of course I can."

"You're pregnant. You—"

"Will you keep your voice down?" She glanced toward Will, who was smoking on the back step as usual.
"I don't want the world to know yet."

"I do," John said. "I feel like standing on the corner
of Soundview and Ocean and telling everyone who

walks by that we're going to have a baby."

"They'll know soon enough."

"Sooner," he said with a grin. "I think your waist-bands are getting a little tight."

"That's ridiculous!" Her hands went immediately to her belly. "It's too soon for me to show." Unless the baby wasn't John's. She pushed the thought away, as she had many times in the week since she'd discovered she was pregnant.

"What gives in here?" Dee popped up in the door-way. "Mrs. Kroger's waiting for her two eggs over easy. Let's get moving."

"He's a bad influence," Alex said, cracking two eggs onto the griddle. "You should tell the boss."

"Dee, you had some roof work done a few years ago, didn't you?"

Dee rolled her eyes. "Don't remind me. Except for my marriage, that was the worst three years of my life."

Alex laughed despite herself. "You paid her to say that, didn't you?" she asked John.

"Did I pay you to say that?" John asked Dee.

"Did I miss something?" Dee asked, looking from Alex to John. "You two should come with subtitles."

Alex added three slices of bacon to the griddle. "He thinks I should move in with him and Eddie while my roof's being repaired."

Dee arched a brow. "Just the roof?" She sounded skeptical.

"And the ceiling," John added. "Don't forget the ceiling."

"Roof *and* ceiling?" Dee turned to Alex. "Pack your bags, honey, and don't look back."

A LITTLE WHILE LATER JOHN went back to the marina and Alex left Will to prep for the lunch rush while she took her break out front.

"I know he paid you to say that," she said to Dee as she sat down on an empty counter stool.

"You'll thank me," Dee said. "I would have moved in with Rush Limbaugh if he'd asked, just to get away."

Dee then proceeded to make her laugh with home-repair horror stories.

"You're right," Alex said. "Rush would look pretty good after that."

"So how's it going for you two?"

"Rush and me?"

Dee tossed a packet of sugar in her direction. "You and John."

Alex looked away to hide her cat-and-canary smile. "I'd say it's going pretty well."

"It must be if you're moving in with him."

"That's only a temporary arrangement," Alex reminded her. "I have a home of my own."

Dee didn't say anything. Her wicked smile said it all for her.

Suddenly Alex wanted to share her news with the first real friend she'd ever had.

"Remember when you asked me if I needed the number of a good gynecologist?"

"Yes," Dee said in a careful tone of voice. "And you need the number of a good gynecologist now?"

Alex took a deep breath, then looked her friend straight in the eye. "Actually I need the number of a good obstetrician."

Dee's shriek could be heard in Atlantic City. She leaped to her feet, then grabbed Alex in a bear hug.

"We're not making it public yet," Alex warned, "so please don't tell a soul."

"They couldn't pry it out of me if they staked me naked to an anthill," Dee said as huge tears of happiness rolled down her cheeks.

"You're not supposed to cry," Alex said, wiping

tears from her own cheeks. "I'm the one who's supposed to be all hormonal and emotional."

"So sue me," Dee said, sniffling loudly. "I am a sucker for happy endings."

Endings? Alex thought. It seemed to her that life was just beginning.

"HERE YOU GO, BRIAN." GWEN, his paralegal, deposited a thick manila folder on his desk blotter. "Sorry it took so long. This is everything I could find on Griffin Whittaker and his wife."

"Nice work," Brian said. "Many photos?"

"A few," Gwen said. "There's one nice portrait of the two of them taken at a charity ball in London."

Gwen was in a chatty mood. It was all Brian could do to keep from tossing her out on her shapely butt; the manila folder was practically burning a hole in his desktop. Finally Gwen went back to her own office, and he dove into the stack of papers.

Griffin Whittaker wins Businessman of Year award . . . Whittaker announces layoffs at London office . . . Mr. and Mrs. Griffin Whittaker of New York City smile for London cameras—

Griffin and his wife were posed before a dark blue backdrop. Whittaker wore a tux. His wife wore a Grecian-styled gown that made her look like a goddess.

There were two more photos, both candid shots of Alex and Griffin in London. According to the accompanying article, the last photo of the Whittakers had been taken on October 1. From that point on, there was no mention of Alex anywhere. It was as if she'd never existed.

Brian continued thumbing through the photocopied pages. He needed something he could sink his teeth into. Something that would wipe the smug smile off his baby brother's face.

Halfway through the stack he found it. Apparently Griffin Whittaker's devoted wife Alexandra had walked out on him suddenly back in October, and her husband had been looking for her ever since. Whittaker had put out discreet, gentlemanly feelers around London and the Continent but had met with no success.

Alex Curry had managed to drop off her husband's radar screen by moving to a nowhere Jersey Shore town. She'd bought the Winslow place for cash, drove a beat-up VW, and worked at the diner in a world that was probably invisible to her Ivy League husband.

Hide in plain sight, he thought. It worked every time. The big question, however, was why she'd walked out.

A woman didn't turn her back on penthouse apartments and chauffeured limousines unless she had a good reason. And a woman didn't move into a rathole like Marge Winslow's place unless she was desperate. No doubt about it: Alex Curry was running scared.

He grinned as he slid the stack of papers back into the manila folder. Greed was a strong motivator, but fear was a stronger one. This was even better than he'd hoped for. Not only did Alex Curry hold a key piece of property in the takeover of Sea Gate, but also she held the key to his brother as well.

When Alex fell, Sea Gate would fall with her.

FUNNY HOW SOMETIMES GOOD NEWS could depress the hell out of you.

Dee was as honestly happy for Alex and John as she'd ever been for any two people in her life. John had been part of her existence since the cradle. They'd shared first teeth, first communions, and first loves. When she'd found out she was pregnant with Brian's baby, it was John who'd volunteered to do the right thing by her. She'd never forgotten that gesture. If she hadn't loved him before, she did from that moment on.

And you wanted the people you loved to be happy. John's life had taken a 180-degree turn from despair to the purest kind of joy. John was one of those rare men who was born to be a father. When Dee was pregnant with Mark, her mother had told her not to expect much from her husband for the first twelve months. "It takes most men at least a year to get used to the idea that the baby isn't going away."

But not Johnny. He bonded with his boys in utero, and the connection between them had grown stronger every day, right up until he lost them in that accident. She'd thought they were going to lose John, too. His pain had been so great there were times she'd almost wished God would take him too so he could be reunited with the family that had been his life.

He deserved a second chance to be happy, and she wondered if Alex had any idea how lucky she was that her baby would have a man like that to look up to.

Mark looked up to John, even if he wouldn't admit it. And God knew, her son adored Eddie. More and more over the last few months she'd found herself wanting to tell Mark the truth, to tell him that he was one of the Gallaghers, too, even if he didn't share the name. Maybe she'd done too good a job of keeping secrets.

Marrying Tony had been the biggest mistake of her life. He'd said he could accept another man's child as his own, but within months she knew that would never happen. Every time her husband looked at her son, he saw Brian Gallagher looking back at him, and that was no way to begin a marriage.

"You've got to tell the kid," Tony had urged her after the divorce became final. "You can't keep a secret like that in Sea Gate."

But she had. Brian was long gone by the time she returned with Mark but without her husband. He'd married the kind of woman she'd always known he would marry, sophisticated and well-connected and rich. The kind of woman who'd never waited tables in a diner to make ends meet. In fact, Dee doubted if Margo had ever set foot inside a diner in her whole privileged life. With Brian out of the picture, the people who'd whispered behind their hands had moved on to other, juicier topics.

She knew it was hard for Eddie to see Mark around town every day and not be able to claim him as his first grandchild, but he did his best. Mark didn't make it easy. Mark had looked up to him from the first day they met, and he'd begged Eddie to take him out on the *Kestrel* any chance he got. Somehow Eddie had managed to be a good friend to the boy without ever hinting that their relationship was one of blood and bone as well.

Dee had settled back into her old life without a ripple, and after a while it was as if she'd never left. After her parents died she moved into their old house, and the money she used to spend on rent now went toward saving for Mark's college education. She'd made it clear to Mark that he would have to help share the burden. He had to keep his marks up in order to qualify for a partial scholarship, and it was understood he'd have to hold down a job to help pay for gas and car insurance and clothes.

She'd done a good job with her boy, a damn good job, but he needed a father now more than ever. She would have known what to say to a daughter, how to guide her through the rough waters of adolescence. The difference between the sexes had never seemed more acute than they did these days as she watched her son take his first steps toward manhood. The sweet-natured boy she used to tuck into bed at night had been replaced by a sullen, angry stranger. She could talk football and baseball with the best of them, but she couldn't show him how to be a man.

She didn't blame Tony for his indifference. Her ex-husband had tried to love Mark the way he would have loved his own child, but it had been like swimming against the tide. The fact that he kept in contact with the boy thirteen years after the divorce meant something, even if it wasn't enough to erase the pain and confusion in her son's eyes every time Tony's name came up. He didn't look or sound or think like Tony and he never would. As Mark grew older, those differences grew more apparent. It seemed to Dee that he looked more like a Gallagher with every day that passed.

And that was the problem. Mark was a Gallagher through and through, and it was time he found out.

She had taken a deep breath the other day and told Sam Weitz the whole story. She'd never done that before. Lots of people knew bits and pieces of her story, but now only Sam knew it all. They'd become lovers the afternoon of New Year's Eve, and now, almost six weeks later, she was feeling cautiously optimistic about the future. She knew that even cautious optimism could be dangerous, but she couldn't help herself.

She'd made more than her share of mistakes with men. Those mistakes had made her cautious and guarded and sometimes downright unapproachable. If Prince Charming decided to sweep her off her feet, he'd better be wearing a flak jacket. *Poor Sam,* she thought. He had no idea what he'd gotten into.

Brian had called a few times since Thanksgiving, and she found his sudden attention disconcerting, to say the least. At first she'd thought he was looking for sex, but by the second phone call she'd realized that was only a small part of it. He persisted in wanting to walk down memory lane with her, reliving high school triumphs and ignoring his one glaring failure until she wanted to wrap the phone cord around his neck.

He acts as if the pregnancy never happened, she had thought. As if Mark belonged to someone else.

"Tell Mark the truth," Sam had urged her over dinner last week. "That's the only part of the equation you can control."

Maybe Sam was right. She wasn't fool enough to believe there would ever be a father-and-son reunion between Mark and Brian. That wasn't what she was looking for. But a grandfather-and-son reunion—well, that was another story.

Whether or not John would admit it yet, something was wrong with Eddie, and Dee was afraid she knew what it was. Her aunt Louise had started the same way. Forgetfulness, followed by disorientation, followed by mood swings, followed by—she couldn't bring herself to think about the way it had ended.

If she was going to give her son the gift of a family, she would have to gather up her courage and do it soon, before it was too late.

SEVENTEEN

~~~~~~~~~~~

THERE HAD BEEN TIMES OVER the past few years when Eddie's faith in God had deserted him. You couldn't watch your wife die a long miserable death without wondering exactly what the Almighty had in mind when He decided who would make an easy exit from this life and who wouldn't. He'd been raised a Catholic and had practiced his faith for almost seventy years without questioning why, but losing Rosie had shaken his belief to the core.

Eddie found his faith again on Valentine's Day when Alex Curry moved in with his son.

John had been smiling nonstop for two weeks now. And laughing. Eddie couldn't remember the last time he'd heard his son laugh as if he meant it. When he told Eddie that Alex was moving in with them while her roof was being repaired, Eddie had been tempted to go to church and light a candle in thanks.

The two of them had shoveled out the house, then applied a little elbow grease where necessary. Dusting. Polishing. Cleaning. Waxing. He wondered if the *Guin-*

ness Book of World Records gave a prize for having a record number of cobwebs. They managed to get the place in shape an hour before John went to collect Alex and her stuff, and then only because Eddie had come up with the idea to stuff some of the junk in the toolshed.

"Whatever works," John had said, and Eddie agreed.

He and Bailey were waiting on the top step when John pulled his truck into the driveway.

"Welcome to our home," he'd said, kissing Alex on the cheek.

"I promise it's only temporary," she'd said, bending down to scratch Bailey behind the ear. "I'll be out of your hair the second the roofers are finished."

"Don't rush on my account," Eddie said, meaning it. "Stay here as long as you want."

She and John exchanged a look that puzzled Eddie, but he let it go. He hadn't been alone so long that he'd forgotten the different ways men and women communicated with each other.

The house felt different with her in it. She'd only been there five minutes, and already it felt more like a home than it had since Rosie died.

"I made coffee," Eddie said as he led the way into the kitchen. "We've got bagels and cream cheese if you want them."

"I'm not much of a coffee drinker," Alex said with a gentle smile, "but I'd love a glass of milk."

"You sit down," Eddie said, gesturing toward the kitchen table. John was busy unloading the truck. "I'll get it for you."

"You don't have to spoil me like this," Alex said, claiming a chair. "I might get used to it."

"So get used to it," Eddie said, opening the refrigerator. "Between the accident and that roof of yours, you've been through the mill the last few weeks."

"The car will finally be ready tomorrow," she said.

"Just in time for me to get back to work."

He handed Alex a glass of milk, then poured himself some hot java. "Don't push yourself," he said.

"I'll bet that's not what you told John when he was a boy," she said, laughing.

"Never had to tell him much of anything," Eddie said. "That one marches to his own drummer. It was Brian we had to lean on, to keep him on the straight and narrow."

Alex opened her mouth as if to say something, then quickly looked back down at the plate of bagels.

"Hope you're not a poker player, Alex," he said, dumping some sugar into his cup. "That face of yours is an open book."

"So I've been told," she said. "I'm sorry. I didn't mean to be rude."

"Brian's been a disappointment," he said honestly. "Family doesn't mean much to him. Not the way it does to Johnny."

"You telling stories about me?" John walked into the kitchen with Bailey at his side. "Let Alex make up her own mind, why don't you." The twinkle in his eyes made Eddie grin.

"Coffee?" Eddie asked.

"Sit down and eat, Pop," John said. "I'll get my own coffee."

"Hell, no," Eddie said. "You did the heavy lifting. I'll do the pouring."

Alex looked up at him. The same twinkle glittered in her eyes. "John's right," she said. "Why don't you sit down, Eddie, so we can tell you something."

"What's going on?" he asked, looking from Alex to John. "You two cooking up some scheme?"

"We have some news for you, Pop," said John, "and we think you'd better be sitting down when you hear it."

His heart lurched, and Alex reached out and touched his hand.

"For heaven's sake, John," she said, "the least you can do is tell your father it's *good* news."

"It's good news," John said.

"Will somebody just spit it out?" Eddie bellowed in exasperation. "I'm almost seventy years old. I don't have all day."

John and Alex exchanged another one of those looks.

Alex nodded. "You tell him," she said.

"Somebody'd better tell me fast or—"

"Pop," said John, "Alex and I are going to have a baby."

The words tumbled around inside Eddie's head like dice. "What?" he asked, trying to make sense of the sounds he'd heard. "What? What?"

"Pop." John knelt down in front of him. "Alex is pregnant. You're going to be a grandfather again."

"What about Libby? What the hell's your wife going to say about that?" Anger bubbled through his veins. "I have four grandchildren already. Four's enough. I don't want any more grandchildren." The blond-haired woman tried to make him smile, but he wasn't buying it. "You trying to shame your parents, miss? Go find yourself some man that doesn't already have a family."

Her golden eyes flooded with tears. "Eddie, this is Alex. You know I would never hurt anybody."

"I don't know anything about you," he said as wild birds flapped crazily inside his chest. His heart . . . was that his heart . . . it couldn't be his heart . . . nobody's heart beat that fast . . . he'd be dead if his heart was really beating that fast. . . .

"POP!" JOHN WAS CROUCHED DOWN in front of him. "Pop!"

"What the hell are you yelling about?" Eddie asked,

puzzled by the look of fear in his son's eyes. "You look like you've seen a ghost." He had the feeling he'd missed something, but he didn't have any idea what it might be. Lately his mind tended to wander, and he couldn't always figure out a way to cover for himself. This was one of those times.

Across the table from him Alex's big golden eyes swam with tears. She and John looked at each other.

"What's with those looks?" Eddie demanded. "Every time I turn around, the two of you are giving each other one of those looks."

"Sorry, Pop," John said. He still looked white as a sheet. "We—uh, Alex and I have something to tell you."

"Yes," Alex said. Her voice sounded shaky, and he felt bad if he'd somehow hurt her feelings, but he didn't know what he might have done. "It's something wonderful, Eddie."

"So tell me already," he said. "I could use some good news."

"Pop," said John. "Alex and I are going to have a baby."

"A baby?" He looked at Alex, and she nodded. The last time he'd seen a woman look so radiantly beautiful, it was when Rosie told him she was pregnant the first time. "The two of you?"

"Yes." Alex reached across the table and squeezed his hand. "Your grandchild."

He thought of Jake and Michael, and a lump the size of a lemon formed in his throat. He missed those boys— Jesus, how he missed them.

"I'm—" He stopped and cleared his throat. "I'm so happy for—" He couldn't manage to get the words out past that damn lump in his throat.

"I know." John's voice cracked on the last word. "I know."

• • •

"I BELIEVE IT'S IMPORTANT TO get to know each other before the examination," Dr. Schulman said as Alex and John took their seats a few days later. "We'll sit here in my office and talk and then we'll do the exam."

"Sounds good to me," John said.

Alex shot him a look. Her hands were clasped tightly in her lap to keep them from shaking. So far it wasn't working. Doctors made her nervous; gynecologists made her crazy. Too many years and too much bad news had conditioned her like one of Pavlov's dogs. Put her within five miles of a table and stirrups, and she started to hyperventilate.

You're pregnant, she told herself. *Really and truly pregnant.* This was a normal, run-of-the-mill prenatal appointment and she had a good man by her side. She'd finally grabbed the brass ring. Now if she could just get herself to believe it.

She held John's hand while the doctor explained the schedule of visits and outlined the costs.

"Susan is our office manager," the doctor said, scribbling something on a pale green legal pad. "Be sure to speak with her before you leave. She'll take down all of your health insurance information."

"I don't have health insurance," Alex blurted out.

The silence in the room was deafening. "No health insurance?" Dr. Schulman sounded as if she couldn't believe her ears.

"No health insurance," Alex repeated. She couldn't quite control the challenging note in her voice. "I'm afraid it's out of my reach." *Did you hear what you said, Alex? If health care is out of your reach, how are you ever going to raise a baby?*

The doctor scribbled furiously. "Susan will help you

work out a payment plan. Hospital charges must be paid in full before delivery.''

"No problem," John said, withdrawing a checkbook from his pocket. "Tell me what the charges are, and I'll take care of them now.''

Alex opened her mouth to protest, but there was something about the look in his eyes that brought her up short. *He needs to do this,* she thought. He needed to take care of her and the baby, to protect them in whatever way he could. And, God help her, she and the baby needed him. She'd never given a thought to health insurance. Now it was quickly becoming the focus of her life.

The doctor outlined what they could expect from each of the prenatal visits. She gave them packets of information about Lamaze classes, breast-feeding, and genetic counseling, then reviewed the forms Alex had filled out in the waiting room.

"You're twenty-eight," Dr. Schulman said. "No family history of cancer, heart disease, or diabetes. This is your first pregnancy. Blood type O-negative. You missed something here, Alex.'' She looked up and smiled. "The date of your last period.''

"I'm not sure when it was," Alex hedged. "It's been a while.''

"Well, this is February," the doctor said. "December, perhaps?''

"No, it was longer ago than that.''

The doctor eyed her with curiosity. "November?''

"I think it was more like March.''

Dr. Schulman arched a brow. "Of last year?''

Alex nodded. "Of last year.''

"Did you have any spotting in the interim?''

"Some," Alex admitted. "But nothing notable.'' Nothing that a normal woman would have considered to be a period.

"Amenorrhea." Dr. Schulman nodded. "Difficult to achieve a pregnancy, but not impossible." She flipped to a new page in her notebook. "When do you estimate the date of conception?"

Her throat constricted as she remembered that terrible October night when her marriage ended.

The night when Griffin raped her.

No, she thought. She refused to believe fate would be that cruel to her or to John.

"Thanksgiving," she said, looking over at John. "It happened on Thanksgiving."

JOHN COULDN'T SLEEP. THE VISIT to the doctor's office had brought back a flood of memories, memories he thought he'd managed to bury in the part of his heart that had died with his wife and children.

But he'd been wrong.

The memories were there waiting for him every time he closed his eyes. He saw Libby's face when she told them they were expecting a baby. He saw Michael's wrinkled red face when he took his first breath and faced the world. He saw Jake when he pulled himself up and took his first steps straight into his daddy's arms.

He waited for the pain to rip through him the way it always did, but it was different this time. The sadness was there, and the regret, but the pain was just a dull ache. It made him feel hopeful and disloyal and disoriented, all at once, the way he used to feel after a bottle of vodka on an empty stomach.

Sorrow had been a part of him for so long that he'd almost forgotten how to be happy, but day by day it was coming back to him. Living with Alex was the closest he'd been to heaven in a very long time. Sleeping with her in his arms. Seeing her face each morning over the breakfast table. Hearing her chat with Eddie about whether they needed more eggs from the grocery store.

It all made him feel alive again, as if the shattered pieces of his heart were somehow moving together.

Next to him she stirred, and he watched, deeply moved, as her hands covered her belly in that age-old gesture. His heart seemed to swell inside his chest cavity with a powerful combination of love and pride and abject terror. The world was a dangerous, unpredictable place. He hadn't been able to protect Libby and the boys. What guarantee did he have that he would be able to protect Alex and their baby from whatever life had in store for them?

Alex stretched slightly, then opened her eyes. "You're still awake." Her voice was little more than a whisper. "Is everything all right?"

"It's the middle of the night," he said, smoothing her hair from her face. "Go back to sleep."

She leaned up on one elbow and looked at him. "You need your sleep, too, John. You're taking out the *Kestrel* in a few hours." He was piloting a group of businessmen on an overnight deep-sea fishing trip out past Montauk Point.

He pulled her into the crook of his arm, where she nestled against his side. "I could pilot the *Kestrel* in my sleep."

She feigned a shiver. "That's not what I want to hear. I want you to be careful."

"I'll be careful."

"Promise me?"

"I promise." For the first time in years he had a reason to be careful.

"Thank you for what you did tonight," she said.

"What I did?" He was genuinely puzzled.

"At Dr. Schulman's office," she went on. "Paying for the hospital and everything in advance. I'll pay you back."

"We're not keeping score here. I don't expect to be paid back."

"I know that," she said, pulling away from him. "It's important to me."

"You're carrying my baby, Alex. It's as much my responsibility as it is yours." The old rules between them no longer applied. The baby had changed everything.

"You don't understand." Her voice was a whisper.

"Then tell me," he said. "Make me understand."

"I think your imagination's running away with you, John. I value my independence."

"It's more than that," he persisted. "I don't know one damn thing about you, Alex. We've been sleeping together for months, you're carrying my baby, and the only thing I know about you is that you were born in New York."

"That's ridiculous. You know a lot about me."

"Half of what I know I learned today in the doctor's office. Twenty-eight years old, O-negative, no family history of diabetes." He pinned her with a look. "Care to elaborate?"

"Is this a job interview?" she shot back. "Will you fingerprint me, too?"

"I'm not blind, Alex. I know you don't belong in a place like Sea Gate."

"I love Sea Gate," she said. "I always have."

He caught her face gently between his hands and forced her to meet his eyes. "What did you say?"

She wanted to look away, but the force of his gaze wouldn't allow it. "I said, I've always loved Sea Gate."

"You've been here before?"

She nodded as ridiculous tears welled up in her eyes. "The summer before my parents died." She told him about the boat trip, about needing repairs, about a magical few days spent in a town she thought she'd never see again. It seemed as if her parents had been on the move her entire life, searching for the magic key that would push her father higher up the ladder of success. Those few days together in a small Jersey Shore town were her happiest memories of being a family.

"You were probably already married and living in New York by then. I used to watch the kids going in and out of the pizzeria and I'd try to imagine how it would feel to really belong somewhere, to be part of something."

"All of that moving around must have been rough on you," John said.

"Oh, it didn't bother me at all," she said with a brittle laugh. "They parked me at boarding school for ten months out of the year. It was the other two months that were the problem."

He looked at her as if he were seeing her for the first time. Maybe he was, she thought. She'd never revealed this much of her past to anyone—not even to Griffin. He had known the details of her parents' death but not of the life she'd led before that point. He'd known nothing of the loneliness, the isolation, the sense that when push came to shove, she was in this life alone.

"How did your parents die?" John asked.

"A plane crash," she said in a voice devoid of emotion. "They were heading off to Aspen or Vail or someplace, and their jet went into the side of a mountain."

"Jesus," John whispered. "I'm sorry."

"They weren't part of my day-to-day life," she said, trying to explain the situation to a man who'd had two parents who loved him. "When the headmistress broke the news, I remember just nodding, then going right back to French class. It wasn't until spring break and everyone else went home that I finally realized I was all alone." A fact that was hammered home with brute force when Alex discovered there wasn't any money left for her to return to school—or to do anything else, for that matter.

"You must have had somebody, Alex. An aunt, an uncle—maybe a cousin somewhere."

She shook her head. "Nobody but bill collectors beating down my door, trying to get me to pay my parents' debts." She was barely seventeen years old and terrified beyond description. "One of my parents' friends recommended that I talk to a man they knew. They said he might be able to make sense of everything for me and maybe help me find a way out of the mess." Again that hollow laugh she couldn't quite turn into the real thing. "He did better than that: He married me."

"You married your financial advisor?"

"Guilty," she said, closing her eyes against the memories. "Is there anything more clichéd than that? He was twenty-five years older than I was, way more sophisticated, and he said he'd take care of everything. I thought I'd never have to worry about anything ever again." Griffin had been husband, father, and safe harbor, and she'd been more than willing to spend the rest of her life as his grateful wife and the mother of his children. Her laugh was bitter. "Apparently I failed at both."

"Life doesn't always work out the way we think it should." John reached for her hand, and this time she didn't pull away. "I thought I'd grow old with Libby and the boys."

"And I thought—" She stopped abruptly. "It doesn't matter what I thought. That was another lifetime. I was another person. I won't make those mistakes again." She'd shared more of herself with him than she ever had with any other person on earth, but it was what she hadn't shared that had the power to destroy them.

He placed her hand on her belly, then covered it with his own. "This isn't a mistake, Alex."

"I know," she whispered. "It's a miracle."

They lay together for a long time, hands pressed to her belly, letting the past drift away from them . . . keeping the future at bay. She loved the way his hands felt against her skin, so warm and strong. So tender. She'd never imagined a man could be tender, but John managed to be passionate and exciting and tender all at once, and he stole her breath away.

He gentled her with his hands, his lips, his body. He grasped her by the waist and positioned her above him so that she straddled his hips. All or nothing or anything in between—it was her choice. Her decision. Her desires that ruled what happened in that bed tonight.

SHE WAS WARM AND WILD, nurturing and demanding. She took him places he hadn't even dreamed about, places he didn't know existed. She gave him her body, but what he really wanted was her heart, and he had the feeling that was the one thing that wasn't hers to give.

EIGHTEEN

"YOU LOOK BEAT," EDDIE SAID when Alex came home from the diner one afternoon later that week. "Take a load off your feet. I'll fix you some tea."

Alex stifled a yawn as she bent down to scratch Bailey behind the ear. "That sounds wonderful," she said gratefully. "But only if you join me."

"Okay if I have a bottle of Bud instead of Lipton?"

She laughed and straightened up. "Of course it's okay." She sat down at the kitchen table and sighed deeply. "I think my feet grew two sizes today."

Eddie popped a cup of hot water into the microwave, then pressed a few buttons. "My Rosie used to say she carried Brian and Johnny in her feet."

"I think Rosie was right. Even my hands are bigger."

"It becomes you," Eddie said with that strange blend of courtly bluntness she found so endearing in him. "You were too damn skinny when you came to town."

She tried to remember the woman she'd been, but it was like crawling into someone else's dreams. She felt so connected, so much a part of life here in Sea Gate, that everything that had come before faded into insignificance. "You're right," she said, reaching for a donut. "I was too damn skinny." And too scared. And too lonely.

Eddie grinned, then turned to answer the call of the microwave. He'd had another one of his "episodes" three nights ago, but apparently it had left no lasting effects behind. She and John had found him on board the *Kestrel*, trying to pilot the boat out of the marina while it was still tied to the moorings. He'd caused a good bit of damage, but fortunately both the *Kestrel* and the marina would survive.

As usual John had blamed it on sleepwalking, but this time Alex refused to play along.

"Eddie isn't sleepwalking," she'd said, forcing him to listen to her. "I think he needs help, John."

"We took him to Dr. Benino," John said. She knew he was deliberately choosing to misunderstand her meaning. "That's who came up with the sleepwalking theory in the first place."

"I think you should take him to a specialist," she went on. She knew she was wading into dangerous waters, but somebody had to force him to face the truth. "Somebody who understands Alz—" She never had the chance to finish the word. John had stormed out of the bedroom they shared, and when she saw him again the next day, neither one mentioned what had happened.

"Here's your tea." Eddie deposited the mug in front of her. "Milk and sugar, just the way you like it."

She thanked him. "You spoil me, Eddie," she murmured, taking a sip. "I'm going to hate to go home after the roof is finished."

"So don't go home," Eddie said, sitting down opposite her. He popped the cap off a bottle of beer. "There's plenty of room for you here."

"I know," she said, "and I thank you for the invitation, but I belong in my own place."

"You belong where you're happy."

"I'm very happy at my place."

He arched a graying brow. "Are you saying you're not happy here?" Occasionally his syntax took on a distinctly Irish lilt for emphasis.

"That's not what I'm saying."

"So if you're happy here, stay put."

"It's not that simple."

"Neither am I," he said with a smile. "So why don't you explain it to me?"

She withheld a sigh. "I wish I could, Eddie. I'm not even sure I can explain it to myself." Part of being a family was caring for each other—and being cared for when that was what you needed. There was a generosity of spirit about John and Eddie that she'd never encountered before, and that generosity extended to her and her baby. *To John's baby,* she corrected herself. She wondered if John would be so willing to open his heart and his home to her if he knew she might be carrying another man's child. She wondered if she'd even have the right to ask him to be.

She took a sip of tea as she tried to push the thought of Griffin from her mind. She'd dreamed about him last night. The details had vanished the second she opened her eyes, but a sense of uneasiness remained. Abandonment didn't suit Griffin's image of himself. She wondered what kind of story he'd concocted to cover up her absence from the London social scene. She had no doubt that his image of himself mattered much more to him than her presence in his life.

Lately she felt as if she was living her days in a kind of suspended animation. Living there in that big Victorian house with John and Eddie and Bailey was as close to heaven as she'd ever expected to come. Knowing she was safe, knowing that her baby would be welcomed into such a place, gave her a sense of contentment so deep it almost frightened her. She'd expected there would be a period of adjustment, a week or two where the three of them—and Bailey—circled around each other as they learned to live together. To her amazement she'd felt at home from the moment she walked in the door. The house felt familiar in the best possible way, and she realized that it wasn't just a question of her needing their help; they needed her as well.

She'd never been needed before, and it was a wonderful feeling. It would be so easy to give herself over to being happy, but Griffin cast a shadow over everything.

She wished she had it to do over again. She'd believed she could leave her wedding ring on the end table and walk out the door, and her old life would be a thing of the past. She hadn't wanted anything from Griffin except her freedom, and she didn't need a lawyer to get it. All she'd had to do was walk out the door.

Well, she'd walked out the door, all right, but fate had the last laugh. Instead of the solitary life of independence she'd expected, she found herself both pregnant and in love—and still tied to the man who'd been both husband and stranger for ten years of her life. Where was the Wizard of Oz when you needed him? As long as she was still married to Griffin, her future remained in shadows.

"Alex." Eddie sounded concerned. "Why so sad?"

She roused herself from her thoughts. "I was wondering why it is we always think of the right thing to do when it's too late to matter."

"If I had the answer to that one, somebody would build a religion around me."

She laughed despite herself. "So what did you do with yourself today, Eddie?"

He took another swallow of beer, then put the half-empty bottle down on the table. "I went to the library."

"The library?" She looked at him in surprise. "I thought you said you weren't much of a reader."

"I'm not." He met her eyes. "I wanted to do some research."

A knot of fear formed in her gut. "Don't tell me," she said, keeping her tone light. "You're going to turn the *Kestrel* into a racing sloop and enter her in the America's Cup."

He didn't return her smile, and the knot of fear grew larger. "I was reading about Alzheimer's."

Tears filled her eyes. "Oh, Eddie. . . ."

"Makes sense, doesn't it?" He held her gaze as if it were a lifeline. "All these crazy things I'm doing . . ." He cleared his throat. "Last week I forgot the Dodgers had left Brooklyn, and that was forty years ago. A man like me doesn't forget something like that unless he—"

"It might not be Alzheimer's," she said. "There could be another reason."

"Maybe," he said, "but the signs are there."

She reached across the table and took his hand. "Have you talked to John about it?"

"He doesn't want to hear it, Alex. Scares him, I'm thinking."

"I know what you mean," she said. "He has this need to protect everyone he cares about."

"Let him," Eddie said. "It's what both of you need, isn't it?"

She sighed. "If I had the answer to that one. . . ."

Eddie laughed, but the look in his eyes came close to breaking her heart. "I want to see him happy," he said. "I want to see the two of you with the baby before—before things get any worse."

"I want that, too, Eddie." She didn't tell him there was nothing wrong. He knew something was, and she loved him too much to lie to him. All she could do was let him know she understood and that she'd be there for him. She took his hands in hers and held it tight against whatever might lie ahead.

BY ST. PATRICK'S DAY, THE secret was out. Alex had been in a losing battle with her rapidly expanding waistline, and she finally had to give in and buy clothes in a size that actually fit her. She wasn't quite ready for maternity clothes, but the loose, shapeless garments she chose might as well have carried the logo "Baby on Board."

As if that wasn't enough, Dee had had to take her off kitchen duty and move her out to the cash register. Morning sickness had finally kicked in with a vengeance, and when Alex suggested they bypass the annual corned beef and cabbage special in favor of fasting, both she and her friend knew the handwriting was on the wall.

She dressed carefully that first day at the cash register, taking extra pains with her hair and makeup in order to attract attention away from her belly to her face, but nobody at the Starlight was fooled. In fact, they seemed downright delighted.

"It's about time you started wearing maternity clothes," Sally Whitton said. "We were afraid you didn't know you were expecting."

"Yeah," said Vince Troisi. "Thought we'd have to take Johnny aside and tell him he's gonna be a daddy."

Alex shot Dee a pointed look. "Did you tell them?" she demanded.

Dee was the picture of aggrieved innocence. "Honey, I didn't have to tell anyone anything. All they have to do is look at you."

The diner erupted with laughter. Alex ducked her head to hide her grin. "Okay," she said, cheeks burning, "so maybe I have gained a little bit of weight."

"Not so much the weight," Nick Di Mentri said. "When you refused to make hashed browns with our eggs last week, we all knew something was up. My wife wouldn't cook onions the whole time she was pregnant."

"Tell me about it," Dee chimed in. "It was either get this girl up front or close down until the third trimester. She told me she wouldn't cook anything with root vegetables."

"You're incorrigible," Alex said, pouring herself a glass of milk at the counter. "I don't know why I put up with the lot of you. It's so much quieter in the kitchen."

"We missed you out here, Alex," Vince Troisi said. "They didn't let you come up for air too often back there, did they?"

"Dee is a slave driver," Alex said with a wink for her friend. "She had me shackled to the grill."

Sally Whitton said she was glad to see Alex out there with the crowd again, but she made no bones about her disappointment that Alex wasn't behind the stove. "Best food I've had in a dog's age," Sally said. "Your pot roast put Will's to shame."

"You should try catering," Dave said. "We're having a first communion party for our granddaughter the second weekend in May. Wish you'd think about handling the food for us."

Alex's cheeks reddened with pleasure. "Are you serious, Dave?"

"The missus asked me to ask you last week, but I didn't think you'd be up to it what with—" He stopped and grinned. "You know."

"I'll give Eileen a call," Alex said. "Thanks, Dave."

"We're all real happy for you and Johnny," Sally

said. "The moment I saw you I said you looked like one of us."

"Get off it, Sal," Eddie chimed in. "The first time you saw our Alex, you said she looked like Princess Di."

"Princess Di?" Alex's eyes widened. "Why Princess Di?"

"Because we never saw anybody like you at the Starlight," Vince broke in.

"And because we sure never thought we'd see you serving coffee," Dave added.

"Life is filled with surprises, ladies and gentlemen." Alex patted her stomach. "Believe me, I know."

CONVERSATION EBBED WHILE THE COUNTER regulars devoured breakfast. Alex sipped her glass of milk and continued working on her list of things she'd need before the baby was born.

Not bad, she thought, totaling up the estimates. If she won the lottery, she might have a chance to break even. John was more than willing to take care of all her bills, but she wasn't going to give in without a fight.

She wondered if Dave had been serious about wanting her to cater his granddaughter's first holy communion. That would be one way to add to her coffers. The simple roofing job on her house had mushroomed into new wiring and new insulation. "This place is a firetrap," her insurance agent had said bluntly. "Either get the repairs done, or we cancel your policy." At the rate things were going, she'd be in debt for the rest of her life.

"So are we on for tonight?" Nick piped up to the group at large. "I got Sarah at the library to let us use their community room."

"We're on," Vince said. "Don't know how many are going to show up but Dee's Sam posted a notice at town hall and got the cable company to run an ad." He turned to Alex. "John will be back up from Cape May, won't he?"

Alex nodded. "John said he'd be home by seven."

"We can't have the meeting without him," Vince said. "He's the only one who can stop this Eagle Management from destroying the town."

Sally Whitton was unimpressed. "You can't stop progress."

"Progress?" Eddie sounded outraged. "They want to turn Sea Gate into a damn parking lot. That's not progress."

"You can't blame people for selling, Eddie." Sally sounded apologetic. "Most of us are getting on in years. We don't get a whole lot of chances to make money."

"You did it, didn't you?" Eddie charged. "You sold out."

"What if I did?" Sally shot back, crumpling her napkin in her hand. "I don't have anyone to take care of me, Eddie Gallagher. I've got to find a way to take care of myself."

A silence fell across the diner as the men seemed to close ranks against Sally. Alex and Dee locked eyes.

"You don't have to apologize, Sally," Dee said. "You did what you had to do."

Which was something Alex understood all too well. She tried to console herself with the fact that she hadn't exactly lied to John, but deep down she knew she was only fooling herself. What would he say if he knew she'd run out on Griffin? What would he say if he knew she not only wasn't divorced, but that she also might be carrying her husband's child?

Twice Dr. Schulman had scheduled Alex for a sonogram, and twice Alex had canceled the appointment.

"We need to pinpoint the date of conception," the doctor had explained once again. "Given your irregular

menstrual cycle, a sonogram is our best tool for deter-
mining your due date.''

Alex couldn't argue with the woman—what the doctor said made perfect sense. Unfortunately there was
more at stake than pinpointing the due date. What if she
found out the baby was Griffin's?

Lately she'd found herself dreaming about him almost
every night. They weren't exactly nightmares, but the
dreams never failed to leave her uneasy.

The dream was always the same: Griffin showed up
on her doorstep to claim his child. He was his usual cool
and sophisticated self. He stepped inside her cottage as
if he were stepping inside a landfill. His eyes took in
every detail. The framed prints on the wall. The ceramic
milk container in the shape of a cow. Disdain rolled off
him in waves. She could feel herself shrinking, growing
more insubstantial by the second. The only thing real
about her was her belly.

She'd wake up in a cold sweat, hands shaking, heart
pounding as if she was in the middle of an anxiety attack. It was only a dream. Dreams couldn't hurt you. If
Griffin hadn't tracked her down by now, the odds were
he never would. In every way that mattered, her marriage was over.

''They're a tough crowd,'' Dee said after the morning
crew scattered. She poured herself a cup of coffee, then
sat down at the counter. ''They cut Sally off at the knees
today.''

''I know,'' Alex said, joining Dee at the counter.
''Sally was crying when she left.''

Dee shook her head sadly. ''When they close ranks
on you, you're done for.''

Alex looked at her. ''You sound as though you've had
personal experience.''

''In a way,'' Dee said, ''although in my case it was
the father they cut off at the knees.'' She met Alex's

eyes. "I suppose you've figured it out by now."

"About Mark?"

"About Mark. John probably told you everything."

"No," said Alex. "Actually John hasn't told me anything at all. But the family resemblance is hard to miss."

"Oh, God, you don't think that John and I—" She looked horrified. "It was Brian."

"I know," Alex said. "I saw the way Mark looked at him on Thanksgiving."

Dee took a sip of coffee, then put the cup back down on the saucer. "Mark doesn't know."

"What?"

"Unless I remember wrong, pregnancy doesn't affect a woman's hearing. I said Mark doesn't know that Brian is his father."

"You must be kidding," Alex said. "How could he not know? Mark practically has the name Gallagher stamped on his forehead."

"One of life's little ironies," Dee said. "Mark thinks my ex is his father."

"You don't really think he believes that, do you?" Alex surprised herself with the blunt statement.

Dee hesitated a moment. "I want to."

"But you don't." She couldn't possibly.

"No," Dee said. "I don't. Tony tried to accept Mark as his own son, but he couldn't do it. Don't ever kid yourself, Alex. That whole blood thing is more important to them than we know. That's why we divorced. I've spent the last thirteen years telling myself that the kid doesn't need a father, but the older he gets, the more sure I am that I'm dead wrong. That's why I've decided to talk to Brian. We made so damn many mistakes, Alex. I want to undo some of them while Mark is still young enough for it to make a difference."

"I don't understand."

"Mark needs to know who his father is. He loves

Eddie and he respects John. I want my son to know that they're his family.''

"And what about Brian?''

"Let's just say I have low expectations.'' Dee forced a smile. "You don't know how lucky you are, Alex. Your child won't have to wonder who his father is. He'll know it's John, right from the start.''

NINETEEN

~

"GALLAGHER, YOU'RE NOT LISTENING TO me."

Brian looked up from his yellow legal pad. "You said something, Mary?" They were having a lunch meeting on the subject of Sea Gate.

"You haven't heard a word I said, have you?"

"Sorry." He pushed the pad to the other side of his blotter. "You were saying?"

She fixed him with the kind of look he associated with schoolteachers and other figures of authority. It was almost enough to make him laugh. "We need your okay to move on to phase two of the Sea Gate project. The storeowners on Ocean Avenue are hanging tougher than we'd expected."

"So offer them more money. Everyone has a price. You'll hit theirs sooner or later."

"Not this time," she said. "They've banded together to fight us."

Son of a bitch, he thought. They were a ballsy group, the people he grew up with. He couldn't help admiring them for fighting the inevitable. And it was inevitable.

They'd been able to close ranks against him when he was young but times had changed. Make no mistake about it, this was one fight he was going to win.

"There's more, Gallagher. Your brother's the one behind them."

"Johnny?"

"You heard it here. I don't know if he volunteered or was drafted, but he's trying to figure out exactly who Eagle Management belongs to."

"Let him," Brian said. "I want him to find out." There was a certain karmic symmetry to the situation that pleased him. John was setting himself up as a savior. Brian would take great pleasure in knocking him back down to earth.

"You don't sound very upset."

"I'm not," Brian said. "Trust me, he'll fuck up. He always does." John couldn't hang on to his wife or his kids or his career. There was no reason to believe he'd manage to hang on to his old hometown.

"They formed a a committee," she said, glancing down at her notes. "It's called Save Sea Gate. Our contact says they'll be taking it to the media once they get themselves rolling."

"You expect me to worry about that, Mary?"

"Somebody has to," she shot back. "We need an emergency meeting of our own. Maybe a conference call tonight to—"

"Listen," he said, "I have another appointment. Why don't we just schedule a strategy meeting for next week."

"Next week?" She pushed back her chair and stood up. "It's almost April, Gallagher. We were talking about a June start-up."

"Schedule something for Tuesday, and I'll be there."

"Your partners aren't going to be happy."

"That's where you're wrong, Mary. After tonight they're going to be downright ecstatic."

He'd been biding his time, waiting for the right moment to play his trump card, and that moment had finally arrived.

ALEX GOT HOME A LITTLE after five o'clock. She'd have the house to herself for another two hours, and she intended to make the most of it. The one bad thing about living with John and Eddie was not having time for "girl" things like long soaks in the bathtub and walking around with mudpacks on her face and deep conditioner on her hair. She might even wax her legs while she was at it. Before too long her belly would be so big she wouldn't be able to do things like that.

She unlocked the front door and stepped inside as a wave of fatigue washed over her. A nap wasn't a bad idea, come to think of it. A real one, complete with a pillow under her head and a quilt pulled up under her chin. The idea was enough to—

"Good to see you again, Alexandra." A tall, well-built man rose from the sofa. He wore a dark gray Armani suit, a Bijan tie, and an insincere smile. "I'm Brian Gallagher. We met at Dee Dee's on Thanksgiving."

She bit back a scream. "Oh, my God! Where on earth did you come from?"

"I used to live here," he said, "although everyone tries to forget that."

"I didn't see your car in the driveway." Her hands were shaking from the shock of finding him in the living room.

"The Porsche's getting a tune-up," he said. "I had my driver bring me down."

"But I didn't see—"

"I sent him off for dinner." He looked at Alex curiously. "Do you always ask so many questions?"

She remained in the archway to the living room. Every instinct in her body told her to turn and run for cover. *Ridiculous,* she thought. John's brother was no threat to her. Still the odd prickling sensation remained. "I didn't know you had a key to the house."

"I could say the same thing."

"I—they're doing some repairs on my house. Eddie—Eddie and John were kind enough—I'm staying here until the repairs are finished. I'll probably be back home next week." *Get a grip, Alex. You don't owe him an explanation.* From what John had told her about his brother, Brian showed up in Sea Gate about as often as Halley's Comet. *Be careful. He's not here to socialize.*

"So where is everybody?" Brian asked.

"Cape May," she said, glancing at her watch. It was only five after five. "They'll be home any minute," she lied.

"What are they doing in Cape May?"

Didn't the man read the newspaper? "The oil spill. They've gone down to help some friends."

"Sounds like something they'd do."

The look in his eyes chilled her to the bone. *He hates them,* she thought in amazement. *He hates everything John and Eddie stand for.*

"If you'll excuse me," she said, "I have a few things to do."

She started toward the kitchen. Brian followed her.

"You're not being very cordial, Alexandra," he said as she filled the whistling teakettle with tap water, then set it on the stove. "I drive all this way to talk to you, and you don't even offer me a cup of coffee."

"I'm not making coffee," she said evenly. "I'm making tea."

"In that case, I'll take a Scotch, no rocks."

"Sorry," she said. "I'm off work. You'll have to serve yourself."

"You're not making this easy."

"Listen," she said, turning to face him. "I'm tired and hungry, and the night isn't half over yet. I don't really know what you're doing here but I know enough to be pretty sure you didn't drive down to Sea Gate for a cup of coffee."

"They've been talking about me, have they?" He almost seemed to enjoy the idea.

"No," she said, taking a cup and saucer from the cupboard. "I figured it out for myself."

He stepped farther into the room. "And what exactly did you figure out, Mrs. Whittaker?"

The cup and saucer crashed to the floor. A shard scratched her ankle, but the sting barely registered. "What did you say?"

"Mrs. Whittaker," he repeated. "Been a while since anyone's called you that, hasn't it?"

She grabbed the counter for support as the kitchen seemed to whirl around her like an amusement park ride gone crazy. He crossed the room toward her. She wanted to move away, but the dizziness was overwhelming.

"Sit down," he said, pulling out a chair from the kitchen table. "My wife had the same problem."

"I don't have a problem," she said as she took the seat. "I haven't eaten, that's all."

"That's not healthy, Mrs. Whittaker, is it?"

"All right," she said, looking up at him. "I heard you the first time. You know who I am."

He sat down opposite her. "You're a long way from home."

"Two or three miles," she said, deliberately misunderstanding him. "A good stretch of the legs."

"Your husband's been looking for you," he continued as if she hadn't spoken at all. "Funny thing. He never thought of looking for you in Sea Gate."

"Is there a point to this, Brian?"

"From what I hear, you left London in a hurry."

She said nothing. Her heart was thundering so hard she feared for the baby's safety.

"Griffin has been worried about you."

He looked to her for a response, but she refused to give him one.

"Does your husband know about the baby?"

The air rushed from her lungs, and she lowered her head. This wasn't happening. It couldn't be happening.

"Take a deep breath," he said, unruffled. "My wife used to get dizzy when she was pregnant, too."

He reached out to take her arm. She swung out at him wildly. *He knows,* she thought. *Oh, God, he knows. . . .*

"You're strong," he said. "John must—"

"Don't." The note of fury in her voice was unmistakable. "Don't bring him into this."

"Protecting little brother," he said, with a nasty edge in his voice. "He seems to inspire that in his women."

"What do you want?" she demanded. "Why are you here?"

"Haven't I made that clear?" His expression was as untroubled as a child's. "Runaway wives usually don't want to be found by their husbands." His gaze lowered to her belly. "Especially pregnant wives. I have a very simple proposition for you, Alexandra: You help me get what I want, and I'll keep your secret."

"And if I don't help you?"

He met her eyes. "I have your husband's private phone number programmed in my cell phone. If he took the Concorde, he could probably be here in seven or eight hours. You can help me out or you can explain that belly to the man you married. It's your choice, Mrs. Whittaker."

BRIAN GALLAGHER WAS GONE BY the time John and Eddie returned from Cape May. They were filled with stories about the oil spill and the impact it was having on sea life, but all Alex did was nod.

"Are you okay?" John asked as he made the salad for supper. "You look pale."

"I—I think I'm coming down with something," she said. "I might not be able to go to the meeting tonight."

"The meeting's not important," he said, placing his hand against her belly. "You and the baby are. Go lie down. I'll call you when supper's ready."

"You know, I don't think I'm very hungry right now," she said, edging toward the door. "Maybe I'll take a nap, then fix myself some scrambled eggs later on."

She hurried toward the bedroom before he could say another word.

Trapped, she thought. *This is how it feels to be trapped.* Brian Gallagher had succeeded beyond his wildest expectations. Whatever decision Alex made, John was the one who would be hurt the most. Nothing on earth could make her go back to Griffin. In a way, she longed for closure, to finally, officially, put an end to their marriage so she could love John the way he deserved to be loved. If it wasn't for the baby, she would welcome the chance.

But the baby changed everything. Griffin was nobody's fool—and he wanted a child of his own more than anything. He would never accept the fact that she was carrying another man's child, not without medical proof.

Brian's proposition was wickedly simple. Just as John had suspected, his brother was the brains behind Eagle Management, the company that was devouring Sea Gate. The only thing that stood between Eagle and the marina was Alex's house. All she had to do was sell her house to the management company, and Brian would forget Griffin Whittaker existed.

"You're asking too much," she had said. "I need time to think."

"Two weeks," he'd said. "Either you sell the house to me by April 1, or your beloved husband gets a call."

"Why are you doing this?" she asked as he turned to leave.

"Because I can," he said. "This fucking town turned away from me years ago. Now it's my turn to even the score."

She knew beyond doubt that he wanted to even the score with John most of all.

But not even Brian knew how well he was going to succeed. If she told John she might be pregnant with her husband's child, she would break his heart. If she sold her home to Eagle Management, she would break his spirit.

The only thing left to do was to pray for a miracle.

THE FIRST MEETING OF THE Save Sea Gate coalition went pretty well. John was heartened by the turnout, even if a percentage of the attendees came to learn how they could profit by the town's troubles. But as long as the marina and the Winslow house remained solid, Eagle Management's plans couldn't move forward.

In fact, things seemed to be picking up at the marina. The long cold winter was over, and the sportfishermen had begun to come back. "Better service," one of them said when John asked what had brought him to Sea Gate instead of one of the other trendier towns. "Don't have to sit in the harbor for two hours, waiting to fuel up. You guys get us up and out fast."

The coalition was scheduled to meet again on March 30. They'd invited a reporter from the *Star-Ledger* to join them in order to get an overview of what was happening in their forgotten Shore town. Maybe the media would be able to do the one thing John hadn't managed:

find out the identities of Eagle Management's top people.

To his surprise, Alex remained strangely aloof from it all. He knew what her house meant to her and why. With the place at the center of the Eagle Management storm, he'd expected her to be more interested in the coalition's plans to keep Eagle at bay.

"Maybe Sally and Rich are right," she had said last night as they lay together in bed. "Maybe it's better to take the money and run." There was so much he could do with it, she pointed out. With the profit from the sale of the marina, he could go anywhere, do anything he wanted.

He heard her words, but he also sensed their meaning. She wasn't talking about the marina; she was talking about her own home. He told himself it was his imagination, that there was no way in hell Alex would think about selling her house, but he couldn't deny the gut feeling that something had changed. He just didn't know what it was.

ALEX HAD A DOCTOR'S APPOINTMENT five days after Brian's surprise visit. She hadn't been sleeping well. Every time she closed her eyes she saw Griffin swooping down on Sea Gate like an avenging warrior, determined to claim her baby.

"You need rest," Dr. Schulman said. "Your blood pressure is slightly elevated, and that intermittent spotting concerns me."

"There was very little," Alex said, clasping her hands tightly together. "I'm fine, Doctor. Really."

"I'm going to have to insist on that sonogram, Alex. If you're worried about the baby, I can assure you the sonogram is a safe procedure."

Alex relented and made an appointment for April 2. She'd keep it if she hadn't already left town.

TWENTY

MAKING UP HER MIND TO confront Brian Gallagher had turned out to be the easy part.

Finding the right time turned out to be anything but.

Either she was working extra hours, or Mark was home on spring break or Mercury had gone retrograde and wasn't coming out until the millennium. All Dee knew was that every time she thought she'd found the perfect time, fate told her exactly what it thought of her plans.

Opportunity finally presented itself in the form of a permission slip from one of Mark's teachers. The science department was organizing an overnight field trip to the Pine Barrens on the same night as the second Save Sea Gate meeting.

Dee took it as a sign from God that she was doing the right thing.

Brian's phone calls had slowed down to a trickle. She supposed it was because he'd finally gotten the idea that she wasn't going to sleep with him again. At first he was cool to the idea of getting together, but she wasn't about to take no for an answer. He might be terrific in the courtroom, but he was no match for a mother out to help her child.

The days until the field trip seemed to pass in slow motion. Rich and his wife left for Florida. Sally began the process of shutting down her bait and tackle shop. Eddie had an incident with a school crossing guard, and Alex moved back into Marge Winslow's old place.

Only Dee seemed to be trapped in a state of suspended animation, waiting.

"SORRY I'M LATE." BRIAN SHRUGGED out of his camel's hair coat and handed it to Dee. Only Brian would wear a camel's hair coat at the end of March. "Traffic's building up down here."

"Tell me something I don't know," Dee said, draping his coat over the back of a chair. "It takes me an hour to get to the community college, and that's after the evening rush."

"The community college?"

Damn it. Why had she mentioned that? Nobody but Mark knew she was taking classes toward a degree. "I'm taking an adult ed course." Basket-weaving. Embroidery. Astrology. Let him think whatever he wanted.

"Margo took a course a few years ago. Cake decorating." He shook his head. "It didn't occur to her she'd have to actually bake a cake in order to have something to decorate."

There was an ugly subtext to his words that made her feel an unexpected kinship with his wife.

"Sit down," she said, gesturing toward the couch.

He glanced around the room. "I could use a Scotch."

"Sorry," she said. "I don't have any."

"Brandy will do."

"I have coffee," she said, sitting down on the chair opposite him. "If you'd like some . . ."

He shook his head, then brushed some cat hair off the sofa cushion and sat down. Apparently the cats in his world didn't shed. The fact that she didn't hit him in the head with a lamp was proof of how much she loved her son.

"Okay," he said. "I'm here. What did you want to talk to me about?"

She met his eyes, then said the words she wished she'd said sixteen years ago. "I want to talk about our son."

"YOU CAN LET ME OFF at the corner," Mark said. "I'll walk the rest of the way." He was the last of the students to be dropped off.

Mr. Carling, his science teacher, pulled over to the curb and stopped the minivan. "Sure you can manage your gear?"

"No prob," Mark said, grabbing his backpack. "See you tomorrow."

The field trip to the Pine Barrens had been a total bust. First it started raining, then the police showed up and said Mr. Carling didn't have the right paperwork from the county. Mark's one chance to look for the Jersey Devil and it got screwed up.

"We have a curriculum planned," the teacher had protested.

"Next time bring the right papers," the cop had said, then directed them back to the highway.

The rain was coming down harder. Mark lowered his head and started jogging toward home. His mom usually had school on Tuesday nights. She was halfway toward getting her associate's degree in business, and he was really proud of her. Maybe he'd make a pot of chili and surprise her when she came home. She'd been acting strange the last few weeks, as if she had something on her mind. He knew she'd been seeing Sam Weitz, but he didn't think she wanted to marry the guy. At least he hoped she didn't. It had just been the two of them for a long time now, and he didn't want some guy coming in thinking he would run the house.

He remembered what had happened to his friend Karl. His mom had married a doctor last year, but the guy turned out to be a real bastard. He didn't want Karl living in the house with them and sent the poor schmuck off to some military school in Vermont. As far as Mark was concerned, it was pretty shitty of the guy to even try something like that, but what had hurt Karl the most was that his mom let him get away with it.

Mark knew his mom would never let some jerk come along and push him out of his own house. Sure they fought about lots of stuff, like why he couldn't get a car of his own or stay out past midnight, but mostly they got along pretty good. It wasn't like he didn't want his mom to find someone and be happy, because he did. But it scared him to think about a stranger coming into their lives and maybe hurting her. She tried to hide it, but Mark knew she'd been hurt by a lot of guys in the past, starting with John's asshole brother.

He didn't want to think about Brian Gallagher. Thinking about him always gave Mark a terrible feeling in the pit of his stomach, as if he was going to puke.

That's weird, he thought as he got closer to the house. Every light in the place was on. His mom had been complaining about the electric bill just the other night. She'd even laid out a plan to help them conserve power. No way would she go switching on all the lights before she went out.

Sweat broke at the back of his neck as he realized her car was still in the driveway. It was only seven o'clock. She wasn't due home from school for another four hours. Maybe she was sick, he thought. There was always some stupid virus going around town. But that still didn't explain the bright red Porsche that was parked next to his mom's Toyota.

He knew that fucking car, and he hated it.

He ducked into some thick rhododendrons at the side of the house and peered in the living-room window. His mother was in Brian Gallagher's arms, and it looked as if he was about to kiss her.

Mark fell backward into the bushes as his world spun out of control. Blood pounded inside his head, almost drowning out his harsh, guttural cry of pain. How could she do it . . . she knew what a bastard Gallagher was . . . he'd never been there for them before . . . why should he be there now? If she hooked up with Gallagher there would be no room for Mark in their lives. He'd end up just like his friend Karl, stuck in some shithole boarding school all alone—

Blindly Mark grabbed for the first thing he could find, a football-sized rock his mother had placed in the garden, and heaved it at the windshield of the Porsche.

The sound of glass shattering made him feel better, as if somebody had released a pressure valve. He grabbed the rock from the front seat, then slammed it against the shiny expanse of hood. He wished it was the bastard's head. His blood beat furiously inside his veins, and the sound drove him on. He slammed that rock against the hood and the trunk and the driver's side door.

It was too late. The son of a bitch couldn't show up now after all these years and take over like he owned them. Maybe Brian Gallagher could fool his mother that way, but Gallagher couldn't fool him. Mark closed his eyes, but the image of his mother crying in the bastard's arms ripped his heart in two.

"I hate you!" he yelled at the top of his lungs. "You bastard, I hate your fucking guts!"

• • •

DEE WASN'T A CRIER. SHE liked to say she was the only kid at Sea Gate Elementary who hadn't shed a tear for Old Yeller or Bambi's mother. It wasn't that she didn't feel things the way other people did. Actually her heart was every bit as soft as the next woman's. She just worked harder to hide it than most women did. You had to when you were a single mother.

But when Brian looked her in the eye and said he refused to acknowledge his son's existence, something inside her broke. Tears made you seem weak and vulnerable. She hated herself for crying, but after sixteen years she couldn't hold the tears back any longer.

"I'm not asking you for money, Brian." She struggled to control the quaver in her voice. "I'm only asking for you to acknowledge Mark as your son. He needs a family. He needs—"

The sound of glass breaking stopped her.

Brian glanced toward the window. "What the hell was that?"

"I don't know," Dee said. "It sounded like it came from the driveway."

"Shit," Brian muttered, releasing his hold on her. "The Porsche—"

The Porsche? She had just poured out her heart to the father of her child, and all he could think about was his fancy car? The son of a bitch should be thankful she didn't keep a gun in the house because if she did, he'd be lying in a pool of his own blood right about now.

He started for the door.

"Brian." Her voice was sharp with anger. "We haven't finished talking."

"In a sec," he said. "This neighborhood isn't the greatest, Dee Dee. I want to make sure the car's okay."

She followed him outside in time to hear him bellow like a bear caught in a trap.

"What's wrong, Brian?" She ran across the driveway

to where he stood, bent over from the waist, trying to catch his breath.

He gestured wordlessly toward the car. The windshield was shattered, and a series of large dents arced across the hood and over the fender.

"Somebody got you pretty good," she observed, walking around the car. *And if I knew who did it, I'd give him an award.*

"Jesus," he said, his voice hoarse and breathy. "Jesus."

"It's only a car, Brian." Her tone was amused and more than a little disgusted.

He wasn't listening. He opened the driver's-side door and grabbed for his cell phone. She watched as he punched in 9-1-1. Anything she might have felt for him, any residual memory of love or longing or hatred vanished, and she felt free for the first time since she was fifteen years old.

THE JOHN GALLAGHER ALEX KNEW worked with his hands. He repaired boats, took rich men out on deep-sea fishing expeditions, and watched over the marina now that Eddie had lost all interest in it.

The John Gallagher who took charge of the Save Sea Gate coalition's second meeting that night was a stranger to her. He was forceful, erudite, downright passionate as he talked about his hometown and why saving that hometown should be important to all of them.

She hadn't wanted to come to the meeting. Moving back into her house had been the first step in breaking away from John. The first of April was just two days away, and she wasn't naive enough to think Brian Gallagher's threat to contact Griffin was anything less than serious. For all she knew he'd already called Griffin, and the two of them were watching her as she spun slowly in the wind.

They had her trapped between a rock and a hard place. For days she'd been telling herself that selling her house to Brian and Eagle Management was the right decision, that anything she did to keep Griffin away from her child was beyond reproach. John would hate her for it, but he wouldn't turn away from the baby, and that had seemed the most important thing of all.

But the more she listened to him talk that night, the more she wondered if she was doing the right thing. A standing-room-only crowd packed the auditorium. It seemed to Alex that everyone in town had gathered there to hear what John had to say about the future.

He'd presented a visual history of Sea Gate from its founding in 1752 to the present, with an emphasis on the glory days. He described the early colonists and the whalers who had helped build the town. The railroad tracks at the far edge of town had been specially constructed to bring Abraham Lincoln to Sea Gate during the Civil War. The address he'd presented hadn't gone down in history the way the one at Gettysburg had, but the original notes still resided behind glass at the local library.

The late nineteenth century had seen the arrival of wealthy New Yorkers and Philadelphians looking for a place to spend the long hot summers. Sea Gate was just the ticket. Elaborate Victorian houses popped up from one end of town to the other, each one more fanciful and expensive than the last. Some houses displayed ocean views, while others faced the verdant town square. Ocean Avenue had boasted one of the first boardwalks in the United States, a wide expanse of wooden planks designed as a promenade by the sea.

Listening to John talk, she could imagine handsome men and beautiful women strolling arm in arm in the summer sun. She'd found herself blinking back tears as a bustling, successful Ocean Avenue flashed across the movie screen he'd set up at the front of the room. Time had been as cruel to the town as it had been to so many of its residents.

"We're not Cape May," he admitted, "but there was a time when we were every bit as popular. We can do it again, but only if we stick together."

They were at a critical juncture. If a few more stores and beachfront houses toppled to Eagle Management, they wouldn't stand a chance, and that suddenly seemed a terrible shame to Alex.

"I'm not saying it'll be easy," he said, pacing the length of the room as he spoke, "but I am saying it'll be profitable."

"When?" one of the local businessmen asked. "I'm on a second mortgage as it is. I don't know how much longer I can hang on."

"Neither do I," John shot back. "But if we give up now, we're not going to get a second chance." It was a cold world out there, he told them. New businesses failed every day of the week. There were no guarantees that any of them would move on to more successful ventures if they turned their back on Sea Gate.

"What difference does it make?" Sally Whitton asked. "Eagle Management's offering us enough money that it doesn't matter."

"Easy for you to say." Margaret O'Neal, a first-grade teacher, cast a sharp look in Sally's direction. "You've already raised your children and enjoyed a career. If you all move away, my husband and I won't get that chance. We don't live down by the water. Nobody's offering us the big bucks for our place, and they probably never will. We're here because we wanted to build a life for our kids, and now you tell us the town is dying. This isn't the way it's supposed to be."

Young families were a town's lifeblood. Without them Sea Gate wouldn't stand a chance. But she couldn't help wondering if John wasn't tilting at windmills. You needed more than pretty pictures to persuade a struggling young family to stay the course. You had to prove to them that there was a future.

She listened, amazed, as John did exactly that.

"Too bad Eddie's not here to see this," Vince Troisi whispered to Alex as John presented a string of facts and figures. "Never thought I'd see Johnny like this again."

"I'm impressed," Alex whispered back. "He's really something, isn't he?"

"He was a damn fine lawyer," Vince said. "Could've been a real success if he'd stuck with it."

He is *a success,* Alex thought. She just wasn't sure he realized it.

An entire town was looking to him for help. He had the ability to shape the lives of three hundred families, to make an impact that would extend far into the future. In the long run John might not win the fight, but if she sold her house to Brian and Eagle Management, everyone in Sea Gate would lose.

There was only one choice she could make. She had to tell John the truth about the baby and pray he would understand.

TWENTY-ONE

"TOO BAD EDDIE WASN'T HERE," Vince Troisi said to John after the Save Sea Gate meeting adjourned. "Nobody knows the docks better than he does."

"*NYPD Blue* night," John said by way of explanation. "A bomb couldn't get him out of his chair."

Vince chuckled. "Haven't seen much of your old man lately. I've been worried about him."

"Pop's doing okay," John lied. "He's just been sticking close to home."

"Wish we could get him down here to talk to some of the newcomers," Vince said. "It's hard to make them understand what it used to be like around here."

"Alex has a few ideas on that subject," John said. "You should ask her about them."

"Good idea." Vince headed across the room to the refreshments table, where Alex was pouring coffee for people.

She glanced John's way and smiled. Smiles like that should be illegal. They made a man forget that life wasn't always good or fair. They made a man believe he could do anything. Her hair was swept off her face with a pair of tortoiseshell combs. It cascaded down her back in soft waves that reminded him of burnished gold. She wore a pair of black silky pants and a loose blouse in a brilliant shade of emerald green.

Her breasts were round and full. Her belly was clearly prominent beneath the folds of her blouse. The doctor estimated that she was well into her second trimester, but couldn't pinpoint a due date without a sonogram.

So far Alex had canceled two appointments. She always had some excuse—she had a cold, she hadn't slept well, she was needed at the diner. The excuses were as transparent as the look of apprehension on her lovely face. Lately she'd become so quiet, so secretive, that he wondered if he knew anything about her at all. He wondered what she did at night alone in that tiny cottage of hers. In that lonely bed.

Did she dream about him? Did she make plans for their baby? Did she lie awake and worry about cleft palates and rare lung diseases and drunk drivers careening across four lanes of traffic? He and Libby had talked all the way through her two pregnancies. Sometimes he thought they'd created those beautiful boys with words as much as flesh and blood and bone.

This baby grew in silence and in secrets.

He had made it clear that he wanted to be with her every step of the way, and for a while he'd believed she welcomed his support. Now he wasn't so sure. Invisible barriers had gone up around her, and by the time the baby was born, he might not be able to reach her at all.

MARK USUALLY SAT ON THE dock on nights like this, but for some reason tonight he boarded the *Kestrel*. He used to spend a lot of time on Eddie's boat when he was a kid, sailing down to the Chesapeake Bay or up to Montauk Point to see the lighthouse, which was older even than Old Barney, the one on Barnegat Island.

Eddie worked Mark's ass off on those trips. There was always something to do on boats, and it seemed that as soon as Mark finished one chore there was another one waiting to be done. He'd be real tired when they finally got back to Sea Gate, but it was a good tired.

He missed those days. He wished somebody had told him how quick the good times could disappear. Everything around him was changing faster than he could handle it, shifting like one of those shape-changers in the fantasy comic books he read when he was a kid. He wished things would slow down long enough for him to think.

Mark walked the boat from prow to stern, glad there was no moon out. He liked the shield of darkness. It made him feel like it was just him and the boat and the ocean. Even without moonlight he could see the repairs John had made to the boat. The fresh paint stood out like a neon Band-Aid on the scarred and weathered surface. Sometimes he wished he'd never seen Eddie swing that axe overhead and bring it crashing down into the brittle wood of the *Kestrel*. If he closed his eyes he could still picture Eddie's face, tears streaming down his lined cheeks, his chest heaving with the effort. And Eddie didn't even remember afterward. He ragged the local kids and threatened to tell the cops every time he saw them within fifty yards of the marina, when he was the one responsible.

It made Mark feel scared and sad all at once, as if there wasn't one damn thing in the entire world that he could count on.

He huddled down beneath a canvas tarp that had been tossed in the stern. A stiff wind was blowing in off the ocean, and it cut right through his jacket and pants. He couldn't count on his mother anymore. Not after what he'd seen tonight through the living-room window.

Brian Gallagher was a first-class scumbag, and the thought that his mom would let him touch her made Mark want to puke.

The moorings squeaked mournfully as the wind rocked the *Kestrel* in its berth. They were having another one of those meetings tonight, one of those Save Sea Gate things that John Gallagher had set up. He wondered if they really thought they had a chance. In another year or two the marina would be gone, and then the houses, and by the time Mark finished college, Sea Gate would be nothing more than an ink dot on an old map.

He wondered if there'd be anyone left to care.

EDDIE WAS RUNNING LATE. THE sun wasn't up yet, but he thought he could make out the beginnings of daylight out beyond the horizon. He was supposed to have been on the *Kestrel* by 4 A.M. to get ready for the trip up to the Stellwagen Bank with a group of deep-sea fishermen from Tuckerton.

The captain set the tone for the trip. If he was late, how could he expect his crew to hop to when he barked out an order? You had to set an example for young people, same way you set an example for your own kids. They had to know the rules, the boundaries, what you wanted them to do and when you wanted them to do it. He treated his crew the same way he treated his own two boys, with discipline and love.

But that didn't mean he was going to take any crap.

He boarded the *Kestrel* and looked for signs of life. The damn boat was silent as the grave.

They'd be shoving off in less than half an hour, and there was still a lot to do before they weighed anchor.

"To hell with the lot of you," he muttered after a moment. He didn't need anybody to help him pilot the *Kestrel*. He'd do it himself.

•   •   •

IT WAS A LITTLE AFTER eleven when Alex and John finally left. John helped her into the truck, and Alex fastened her seat belt. They hadn't exchanged more than a few words with each other since the meeting ended. The images and words of his presentation lingered with her as John drove down Ocean Avenue, and she felt as if she were seeing the town's potential for the first time. A heavy fog had rolled in off the ocean. It tumbled across the road, softening the harsher realities, making it easier for Alex to imagine Sea Gate the way it used to be.

The way John wanted it to be again.

There would never be a good time to tell him about the baby, same as there would never be a good time to tell him that his brother was behind Eagle Management's plans to turn Sea Gate into a giant parking lot.

The one thing she knew was that if she didn't do it now while she had the nerve, she would never do it, and John deserved better than that.

BY THE TIME THE COPS arrived at Dee's, Brian was almost foaming at the mouth.

"Will you calm down?" Dee asked as the squad car pulled into her driveway. "They got here as fast as they could."

Brian was beyond rational thinking. He pushed past her as if she wasn't even there. She couldn't help but wonder what he'd be like in a real emergency. "What the hell took you so goddamn long?" he demanded as Dan Corelli and a rookie climbed out of the car. "Now you don't have a chance in hell of catching the bastard who did it."

"Nice talk from a hotshot lawyer," Dan said after greeting Dee. "You wanna cool down and tell me what happened?"

"Someone took a swing at his car," Dee said, biting back a grin.

"Looks like someone got a home run," Dan observed. He glanced over at Brian. "Hope you got insurance."

"Of course I've got insurance," Brian roared. "What the hell kind of question is that? Shouldn't you be dusting for prints or something?"

Big mistake, thought Dee. Dan Corelli had never liked Brian. This would really push the veteran cop over the edge. In a way she almost felt sorry for Brian. For all of his education and success, he still didn't know the first thing about how to get along with people.

Dan gestured for his young colleague to get something from the squad car. "All right, Gallagher," he said, leaning against the door of the Porsche. "Why don't you tell me how it's done."

MARK AWOKE WITH A START. The boat was listing to starboard as a wicked, wind-powered rain sluiced across the deck. He felt groggy, his brain fuzzy with sleep, but it only took a second for him to realize the *Kestrel* had broken free of the dock and was drifting away from the marina.

The boat's lights blazed, although he couldn't remember switching them on; he wasn't even sure he knew how. He jumped up, and his feet nearly slipped out from under him on the wet deck. Heart pounding, he tried to peer through the rain and fog. He thought he could make out some lights toward port, but he wasn't sure. Eddie had told him a long time ago that weather could play tricks on even an experienced sailor, make him think he saw things that weren't there.

Could it make you *hear* things, too? The sound of wood splintering filled the air. The fog was so thick he couldn't see the other side of the boat. He moved slowly across the slick wooden deck in the direction of the sound. His heart thudded at the base of his throat, in his ears, behind his eyes. A form began to take shape near the prow.

"Jesus," he muttered, feeling like he'd been kicked in the gut. Eddie . . . it was Eddie . . . Eddie swinging an axe in a wide glittering arc overhead . . . bringing that axe down into the side of the boat—

"Eddie, stop it!" His voice rang out. "We're taking in water." It swirled around his ankles, lapping up toward his calves.

Eddie brought down the axe again. It slammed into the wood with a sickening crack. Splinters exploded in every direction. One bounced off the old man's cheek, but he barely seemed to notice. Nor did he seem to know Mark was there. He grunted as he raised the axe again. Mark tried to lunge for the handle, but Eddie dodged him. The air next to Mark whistled as Eddie swung the axe. Mark was so scared he almost peed his pants.

"You've gotta stop this," he cried out as the water reached his knees. "The *Kestrel's* gonna sink, Eddie. You're killing her!" He could hear the sound of dishes and pots crashing to the floor of the galley down below as the boat listed to starboard.

Eddie pushed him hard, and Mark fell against the railing. "I didn't raise my son to talk to me that way," Eddie roared. "Bad enough Brian broke his mother's heart. I won't have you bringing her shame, too."

"I'm not John," he cried, desperate for Eddie to recognize him. "I'm Mark, Eddie! I'm Mark!"

Eddie looked at him with wild, drowning eyes. He raised the axe overhead, then started for Mark.

"Jesus, Eddie, stop! I'm Mark . . . I'm Dee's son, Eddie. Please don't—" He ducked as Eddie lunged forward, slipped on the slick deck, then tumbled over the railing into the icy black water.

Mark's mind went blank. He called Eddie's name, but there was no answer.

No! He refused to believe it. Not Eddie. Not like this. There had to be a chance for him. For both of them. There had to be something he could do. Mark made the sign of the cross, then followed Eddie overboard.

"WE NEED TO TALK," ALEX said as John swung his truck into her driveway.

Her words didn't surprise him. Neither did the sense of sadness that seemed to hang over the two of them, as thick and impenetrable as the fog rolling past the windshield.

"Seems like I did nothing but talk tonight," he said, turning off the engine. "Didn't you hear enough of me?"

"You were wonderful," she said, "but that's not what I meant. There's something I need to tell you."

"Your roof's leaking and you want to move back in with me."

Her smile was gentle and sad, and it made him want to kiss her until she forgot everything but him.

"So talk," he said, leaning back in his seat.

"Not here." She opened the door to the truck. "Inside."

"Sounds serious."

"It is," she said, her voice soft. "Very serious."

He climbed out of the truck, then went around to the passenger side and helped her down. "I'm not getting a good feeling about this, Alex. What's wrong? Is it the baby?"

"Inside," she repeated. She turned away, but not before he saw the shimmer of tears in her eyes.

He followed her to the front door and waited while she rummaged in her bag for her keys. The urge to throw her over his shoulder and head for higher ground was almost too strong for him to resist.

He looked out toward the marina. It hardly seemed possible, but the fog had grown even thicker. A slight movement caught his eye, and he felt an answering stab of apprehension in his gut.

"Alex." He placed a hand on her shoulder. "Look over there. Near slip number one."

"John, I—" She stopped. "It's Bailey!"

"Jesus," he muttered. "I thought she was home with Pop."

Alex didn't say anything. She didn't have to. They both knew that with Eddie anything was possible these days.

"Bailey!" His voice rang out through the drizzle and fog. "C'mere, girl!"

They heard two barks, then the sound of her paws hitting the wet, sandy earth as she ran toward them.

"Hey, girl!" John buried his face in the fur of her neck. "What the hell are you doing here?"

Bailey licked his hand, then turned to Alex, who kissed the top of the dog's head. Suddenly Bailey pulled away from both of them and ran full speed toward the marina.

"Oh, God," Alex whispered. Her hands covered her stomach in a gesture that had become as natural as breathing. "Eddie."

"Stay here," John ordered, then took off after Bailey. *Bad moon rising.* He couldn't get the words to the old song out of his mind. *There's a bad moon on the rise.* His old man usually didn't start sleepwalking until three or four in the morning.

Bailey didn't slow down when she reached the dock. John heard her nails clicking against the wooden planks as she ran.

"Bailey!" His voice cut through the fog. He was less

than thirty feet behind the dog, but he could barely see her. There were no barriers at the end of the dock, just a drop-off. If she kept running like this, she was going to tumble straight into the water.

At least there was no sign of his old man. Nick Di Mentri's boat was in slip three, where it had been for the last twenty years. Vince's garvey bobbed up and down in slip eight. Everything seemed the way it should be. Bailey skidded to a stop on the slick surface, then threw back her head and let out a bloodcurdling howl that stopped John cold.

Slip fifteen, the last one before the end of the dock, was empty.

The *Kestrel* was supposed to be in there. Eddie had claimed that spot the day he bought the boat, and he'd never relinquished it to anyone. The *Kestrel* should have been there right now.

"Eddie!" The fog curved John's voice right back at him. "Where are you, Pop?"

The only other sound was Bailey's keening cry.

IF JOHN ACTUALLY BELIEVED ALEX was going to stay put, he didn't know her half as well as he thought.

She loved Eddie almost as much as he did, and if the man was in trouble, she wanted to help. He'd opened his house to her, a total stranger, and made her feel as if she was part of a real family. It was something she would never forget. There was nothing she wouldn't do for him.

"Eddie!" John's cry pierced the fog. "Where are you, Pop?"

The ground was slick with rain and badly rutted from the long hard winter. The fog curled around her ankles and calves, making it impossible to see where she was walking. Twice she'd barely managed to save herself from a nasty fall.

She cupped her hands around her mouth. "John! Where are you?"

"Go back home, Alex. Eddie took out the *Kestrel*. I'm going after him."

"No!" She broke into a run. "It's too dangerous. Let me call the police."

The lip of the dock knocked her off balance, and she fell to one knee. A sharp pain knifed its way up toward her hip, but her fear outweighed her pain.

"Please stop, John!" She scrambled to her feet and ran down the dock in the direction of his voice. "Let the police handle it."

He stepped out of the fog toward her and grabbed her by the forearms. "I have to do this," he said, gripping her tightly. "I can't lose him the way I lost Libby and the kids. . . ."

"But it's not the same thing," she protested. "I have a bad feeling about this."

He untied Vince Troisi's boat from its mooring and jumped in. "Take Bailey back to the house and call for help. I'm going to find Eddie."

He vanished into the fog before she could say another word.

TWENTY-TWO

DAN CORELLI WAS FINISHING UP his report when the call came in.

"Shit," said Dan, a frown pleating his forehead. "There's trouble at the marina."

That piqued the rookie's interest. "Vandalism again?"

"Not this time." Dan looked from Dee to Brian. "Looks like your old man decided to take the *Kestrel* out in this mess."

"Oh, God!" Dee said. "Is he all right?"

"Don't know," said Corelli. "John called for help. "

Brian's neutral expression twisted into a scowl. "Surprised he didn't start swimming out to the boat to save the day."

"Brian." Dee's tone was sharp. "This is your father we're talking about."

"I know who we're talking about," he said, not at all chastened or embarrassed. "I'd say I'm the only one who sees the situation for what it is."

"What's that supposed to mean?" Dee demanded,

aware of Dan Corelli's interest. The conversation would be all around town by morning, but she didn't care.

"The old man's lost it," Brian said bluntly. "We're not talking normal behavior here." He listed some of Eddie's more recent midnight rambles, a few of which Dee hadn't been aware of.

"Who told you about his sleepwalking?" she asked.

"Sleepwalking?" He laughed out loud. "Is that what they're calling it?"

"That's what Dr. Benino called it."

"Benino's an old-timer who doesn't know his butt from a hole in the ground. Maybe it's time to put Eddie in a home. I offered Johnny the money, but he didn't seem to see things my way. Too bad. I don't offer twice."

She raised her hand to slap his face, but some shred of reason stopped her at the last second.

"Smart move," he said, his voice steely.

"Smarter than you'll ever know," she shot back.

"Sorry to interrupt," Corelli said, a half-smile on his face, "but we're gonna have to save this for another day. We're on our way to the marina." He looked at Brian. Even though his expression never changed, his dislike was clearly visible. "Don't suppose you want to come with us?"

The telephone rang before Brian could answer. Dee crossed the room to answer it.

"This is Mr. Carling, Mark's science teacher. Sorry to bother you so late, Ms. Murray, but Mark left his wallet in my car. I didn't want him to worry."

"Mr. Carling?" A nervous twitch erupted beneath her left eye. "Aren't you supposed to be in the Pine Barrens with your class?"

Mr. Carling was silent for a good ten seconds. "I'm afraid the field trip was called off, Ms. Murray. I drove Mark home myself."

"Oh, God." She sank into the chair by the phone.

"Are you telling me he's not there?" Mr. Carling sounded horrified.

"When did you drop him off?"

"About an hour and a half, two hours ago."

Which was right around the time someone trashed Brian's Porsche.

MARK DIDN'T KNOW HOW LONG he'd been in the water, but it seemed like forever. He'd given up trying to swim for shore. Every time he struck out in what he thought was the right direction, he seemed to drift farther out into the ocean. He could feel all sorts of currents pulling at him, and he worried that the riptide was going to get him. It was pitch black out there and cold as hell. He tried his best not to think about what might be lurking beneath the surface of the water. He had to concentrate on staying alive . . . on keeping Eddie alive.

Eddie must have hit his head when he fell into the water. Mark had found him floating face down, right near the stern of the *Kestrel*. The first thing Mark did was feel for a pulse, even though it was real hard to tread water and hang on to Eddie's wrist. He felt like crying with relief when he finally located a heartbeat.

Eddie couldn't die. Eddie was the most important person in Mark's life, except for his mom. It was Eddie who'd taught him how a man was supposed to act. Eddie who'd taught him to respect the power of the sea and everything that lived in it.

And he did respect the sea. He knew that the sea won almost every battle, and that you had to use your head if you wanted to survive. You couldn't waste your energy screaming or thrashing around. You had to conserve your strength for when it mattered.

He had Eddie in a lifeguard's hold. He tried treading water for a while, but his muscles quickly began to tremble with exhaustion from the effort. He rolled three-quarters of the way onto his back with Eddie cradled against his chest and prayed he'd be able to keep the two of them afloat until daybreak, when he might have a chance to strike out for shore.

Maybe if he left Eddie behind he'd be able to make it to shore right now. If he didn't have to cart one hundred and sixty pounds of dead weight, he'd have a chance to get out of this mess. He thought of his mother and how much she'd done for him all these years, and he felt like crying. If he died, a part of her would die, too, same as a part of John had died after his kids were killed in that car crash.

John had aged right in front of them, his face crumbling in on itself at the funeral when those little white caskets were carried up to the altar and placed on either side of Libby's big mahogany casket. He'd never realized a human face could look like that, as if all of the pain in the entire world was right there in his eyes.

He didn't want that to happen to his mother. If he died, she'd be left alone. Maybe she'd even turn to that bastard Brian Gallagher if Mark wasn't there to stop her. It wasn't so hard to imagine it happening. Hell, he'd seen them together tonight through the living-room window.

All he had to do was leave Eddie to fend for himself. They were out beyond the breakers. Eddie could probably float on his back for a good half hour or so. That would be plenty of time for Mark to get to shore and find help before anything awful had a chance to happen.

That wasn't being selfish, was it? He was only sixteen years old. He hadn't even slept with a girl yet or bought his first car. He was too young to die. Eddie had lived his life. He wouldn't want Mark to sacrifice himself so an old man could have a few more years.

But what kind of man would he be if he saved his own ass and let his own grandfather die?

JOHN ROWED HIS WAY BLINDLY through the dark, fog-shrouded waters. The flat-bottomed garvey moved noiselessly. The only sound was his heart double-thumping inside his chest. He could feel his pulse beating crazily at the base of his throat, in his ears, at the top of his skull.

They'd tried to tell him something terrible was going to happen to Eddie, but he wouldn't listen. He'd clung to Dr. Benino's sleepwalking diagnosis as if it were a lifeline, clung to it for so long that it had managed to turn into a hangman's noose.

The fog clung to his skin like a damp spider's web. He knew he couldn't be more than a few hundred feet away from the end of the dock, but already the structure had disappeared into the darkness. He stopped rowing and closed his eyes, trying to regain his bearings. There was no moon, no stars to help him. No landmarks on shore. Nothing but his powerful, bone-deep need to save his father's life.

He wondered how long Eddie had been gone. If he'd left right after John went to the Save Sea Gate meeting, he could be long past Cape May, on his way down to the Chesapeake. John wouldn't stand a snowball's chance in the garvey.

He'd told Alex to go back to the house and call for help. He should have told her to call the coast guard. The cops wouldn't be able to help him out here. Why the hell hadn't he thought of that before he jumped into the boat? All he'd been thinking of was Alex and whatever it was she wanted to talk to him about. She'd looked so serious . . . so sad—

He pushed the image from his mind. He had to stay focused for Eddie's sake. He had to try to think like

Eddie, figure out where he would go. When John's mother was alive, Eddie used to like to take her up to a little cove near Old Barney, the lighthouse on Barnegat Island. It was their spot, one of those Shore secrets that the old-timers knew about and refused to share.

The last few days Eddie had been doing a lot of reminiscing about Rosie and the early days of their marriage. The cove near Old Barney was as good a place as any for John to start his search. Now, if he could only figure out which goddamn way was north, he might stand a chance. Based on the direction of the current, he made a calculated guess, and had rowed a good thirty feet when he heard a sound.

He stopped rowing and listened.

Nothing.

He picked up the oars and began rowing again.

"Help!" The voice was shadowy, indistinct. It could belong to anybody. "We need help!"

John lowered the oars once again and cupped his hands around his mouth. "This is John Gallagher. Where are you?"

He couldn't make out the words, but the sound was coming from his left. A sense of foreboding snaked its way up his spine. He grabbed the oars one more time and prayed he wouldn't be too late.

ALEX LOCKED BAILEY IN HER house, then ran as fast as she could to the marina. She tried to ignore the tearing pain in her hip, but it put a hitch in her step that slowed her down even more than her growing belly.

"Thank God," she whispered as the flashing lights of a squad car cut through the fog.

The car screeched to a stop a few feet away from the door to the marina office. Dan Corelli and a rookie leaped from the front, and to her shock Dee and Brian Gallagher climbed out of the backseat.

Her shock must have been obvious, because Dee immediately came to her side.

"I think Mark's out there with Eddie," Dee said without preamble.

Alex grabbed her friend's hand. "I thought he was on a field trip."

Dee's lower lip began to tremble. "He was," she said, somehow managing to keep her voice steady, "but it got called off. I think he saw Brian's car in our driveway and got the wrong idea." She stopped abruptly and looked down.

Alex's gaze strayed toward Brian Gallagher, who was keeping step with the cops as they strode to the end of the dock.

"It's not what you think," Dee said. "I wanted to talk to Brian about Mark. My son deserves to know that Eddie is his grandfather, that John's his uncle—all I wanted was to give Brian the opportunity to be part of my son's life. You can probably figure out what he thought of that idea."

She told Alex about the tears she'd shed and Brian's slick attempt at comforting her. "The bastard tried to put the moves on me ten seconds after he told me he didn't want anything to do with my son. I was so shocked I stood there for a moment until we heard a noise in the rhododendrons by the side window. I think it was Mark, Alex. I think he saw me in Brian's arms and lost it." A grin pierced the sadness on Dee's face. "Somebody smashed the crap out of Brian's Porsche."

"You're kidding," Alex said.

Dee shook her head. "Somebody pitched a rock through the windshield and did a number on the paint job."

Despite herself, Alex began to laugh. "Did he sign his name to his handiwork?"

"My kid's smarter than that," Dee said. "You've got

to admit he knows how to pick his battles." Mark would be grounded big time for what he did, but there was a part of Dee that obviously wanted to send up three cheers for teenage rebellion.

They joined the cops and Brian at the end of the dock.

"John's out there right now," Alex said, ignoring Brian totally. "He took one of those little flat-bottomed boats."

"He won't be able to do squat with a garvey," the rookie cop said. "Better contact the coast guard for help."

"You do that," Dan Corelli said, "and see if we can get anyone from the Beach Patrol out here."

It all seemed so primitive, Alex thought. Two men and a boy were out there somewhere in the dark, unforgiving sea, and none of the modern conveniences they took for granted could help them.

"It's bad, isn't it?" Dee asked Corelli. "Tell me the truth."

"It's bad," Corelli said. "We've got a real nasty riptide going about three hundred yards offshore. They had problems up as far north as Brigantine and down by Absecon. That wouldn't have been a problem in the old days. Back then Eddie could pilot the *Kestrel* through a gale."

Alex leaped on his words. "You mean the *Kestrel* is strong enough to survive a riptide?"

"The *Kestrel* will outlive us all," Corelli said. "It's John I'm worried about. Superman couldn't row his way out of the tide we've got going tonight."

A hand seemed to grip Alex's midsection, and she doubled over from the waist.

"You better go back home," Corelli said, not unkindly "It's gonna be a long night."

"No." She forced herself to straighten up. "I'm staying here."

He looked at her. "That baby of yours isn't due yet, is it?"

"No," she said. "Not for a good while."

"You don't look so good."

"I hurt my hip before," she said, brushing away his concern. "I'm fine."

Next to her Dee lit a cigarette. Her hands were shaking, and the glowing ash moved up and down like a signal. How must it feel to know, Alex wondered, that your son, the child of your body, was in danger and there was nothing you could do to help? She wished she had some words of comfort to offer, but her mind was filled with nothing but terror.

Only Brian seemed unconcerned. He stood near the end of the dock, smoking a cigarette and looking out at the ocean.

Dee followed Alex's gaze. "Next time anyone says blood is thicker than water, kick them for me. The guy's father, brother, and son are out there somewhere, and all he can think about is his Porsche."

But Alex knew better. Brian was thinking about more than his Porsche.

He was thinking about how to destroy the town.

WATER WAS EVERYWHERE.

Swirling black cold water pounding against him, trying to pull him down down down. . . .

Mark's arms and legs trembled with fatigue. He'd done everything he could to save himself and Eddie, but it looked like it was too late. The tide had them in its clutches and was pulling them out beyond the breakers, and once that happened, they'd be goners.

He could have managed to swim against the tide an hour ago, but that was then.

He was even hallucinating—a while ago he thought he'd heard John's voice floating toward him through the darkness. It was so cold . . . the cold was screwing up his brain . . . making it hard for him to think.

If only he could concentrate, maybe then he could come up with the right thing to do, but the thoughts just wouldn't come.

Eddie sputtered, then coughed. "What—what the hell . . . ?"

"Don't move," Mark said in a hoarse voice. "I've got you, Eddie."

"Jesus . . . sweet Jesus . . ."

"We went overboard," Mark said, feeling his strength ebbing as he spoke. "We gotta keep afloat till someone comes to get us."

Nobody's going to come, asshole. It's over. You tried to save the old man and yourself, and now you're both going to buy the farm.

He should have used the radio on the *Kestrel* to summon help before he jumped overboard. Maybe then they would have had a chance.

It was over . . . over . . . over—

"Mark, is that you?"

A deep familiar voice penetrated the cold empty place where his brain had been. *Don't pay attention to it, jackass. It's just your imagination.*

"Mark," the voice called out again. "Can you hear me?"

His eyes burned with tears. It sounded like John. But not even John could get him out of this mess. Good thing it was only his imagination talking. He didn't want John to take the blame if he and Eddie drowned out here. It wasn't John's fault.

Suddenly a garvey appeared from nowhere, its wide flat bottom bobbing in the choppy water. Garveys were weird boats. They were built real deep, and the seats were so low you were practically sitting on the floor. Duck hunters liked them because they cut through the water without a sound, and only the hunter's head was visible above the boat line.

From that angle, the garvey looked empty. He wondered if it had broken free of its moorings and been caught by the same squirrelly currents.

He looked again, and his heart tried to punch its way out of his chest.

A man stood in the prow of the boat with the fog swirling all around him like something out of one of those fantasy movies where the hero appears in a puff of smoke to save the day.

Except this time it wasn't a movie. And he wasn't imagining it. It was really happening.

John had come to save them.

TWENTY-THREE

THE COAST GUARD SAID IT would take them at least two hours to reach Sea Gate. They had other, bigger problems to deal with up and down the coast, and the problems of one small town on the Jersey Shore would just have to wait in line.

Up until that point adrenaline had been holding Alex together, but the second she heard about the coast guard, she felt her tightly held control begin to loosen. *They're going to be all right,* she told herself over and over, a mantra against her fears. *John will find them. They'll all be okay.*

But what if they weren't? She heard them talking about the wicked riptide and the unpredictable currents. What if John couldn't find them? He was out there alone in the fog in that strange flat boat—he wouldn't stand a chance if the surf got rougher.

Dee looked at Brian. "You've piloted a boat before, Brian. Do something."

"What's there to do?" he asked. "You can't see two feet in this fog. Let the coast guard handle things."

Dee's voice was low and deadly calm. "Your son is out there with your father and your brother. Don't you give a damn what happens to them?"

Alex watched Brian's face for any sign of human emotion, but saw nothing. He turned away from Dee as if she weren't there and continued to look out toward the invisible horizon.

"Go to hell," Dee said, tears streaming down her face. "I'll take a boat out myself."

Dan Corelli blocked her way. "Don't do it," he said. "We're having enough trouble finding the three of them. Don't make our job any harder."

"I don't care about your job," Dee said, her tears turning into gut-wrenching sobs. "My son and two dear friends are out there, and nobody's doing a damn thing—nobody!"

That sense of being powerless was worse than anything. Alex had spent most of her life in a position of weakness, and she knew exactly what Dee was feeling.

"I'll go with you," she said. "I'd make a good second mate."

"You're pregnant," Dee managed. "You can't take a chance like that."

"And you can't go out there alone."

"I'm scared," Dee said. She was a strong woman. Alex could imagine what that admission cost her.

"Mark might not be out there, Dee. Maybe he went to a friend's house."

Dee shook her head. "His shoes," she said, her voice a whisper. "I found them at the end of the dock."

Alex's pulse rate increased. "How can Dan Corelli just stand there waiting for the coast guard? He should be doing something."

Dee's gaze drifted past Alex. Her eyes widened. "Alex," she said, "look!"

Alex spun around, and the sight she saw made her

spirits soar. It seemed like half of Sea Gate was running toward them. Vince Troisi and Nick Di Mentri. Rich and Sally and Dave. Scores of people she knew from the diner and others she'd never seen before but who would now hold a special place in her heart. The old and the young, come together to help their own.

"How did you know?" Alex asked as they crowded around her and Dee.

"Police band radio," Vince said. "I called Rich, and he called Nick—you know how it goes."

She didn't, but she was learning. This was what it meant to be part of a real community, a family that went beyond connections of blood to include everyone who needed to know there was a place for them in the world.

"We're going to find them," Vince was saying. "You can bet the farm on it."

They began untying boats from their moorings, setting up searchlights to cut through the fog. Dee seemed to be everywhere. She knew what needed to be done before anyone had a chance to bark out an order.

Alex sat near the *Kestrel*'s empty slip, hands cradling her belly. Sally Whitton came and sat down next to her. For once Sally didn't talk. She just reached over and patted Alex awkwardly on the shoulder, and that simple touch was all it took to release months of pent-up emotion. Alex lowered her head and started to cry.

"There, there," said Sally, putting an arm around her and pulling her close. "You cry all you want. It's good for you."

Nobody had ever said that to her before. Her mother had used tears as a weapon in the war between the sexes, while Griffin had considered them a lower-class affectation. Tears were normal and natural to Sally, same as they were to Dee and everyone else gathered there on the dock.

Sally patted her on the back from time to time, and

after a while Alex's tears subsided. Sally had done more than just comfort a crying pregnant woman—by sitting down with her, she had officially acknowledged that Alex was one of them.

They were a family, all of them, joined together to help their own.

Only Brian stood apart from the rest. He looked out of place in his expensive suit and handmade shoes, like someone from her old life. He smoked one cigarette after another, alternately looking bored and annoyed, as he scanned the horizon. Nobody spoke to him. Nobody tried to include him in the rescue operation. He had been born and raised in Sea Gate and yet he was a stranger to everyone there.

He turned slightly and met her eyes.

You lost, she thought, not turning away. Even if he managed to turn Sea Gate into the world's biggest parking lot, he would still be the loser. She almost felt sorry for him. He'd isolated himself from everything that really mattered and he didn't even know it.

"I see something out there." Nick trained his searchlight at a point north of the marina.

Dee grabbed his binoculars and peered out through the fog. "I don't see anything."

"A little more that way," Nick said, angling the searchlight.

"Oh, God!" Dee's voice went high with excitement. "It's a boat—I think it might be a garvey!"

Alex rose to her feet, then drew in a sharp breath as pain radiated across her belly from hipbone to hipbone.

"What's wrong, honey?" Sally took her by the elbow. "It's not the baby, I hope."

"I'm fine," Alex assured her. "I slipped before and must have twisted something."

Sally looked as if she didn't quite believe Alex, but there was no time to quibble. They hurried to the end of the dock where everyone had gathered to wait. Dee stood next to Nick. They made way for her as Alex approached, patting her on the shoulder, murmuring words of friendship and support, making sure she was there at the edge of the dock with Dee where she belonged.

Let them be safe, she prayed. *Let them all be safe.* She knew that John had a score to settle with himself, a very personal score that had to do with the deaths of his wife and sons. She'd seen it in the way he took care of her, the way he shouldered burdens another man would have turned away from. He showed his love for her in everything he did, and yet he had never once said the words.

I love you, she thought, letting the words cut deep into her heart. Not just sexually, although that was a big part of it. Not just because she prayed he was the father of the child she carried. She loved him in a deeper way, spiritually, physically, emotionally. Sometimes she thought she'd been born loving him and it had taken her twenty-eight years to figure it out.

He deserved to be happy. He deserved a woman who came to him without entanglements. He deserved children. He could give so much to a child, she thought. He knew what was important in life. He could teach a child the things Eddie had taught him, about honor and courage.

About love.

"Any second now," Vince said, keeping the beam of light focused on the approaching boat. "We'll know what's what any second."

The ache in her belly grew stronger. *Think about the baby,* she told herself. Getting this upset wasn't good for the child growing inside her womb. No matter what happened between her and John, there would always be the baby.

John was safe. He had to be. The world needed people like him, a good man in a world where goodness was in short supply.

"I think it's a garvey," Nick said. "Sweet Jesus, I think it is."

Dee's fingers dug into Alex's hand. Alex closed her eyes, too afraid to watch.

Next to her Dee let out a cry, a sharp explosion of sound that Alex felt in her bones.

"Please, God," she whispered. "Please."

She opened her eyes. The men were grabbing for the boat, pulling it close to the dock. She saw it all, the boat and the men and the dock. She saw Brian tossing a cigarette into the water, heard the sizzle as it broke the surface. She saw Dee's face, alive with happiness. She saw Mark, wet and skinny, struggling to man an oar. And she saw Eddie sitting next to Mark, a rock for the boy to lean against.

But she didn't see John.

A terrible silence fell across the dock. A single sound rose out of that silence, a low keening wail, and she realized in some distant part of her mind that it was coming from her. Her knees buckled, and she felt someone put an arm around her to catch her. Cold . . . so cold . . . she wondered if she would ever be warm again. This wasn't really happening. She was dreaming, trapped in the middle of a nightmare, and all she had to do was wake up and it would all go away.

Dee turned to her, and their eyes met. The look they exchanged was one of triumph and despair and a deep understanding that transcended even sorrow. Dee opened her arms and reached out to her son, gathering him to her breast the way she had when he was a little boy.

Nick and Vince grabbed Eddie and pulled him out of the garvey. They pounded him on the back, ruffled his wet hair, did all the things men did to express emotion without words.

Brian tossed another cigarette into the water. Mark looked toward the sound. His youthful features hardened into something fierce and ugly, and before anyone realized what was happening, he hurled himself at Brian, ramming his head into the man's gut, knocking him to the ground. The look of shock on Brian's face would have been comical if the situation had been different. He lay there on his back in his big-city clothes while his son hammered at him with his fists.

"You son of a bitch!" Mark cried as Brian covered his face with his arms. "Leave her alone! Nobody wants you here!"

Something inside Brian seemed to explode. One second he was the passive victim, and the next he was a lethal weapon. He threw Mark off him as if the boy was made of feathers. He jammed his thumbs into the soft spot in Mark's throat, and Dee screamed as her son dangled from Brian's hands like a rag doll.

"This is the little fuck who wrecked my car," Brian said to Dan Corelli, who seemed too shocked to move. "I'm pressing charges."

"He's a juvenile," Dan said, still motionless. "And you don't have any proof."

"Call it intuition," Brian snarled. He shook the kid until the boy's feet left the ground again. "Tell the nice man what you did, you bastard."

Mark's face was bright red, and he was struggling to breathe, much less talk.

"Put him down," Dee shrieked, landing a blow to Brian's shoulder.

"Put him down?" Brian abruptly released Mark, and the boy fell in a heap at his feet. "You did a great job with him, Dee Dee. You should be proud."

"You bastard," she said, bending down to help her son.

Alex watched through a haze of sorrow as Brian turned again to Dan Corelli. "I'm not bullshitting you, Dan. This kid is going to learn discipline if you have to beat it into him."

"A little late, isn't it, big brother?" That voice—that wonderful beloved voice!

Years later Alex would remember the moment she saw John stepping out of the shadows as the moment her life began again. Relief flooded through her body, and she sagged against Sally Whitton, but there wasn't time to savor the joy. What had started as an uncomfortable situation was quickly turning violent.

Brian turned toward the familiar voice. "Stay out of it," he warned. "It's none of your business."

"More my business than yours," John said, advancing on him with slow, measured steps. He was dripping wet. His jeans and fisherman's sweater clung to his body like a second skin. Behind him Alex could just make out the lines of the *Kestrel*, bobbing near slip number one. It wasn't hard to see she had taken some heavy damage.

But, as she thanked God a thousand times, it was easy to see that John hadn't.

"Stand up," Brian barked at his son.

"Fuck you," Mark said, a scared kid talking tough to hide his fear.

Brian grabbed him by the arm and pulled him to his feet. "You busted up my car, didn't you?" Anger stripped away his cultured city tones. "Tell them."

John loomed over the two of them. "Touch that kid again, and I'll kill you," he said to Brian.

"Go to hell," Brian said. "Tell them what you did," he ordered Mark again.

Mark pulled away from him. Hatred poured off him

in waves. "I threw a rock through your fucking wind-shield!" His voice cracked and broke mid-sentence. "I wish I'd set fire to it! Why don't you leave us alone?"

Brian turned coldly to Dan Corelli. "You've got your confession," he snapped. "What more do you need?"

"Not much," Dan conceded. He turned to the boy. "You admit you wrecked his car?"

"Yeah, I wrecked his car."

"Do something," Dee said to John. "Shouldn't he have a lawyer or something?"

John stepped between Dan and Mark. "You don't have to answer his questions," he said to the boy. "You have rights in this situation, too."

Dan, however, seemed less amenable than before. "It's starting to come together now," he said, pulling a notepad and pen from his pocket. "What about the vandalism here?" He gestured toward the boats moored in the various slips. "We're called out here three times a week. I always thought it was one of you kids, and now I got proof."

"You don't have any proof at all," John protested. "Just because Mark said he smashed Brian's windshield doesn't mean he had anything to do with what happened here."

"Figure it out," Brian said, disdain dripping from each word.

John turned to Mark. "Did you trash any of the boats?"

Mark stared down at the ground.

"Mark." John's voice toughened. "I'm asking you again: Did you trash any of the boats?"

Mark continued to maintain his silence.

"Good as a confession to me," Brian said to Dan Corelli. "I'd haul his ass into jail and—"

"Shut up."

All eyes turned to Eddie as he entered the fray. "Drop it, Brian," he ordered.

"Stay out of it, Pop," Brian said. He turned back to Mark. "You wrecked the boats just like you wrecked my car. Tell them."

"You're making a mistake," Eddie said. "You don't know what you're talking about."

Brian laughed out loud, then gestured for the crowd. "I don't know what I'm talking about? This from a man who wanders around in his pajamas?"

John opened his mouth to speak, but Eddie silenced him with a look. "I did it," Eddie said quietly. "I took a sledge to the *Kestrel* and most of the boats here."

"No," Mark cried. "Don't say that."

The look Eddie gave the boy warmed Alex's heart. The connection between them was strong and vibrant. "You've been covering up for me for too long, Mark. It's time I faced up to what's been happening. I've got a real problem," he said simply, "and it's scaring the hell out of me."

"You don't have to do this, Pop," John said. "You can talk privately with Dan."

"No." Eddie's voice was firm. "My grandson has been cleaning up behind me for a long time now, and I don't want him taking the blame for something that wasn't his fault."

Grandson.

Tears streamed down Mark's face. "You called me your grandson."

"About time, I'd be thinking." Eddie's eyes were filled with love and pride. "You saved my life out there tonight, Mark. You risked your own neck to save mine."

Mark's expression veered between embarrassment and pride. "You needed me."

"And you were there for me," Eddie said. He leveled

his gaze at Brian. "More than I can say for my own son."

Brian reached into his pocket and withdrew a thick stack of currency. He flung it in his father's direction. "Johnny wouldn't take it. Maybe you're smart enough to use it to put yourself in a home, where you won't get into trouble."

It was all Alex could do to keep from leaping for Brian's throat. Mark, however, didn't hesitate.

"It's all your fault! Nobody wants you here. Why don't you go back where you came from and leave us all alone?"

"Mark is a good boy," Eddie said to Dan Corelli. "I think we can work this out."

"It's up to Brian," he said. "He's the one who's pressing charges."

"Do the right thing, Brian," Eddie said to his son. "You owe the boy."

"I don't owe any of you jack," Brian said. "What the hell have any of you ever done for me?"

"If you have to ask that," John said, "you're more pathetic than I thought."

"You've got it wrong, little brother. Everyone here knows who's pathetic. I'm not the one who couldn't hang on to his wife."

Alex stiffened with fear. She knew Brian was capable of anything.

"Nothing to say?" Brian taunted as John watched him. "No wonder Libby took off—"

John grabbed him by the collar and came close to lifting him off his feet. "You don't know anything about it."

"I know she was sick of living with a loser, little brother. I know she wanted more from life than being trapped in this poor excuse for a town. I knew exactly what she wanted and how to give it to her."

John's roar of fury tore through Alex.

"Don't like the truth, do you, little brother?" Brian went on. "Why don't you admit that Libby was leaving you for good that day, not just going back to New York? She'd had enough of life here in this Jersey Shore version of Mayberry. She wanted to be with someone with a little ambition, someone who wasn't satisfied with just treading water." John tightened his grip, but it didn't stop Brian. "Come on, Johnny. Show me what the big hero can do."

"He's not worth it," Eddie said, placing a restraining hand on John's arm. "Let it go."

Alex couldn't take it anymore. Too many lies. Too many secrets. She had to put an end to them now before they destroyed everyone. She took a step forward, then froze as Brian's attention turned to her.

"Two more days, Alexandra," he said, meeting her eyes. "That's all you've got."

She straightened up, ignoring the pain shooting between her hipbones. John was watching her. So was everyone else at the marina. "I won't be needing the two days," she said calmly and clearly. "And I won't be selling my house to you and Eagle Management."

The crowd exploded. They started lobbing questions at Brian like hand grenades. She stood there, eyes locked with his, and knew she would pay for what she did. She also knew it was the best decision she'd made in a very long time.

She turned away as John reached her side.

"How long have you known he was behind Eagle?" he asked her, brushing a lock of hair back from her forehead.

"A few weeks," she said.

"You should have told me."

"I wanted to but—"

"He was blackmailing you?" She could see the

shadow of fear in his beautiful deep blue eyes.

"Yes," she whispered. "I tried to tell you before, but we saw Bailey and—" She stopped and drew in a deep breath. "There's something you need to know, John, something I've been too afraid to—"

"Alex?" He gripped her by the shoulders. "What is it?"

"I-I don't know." She swayed against him. "Dizzy . . . I've been having this pain—"

He gathered her close, and she heard his low intake of breath against her ear. Suddenly she found herself swept up into his arms, held tight against his broad chest. "We need help here, Corelli," he called out. Dan turned and looked toward them. "We need the hospital, *fast*."

"The hospital?" She struggled against him, trying to see his face. "I don't need the hospital. I twisted a muscle, that's all. I'm fine. I—"

"You're not fine, Alex," he said. "You're bleeding."

TWENTY-FOUR

～

"FASTER," JOHN URGED CORELLI AS the squad car rocketed toward the hospital in the next town. "I'm afraid she's hemorrhaging."

"I'm going as fast as I can," Dan said. Beads of sweat dripped down the sides of his face. "This fog is a bitch and a half to drive in."

"Did you call Dr. Schulman?"

"She'll be waiting for us at the entrance to the emergency room."

"Just go faster," John said again, feeling powerless to stop what was happening.

"I'm doin' the best I can, Johnny."

Alex gripped his hand tightly. "Leave him alone, John," she said, her beautiful face pale and frightened. "The last thing we need is an accident."

He knew she was right, but the blood—

"You're going to be fine," he told her over and over again. "This isn't anything serious."

They both knew better, but there were times when a lie was exactly what you needed.

297

"Listen to me," she said as the car careened around a corner. "I have to tell you something, and it can't wait."

"It's going to have to wait," he said. "We're at the hospital."

"No!" Her voice seemed to fill the car. "Now, John. I have to tell you now."

"We're here," Dan said, screeching to a stop. "I'll go get a stretcher."

Alex waited until the car door closed behind Corelli. "Remember what I told you about my husband?" John nodded. His gut knotted with apprehension. Sentences like that rarely preceded good news. "That wasn't all of it, John." Her words spilled out in rapid-fire succession. "I—I couldn't get pregnant. We tried for ten years, and I just couldn't manage."

"You managed now," he pointed out, hanging on to her hand as if it were a lifeline. "You're pregnant, Alex. You're carrying our baby."

Her amber eyes filled with tears. "It never happened with Griffin." She told him about the endless visits to expensive doctors, the joyless sex, the husband who sought comfort in the arms of a string of mistresses while his wife slept alone in their king-size bed.

"All of that's over," he said as the doors to the emergency room swung open. "It's nothing but a memory, Alex. Part of the past."

"But it's not part of the past, John. We're not divorced." Her voice broke, and she looked down at her hands. "He had a mistress named Claire Brubaker. We'd moved to London to get a fresh start. He swore to me that he wouldn't see Claire anymore. We were going to make the marriage work even if I never managed to get pregnant." Her soft laugh was filled with pain. "Back then I used to shop a lot. There wasn't much else for me to do. I went into Harrods to buy a new Filofax, and

Claire was standing at the next counter.'' Claire who was supposed to be in New York. Claire who wasn't supposed to be pregnant with Griffin Whittaker's child.

''He didn't deny it,'' she continued. ''The look in his eyes—'' She shook her head sadly. ''I'll never forget that look. That baby meant everything to him, John. Everything.''

''The stretcher's coming, Alex,'' he said. ''We've got to get you inside.''

''I have to finish this,'' she said. ''I want to say it once and never think about it again.''

''You left him,'' he said. ''I know that, Alex. You learned about the baby and you left.''

''I stayed.''

He felt like he'd been gut-punched. ''You stayed?''

''He said the baby wouldn't affect our lives.''

''You believed that?''

''He was my entire world, John. I had no place to go, no one to turn to, nothing to call my own.''

''But you're here,'' he said. ''What changed your mind?''

The car door opened, and a technician popped his head inside. ''Ready when you are.''

''Wait,'' she said, a note of hysteria in her voice. ''I need a minute.''

''You can't wait,'' John said, gesturing for the tech to go ahead. ''The baby can't wait.''

And the truth was he had the feeling he didn't want to hear what was coming next.

''NO SIGN OF PLACENTA PREVIA,'' Dr. Schulman said.

''That's a good thing?'' John asked.

''A very good thing,'' the doctor said. ''I want to do a sonogram, and then we'll talk about what to do next.''

''You're doing good, kid,'' John said to Alex after

Dr. Schulman disappeared to see if the equipment was available. "Looks like you're finally going to get your sonogram. Now we'll know exactly when the baby's due."

"Claire Brubaker lost Griffin's baby."

John's attention was galvanized. "What?"

"She lost the baby in October. Griffin came home drunk—" She stopped and took a deep, shuddering breath. He noted the small muscle twitching beneath her right eye. "He raped me, John. He was drunk and filled with pain—I tried to fight him, but he overpowered me."

The buzzing in John's head all but drowned out her words. In a way he wished it would. The images her words painted would be seared in his brain forever. *I'm capable of murder,* he thought as she spoke. He'd always wondered. Now he knew.

"I walked out that night," she was saying. "I took my jewelry and some clothes and I walked out the door and never looked back." She'd left her wedding ring on the end table, silent testament to what had happened between them. "I didn't care about a divorce. Divorce meant I'd have to see him again or speak to him, and I didn't want that. All I wanted was my freedom, and I didn't need a piece of paper to give it to me." She hadn't expected to fall in love. She certainly hadn't expected to get pregnant.

'This is what Brian was threatening you with, isn't it?"

She nodded, a look of such misery in his eyes that it hurt to see it. "Brian said if I didn't sell my house to Eagle Management, he would call Griffin and tell him where I am."

"You could have sold him your house." She could have protected herself with one simple action.

"I thought about it," she said, "but then I saw you

in action, John. I saw how much this town means to you—I saw how much you mean to this town, and I knew I couldn't do it." *And I love you, John. I just don't have the courage to tell you.*

"Even if it meant bringing your husband back into your life."

"I love this town," she said. "It deserves a second chance."

"What about your husband? Does he deserve a second chance, too?"

"No," she said in a voice that brooked no argument. "He deserves nothing at all."

"We can handle this," he said, taking her hands in his. "Whatever happens, we can handle it."

"John." Her eyes brimmed with tears. "What if the baby isn't yours?"

AND THERE IT WAS. THE MONSTER in the closet. The creature under the bed. If Alex lived another fifty years, she prayed she would never see a look of such sorrow on anyone's face again. Pain was visible in every line, every angle of his face. His eyes were saturated with pain. His mouth was twisted with it.

The seconds stretched into minutes. The minutes would turn into hours if someone didn't break the terrible silence.

"I'm so sorry," she whispered, "but you had to know."

He nodded, the movement slow, like the movement of an old man. "That's why you kept putting off the sonogram, isn't it?"

"Yes, it is. This is my problem, John," she said, meeting his eyes. "I'll understand if you walk out that door and don't come back."

He lowered his head and buried his face in his hands. She longed to reach over and stroke his hair, trace the curve of his ear with the tip of her finger, but she wasn't sure she still had the right. That terrible silence was back again, and she was afraid that the answer she feared most was hidden within it.

"John, if you—"

"I love you, Alex."

The words stopped her cold. Was she just hearing what she wanted to hear? "Did you say s-something?"

He looked up and met her eyes. "I said I love you, Alex."

She opened her mouth to speak, but he raised a hand to silence her.

"I won't lie to you and say I wouldn't give anything for that baby in your belly to be mine, but that doesn't change anything. I've loved you from the moment you walked into the Starlight that morning with your black raincoat flapping around your ankles—" His voice broke, and he cleared his throat. "I didn't want to fall in love again. I didn't think I could. But there you were, and there I was and"—he gestured with his hands—"here we are."

Tears spilled down her cheeks and splattered on her thin hospital gown. "Here we are," she echoed. "I won't lose the baby, John. No matter what, I can't lose the baby."

"I know," he said. "I understand."

"You say that now, but what if Dr. Schulman tells us I conceived in October? How can you be so sure you'll feel the same way then?"

Again that silence.

"Because the baby is yours," he said at last. "Because I love you and I love what belongs to you. Because if I met you two years from now, I would love your child the way I loved my own."

She held onto his words like a talisman as an aide wheeled her into the examination room for the sonogram. John walked next to the stretcher, holding her hand.

Dr. Schulman greeted them, but Alex barely heard her description of what was about to happen. She was vaguely aware of a gel being applied to portions of her belly, of sensors being attached, but her thoughts were far away. For all she knew Brian had already contacted Griffin and told him where he could find his runaway wife. What Griffin would do with that information was anybody's guess.

Conversation flowed around her. She caught bits and pieces of it.

"Over there . . . move that sensor . . . a little more gel . . . there you go . . . okay, there it is . . . are you looking, Alex?"

John's attention was riveted to the monitor. A look of wonder lit up his face.

"Oh, my God," Alex said as the image on the screen came together for her. "The baby!"

Tiny hands. Tiny feet. The sweet curve of the baby's spine.

She clutched John's hand even tighter than before. "Do you see that?" she asked, her voice high with excitement. "Can you believe it?"

He bent down next to her and kissed her on the mouth. "A miracle," he said. "It's always a miracle."

Dr. Schulman watched the monitor carefully, exchanging opinions with the technician, speaking her notes into a hand-held tape recorder.

"Your baby is being coy," she said with a laugh. "I can't tell if we have a little boy or a little girl."

"I don't care," Alex said, tears of joy flowing down her cheeks. "Is the baby healthy?"

"So far, so good," said the doctor. "But, I think you need some bedrest, for starters. We'll monitor you for a few days, see if we need to do anything to your cervix, then proceed from there."

"The due date," John said.

"Oh, of course." The doctor glanced at her notes. "I'd say we're looking at a Labor Day baby."

"Labor Day." Alex tried to do the math, but she was too nervous. "The date of conception—?"

"Your Thanksgiving Day guess was pretty close, but I'd put it closer to the beginning of December."

"And you're sure of that?" Alex asked, her heart thundering crazily inside her chest. "You're positive?"

"As positive as I can be without a menstrual chart to guide me."

"And it couldn't have happened in October?"

"Absolutely not."

She looked at John and saw her future in his eyes. She saw a chain of days stretching into months, months moving into years, all of them spent together as a family.

Some women dreamed of jewels.

Some women dreamed of designer clothes.

Some women dreamed of a family to call their own.

Alex's dream was finally coming true.

"Your baby," she said as he kissed her again. All of his goodness, his strength, his courage—it would all be part and parcel of the child growing inside her womb. The child who would make them a family.

"*Our* baby," he said.

"I love you." The words came hard for her. It was so much easier to show him how she felt, but she knew he needed to hear those three words as much as she needed to say them. "I love you so much that it scares me, John, because I can't imagine my life without you in it."

The look he gave her was enough to break her heart. "So if you love me so much, why don't you marry me?"

•   •   •

OF COURSE, THEY BOTH KNEW the answer to that.

Until Alex and Griffin divorced, there could be no wedding.

Alex was to spend four nights in the hospital. It seemed to her as if everyone in Sea Gate passed through her room to see how she was doing and wish her well. Dee knew about her lack of health insurance, and she took up a collection at the diner and presented Alex with a check. Alex was overwhelmed by the gesture.

"Don't go thinking this is out of the goodness of my heart," Dee said with mock severity. "I expect you back at the Starlight ASAP."

"I can't wait," Alex said. "Would you believe I miss everyone, and I've only been gone a couple of days."

"I still believe in Santa Claus," Dee said. "I guess I can believe just about anything."

The movement to save Sea Gate from developers had exploded into action since that night at the marina when Brian Gallagher was revealed as the power behind Eagle Management. Family didn't do that to family. Brian had violated an unwritten code of behavior, violated it in a way that good people like Sally and Rich and Vince couldn't condone. Sally backed out of her deal the morning after the incident. Rich and his wife were seeing a lawyer about reneging on their deal. Rumor had it the other members of Eagle Management were rethinking their position on Sea Gate and looking to target another Shore town.

"Nothing is certain yet," Dee said, "but things are finally looking up for all of us."

John, Alex thought happily. It was all thanks to John. His passion. His persistence. His courage.

"So when's the wedding?" Dee asked. "They're taking bets again. Sally has the July Fourth weekend covered, but Vince is pushing Memorial Day."

"You know the story," Alex said. "First I have to get a divorce."

"So get a divorce."

"It's not that easy." She'd spent the last three days waiting for the phone to ring, and every time it did, she expected to hear Griffin's cultured, disapproving tones. "Brian must have called him by now," she said.

"You've taken the fun out of his revenge," Dee said. "With the Sea Gate deals falling apart, he has other things to think about."

Which meant it could drag on forever. "That's it," Alex said, reaching for the telephone on the stand next to her hospital bed. "I'm going to call him."

"Are you sure you want to do that?" Dee asked. "Maybe you should have a divorce attorney make the call. These things can get pretty sticky."

Alex pressed 9 for an outside line, then began to dial the city and country codes for London, England. "I didn't bring anything into the marriage," she said, "and I don't want to take anything out of it except my freedom. The whole thing should be cut-and-dried."

It was all academic. His secretary told Alex that he was out of town on business, and she didn't know when he was expected back.

"I'm going to let you rest," Dee said. "Once you're home, you'll be thinking about this interlude with longing."

"I'll be home tomorrow," Alex said. "I should be back at the Starlight by Monday."

"Don't rush things," Dee warned. "Take your time. The Starlight will still be there."

Alex smiled. That was one of the best things about Sea Gate. You could count on things and people being there when you needed them.

She felt restless after Dee left, unsettled. John was busy repairing the *Kestrel* for a weekend trip down to

the Chesapeake. He wouldn't be in for a few hours. She
hated daytime television. The thought of being reduced
to watching Jerry Springer made her break out in hives.

Closure, that's what she was looking for. She was
anxious to get on with her life, to move forward. She
wanted to marry John, to stand up before God and make
those beautiful promises. She wanted—

"Alexandra."

She turned toward the door. "Griffin!" She recognized his suit; it had cost almost as much as her new
roof.

He stepped into the room. "I would have telephoned,
but some things are best done in person."

JOHN LEFT THE MARINA AROUND four o'clock. He
hadn't finished the repair work on the *Kestrel,* but the
need to see Alex, even for a few minutes, was too strong
to ignore. He got to the hospital a little after four-thirty
and was striding through the parking lot toward the entrance when he bumped into Dee as she was about to
climb into her car.

"Look at you," she said with a shake of her head.
"You're so much in love it's disgusting."

He grinned and tugged at a lock of red hair. "Your
turn's coming, pal," he said. "You and Sam seem to be
hitting it off pretty well."

"He has possibilities." She gave John a quick hug.

"What's that for?"

"For being happy," she said. "I've waited a long
time to see that smile on your face again."

"I'm as surprised as you are," he said to his old
friend. "Guess I'm proof that anything can happen."

They chatted for a couple of minutes about Mark and
Eddie, then John said he'd better go in and see Alex.

"Some Cary Grant type stopped me in the hall when

I was leaving,'' Dee said. ''He asked which room was Alex's.''

''A Cary Grant type?''

Dee wrinkled her nose. ''You know the type I mean. Tailored up the yin-yang, too good for the rest of us.''

John took off at a run. He didn't bother waiting for the elevator; instead he took the stairs to the third floor two at a time. Brian had made good on his threat, and now Griffin Whittaker had come to town to claim his wife. A nurse gave him a fish-eyed look as he barreled down the hallway toward Alex's room, but he didn't give a damn.

A red mist of rage exploded behind his eyes as he thought of the last night Alex had spent as Griffin Whittaker's wife. He wanted to get his hands around the son of a bitch's throat and make him pay for what he did to her.

The door to her room was closed. He didn't bother to knock. He grabbed the knob and swung the door wide. Alex was sitting on the edge of her bed, a glass of orange juice in her hand.

''John.'' Her face lit up with her smile. ''I wasn't expecting you.''

He stepped into the room. ''Whittaker,'' he said. ''Where is he?''

''You're too late.'' She motioned for him to sit down next to her, and he did. ''He's gone.''

''Are you okay?''

''Yes,'' she said, her smile growing brighter. ''You could say that.''

It was hard to shift down from anger to relief. ''He didn't stay long.''

''He didn't have to. We settled our business pretty quickly.'' She met his eyes. ''He doesn't want me, John. I'm free.''

It took a second for her words to penetrate, and even

then he couldn't quite believe it was over. "You're free?"

"He has a new pregnant mistress. He wants to marry her. My belly and I are a major embarrassment to him, and he wants me out of his life ASAP."

"He'll give you a divorce?"

"At the speed of light." She looked a little sheepish. "Remember what I said about not taking a settlement from Griffin?"

He nodded.

"Apparently his guilty conscience got the better of him, and he made me an offer I couldn't refuse. Six months from now I'll be a free woman with seed money for the catering business I'd like to start with Dee."

"You and Dee?"

"We'll make a great team. She'll keep the books; I'll cook the food. I had to depend on Griffin for everything," she said, "even my self-esteem. That's too much to ask of a marriage, John."

"So what are you saying?" He couldn't keep the uncertainty from his voice. Maybe when push came to shove she didn't believe marriage was a viable option for her.

"I'm saying I'm a different person now. I've learned I'm not weak or powerless or any of the things I thought I was when I was Griffin's wife. I'm strong and I'm smart and I can handle just about anything life throws my way."

"And where does that leave us?"

"Married," she said, "if you'll ask me again."

He met her eyes. "I'm asking."

"And I'm saying yes," she said, placing his hand on her belly. Their baby stirred beneath his palm, tiny hands and feet kicking hard, and he knew a moment of profound happiness he'd never expected to feel again. "We both say yes."

One word.

One syllable.

And a new family was born.

TWENTY-FIVE

MARK DIDN'T MUCH CARE FOR weddings, and for the most part babies were invisible. But when the wedding was John and Alex's and the baby was their brand-new Emilie Rose, even Mark had to make an exception. Besides, you didn't often go to a wedding and christening on the same day.

Although he wouldn't admit it to anyone, he'd gotten a little misty when Father O'Laughlin made that speech about love and families and how sometimes God sent happiness your way after you'd stopped believing He even remembered your name.

It almost hurt to look at John, as if you were invading his privacy. He'd never seen a happier man. And Alex. Well, she always looked beautiful, but there was something real special about brides, and she was no exception. When she'd walked down the aisle carrying six-week-old Emilie Rose, there hadn't been a dry eye in the church. Even tough Vince Troisi had blubbered into his handkerchief.

"Come on," Eddie said, waving to him from the

church steps. "They're taking a family picture."

Mark looked from his grandfather to his mom. She and Sam Weitz were standing on the top step with the Gallaghers, smiling like they'd won the Lotto. *My family,* he thought as he joined them. Sometimes he still couldn't believe it.

It had felt funny at first, calling Eddie "Grandpa," but he got used to it real fast. Nobody had expected Brian to show up for his brother's wedding, and he didn't disappoint them. But it didn't matter that much to him anymore. He was one of the Gallaghers now, and he didn't need Brian to make it possible.

He knew where he belonged.

He was connected to all of them. To Eddie and John. To Alex and Emilie Rose. To his mom and maybe even to Sam Weitz, if things kept going the way they'd been going. No matter what happened in his life, they would be there for him, because they were his family.

He would be there for them, too. Not because he had to be, but because being part of a family was a whole lot better than being alone.

He took his place between his mom and Eddie. She smoothed his hair with her hand, and the look of love in her eyes made a big fat lump form in his throat.

"C'mon, Ma," he said, pretending to be annoyed. "There's nothing wrong with my hair."

She smiled at him, and he knew that she understood what he was really saying. There were limits to just how sappy a guy was going to get with his mom.

"You're looking pretty impressive," Eddie said with a grin. "You clean up good."

"So do you, Grandpa," Mark said. There was a rough road ahead for Eddie, but Mark was going to be there for him every step of the way, same as Eddie had always been there for him.

"Remember we've got that fishing trip tomorrow

morning. Don't stay up partying too late. I'm going to work your butt off on the *Kestrel*."

"Okay, everybody." The photographer positioned himself and raised his camera. "Get your game faces on. On the count of three, I want you all to say—"

"Family," John broke in. He looked down at his bride and his new baby, and the smile he gave them made Mark happy to be alive. "The most beautiful word in the English language."

Mark couldn't have said it better himself.